D0032044

He was on the tall side, and whipcord lean.

His hair was black as a raven's wing, falling around his face and over the high collar of his doublet in unruly waves. He impatiently pushed them back, revealing high, sharply carved cheekbones and dark, sparkling eyes.

Eyes that widened as they spied her standing there, staring at him like some addled peasant girl. He handed the lady his empty goblet and moved toward Rosamund, graceful and intent as a cat. She longed to run, to spin around and flee back into the woods, yet her feet seemed nailed into place. She could not dash off, could not even look away from him.

"Well, well," he said, a smile touching the corner of his sensual lips. "Who do we have here?"

* * *

The Winter Queen
Harlequin® Historical #970—November 2009

THE
WINTER
QUEEN

AMANDA
McCABE

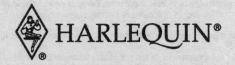

HARLEQUIN®

TORONTO • NEW YORK • LONDON
AMSTERDAM • PARIS • SYDNEY • HAMBURG
STOCKHOLM • ATHENS • TOKYO • MILAN • MADRID
PRAGUE • WARSAW • BUDAPEST • AUCKLAND

Recycling programs
for this product may
not exist in your area.

ISBN-13: 978-0-373-29570-8

THE WINTER QUEEN

Please address questions and book requests to:
Harlequin Reader Service
U.S.: 3010 Walden Ave., P.O. Box 1325, Buffalo, NY 14269
Canadian: P.O. Box 609, Fort Erie, Ont. L2A 5X3

Chapter One

December, 1564

> *…it is our deepest hope that, once at Court, you
> will see the great folly of your actions and rejoice
> at your happy escape from this poor match. The
> Queen has done our family a great honour by ac-
> cepting you as one of her maids of honour. You
> have a chance to redeem yourself and our family
> name through service to Her Grace. To discover
> what will truly make you happy. Do not fail her, or
> us.*

Lady Rosamund Ramsay crumpled her father's letter in her gloved hand, slumping back against the cushions of the swaying litter. If only she could crush his words out of her memory so easily! Crush the memory of all that had happened since those sweet, warm days of summer. Was it all just months ago? It felt like years, vast years, where she had aged far beyond her nineteen years to become an old, old woman, unsure of herself and her desires.

Rosamund shivered as she tossed the crumpled letter into her embroidered bag, curling her booted feet tighter around the warmer that had long gone cold. The coals weren't even smoldering embers now. It made her think of Richard, and their professed feelings for each other. The kisses they had stolen in the shade of green, flowering hedges. He hadn't even tried to see her when her parents had separated them.

And now she was being sent away from Ramsay Castle, pushed out of her home and sent away to serve the Queen. No doubt her parents were sure she would be handily distracted there, in the midst of a noisy, crowded Court, like a fussing babe handed a glittering bauble. They thought that, with Queen Elizabeth's patronage and all the fine, new gowns they had sent with her, Rosamund would find another match. A better one, more suited to the Ramsay name and fortune. They seemed to think surely one handsome face was as good as another in a young lady's eye.

But little did they know *her*. They thought her a shy little mouse. But she could be a lion when she knew what she wanted. If only she knew what that was…

Rosamund parted the curtains of the litter, peering out at the passing landscape. Her parents' desperation to send her away was so great that they had launched her out into the world as soon as the Queen's letter had arrived, in the very midst of winter. The world beyond the narrow, frost-rutted roadway was one of bare, skeleton-like trees stretching bony branches towards a steel-gray sky. Thankfully, it was not snowing now, but drifts of white lay along the roadside in lumpy banks.

A sharp wind whistled through the bare trees, bitterly chilling. Rosamund's escorts—armed guards on horseback, and her maid Jane in the baggage cart—

huddled silently in their cloaks. She had not heard a single word since they had stopped at an inn last night, and likely all would be silent until they at last made it to London.

London. It seemed an impossible goal. The palace at Whitehall, with its warm fireplaces, was surely just a dream, as the cozy inn had been. The only reality was this jolting, jarring road, the mud, the never-ending cold that bit through her fur-lined cloak and woollen gown as if they were tissue.

Rosamund felt the hollow sadness of loneliness as she stared out at the bleak day. She had lost her parents and home, lost Richard and the love she had thought they shared. She had no one, and was faced with making a new life for herself in a place she knew so little of. A place where she could not fail, for fear she would never be allowed home again.

She drew in a deep breath of the frosty air, feeling its bracing cold stiffen her shoulders and bear her up. She was a Ramsay, and Ramsays did *not* fail! They had survived the vicissitudes of five Tudor monarchs thus far, and had escaped unscathed from them all, with a title and fine estate to show for it. Surely she, Rosamund, could make her way through the Queen's Court without getting herself into more trouble?

Perhaps Richard would soon come to her rescue, prove his love to her. They just needed a plan to persuade her parents he was a worthy match.

Rosamund leaned slightly out of the litter, peering back at the cart rumbling along behind her. Jane sat perched among the trunks and cases, and she looked distinctly grey and queasy. It had been hours since they had left the inn, and Rosamund herself felt stiff and sore, even tucked up among the fur robes and cushions. Feeling suddenly wretched and selfish, she gestured to the captain of the guard that they should stop for a moment.

Jane hurried over to help her alight. 'Oh, my lady!' she gasped, fussing with Rosamund's white-wool cloak and gloves. 'You look frozen through. This is not a fit time for humans to be out and about, and no doubt about it!'

'It is quite all right, Jane,' Rosamund said soothingly. 'We will soon be in London, and surely no one can keep a warmer household or finer table than the Queen? Just think of it—roaring fires. Roasted meats, wine and sweets. Clean bedclothes and thick curtains.'

Jane sighed. 'If we only live to see it all, my lady. Winter is a terrible thing indeed. I don't remember ever seeing a colder one.'

Rosamund left the maid straightening the litter's cushions and headed into the thick growth of trees at the side of the road. She told Jane she needed to use the necessary, but in truth she really needed a moment alone, a moment of quiet, to stand on solid ground and be away from the constant sway of the hated litter.

She almost regretted venturing away from the road, as her boots sank into the slushy snow-drifts and slid across frozen puddles. The trees were bare and grey, but so closely grown she soon could not see her party at all. The branches seemed to close around her like the magical thicket of a fairy tale, a new and strange world where she was alone in truth. And there were no valiant knights to ride to her rescue.

Rosamund eased back her hood, shaking her silvery-blonde hair free of its knitted caul. It fell in a heavy mantle over her shoulders, blown by the cold wind. She turned her face up to the sky, to the swirling grey clouds. Soon enough, the crowds and clamour of London would shut out this blessed silence. She would surely not even be able to hear her own thoughts there, let alone the shriek of the wind, the rattle of the naked branches.

The laughter.

The *laughter*? Rosamund frowned, listening intently. Had she stepped into a story indeed, a tale of fairies and forest sprites? Aye, there it was again, the unmistakable sound of laughter and voices. Human voices too, not fairies or the whine of the winter wind. Still feeling under an enchanted spell, she followed the trail of that merry, enticing sound.

She emerged from the woods into a clearing, suddenly facing a scene from another world, another life. There was a frozen pond, a rough circle of shimmering, silver ice. On its banks crackled a bonfire, snapping red-gold flames that sent plumes of fragrant smoke into the sky and reached enticing tendrils of heat toward Rosamund's chilled cheeks.

There were people, four of them, gathered around the fire—two men and two ladies, clad in rich velvets and furs. They laughed and chattered in the glow of the fire, sipping goblets of wine and roasting skewers of meat in the flames. And out in the very centre of that frozen pond was another man, gliding in lazy, looping circles.

Rosamund stared in utter astonishment as he twirled in a graceful, powerful arc, his lean body, sheathed only in a black, velvet doublet and leather breeches, spinning faster and faster. He was a dark blur on that shining ice, swifter than any human eye could follow. As she watched, mesmerised, his spin slowed until he stood perfectly still, a winter god on the ice.

The day too grew still; the cold, blowing wind and scudding clouds held suspended around that one man.

'Anton!' one of the ladies called, clapping her gloved hands. 'That was astounding.'

The man on the ice gave an elaborate bow before launching himself into a backward spin, a lazy meander towards the shore.

'Aye, Anton *is* astounding,' the other man, the one by the fire, said. His voice was heavy with some Slavic accent. 'An astounding peacock who must show off his gaudy feathers for the ladies.'

The skater—Anton?—laughed as he reached the snowy banks. He sat down on a fallen log to unstrap his skates, an inky-dark lock of hair falling over his brow.

'I believe I detect a note of envy, Johan,' he said, his deep voice edged with the lilting music of that same strange, northern accent. He was not even out of breath after his great feats on the ice.

Johan snorted derisively. 'Envy of your monkeyish antics on skates? I should say not!'

'Oh, I am quite sure Anton is adroit at far more than *skating*,' one of the ladies cooed. She filled a goblet with wine and took it over to Anton, her fine velvet skirts swaying. She was tall and strikingly lovely, with dark-red hair against the white of the snow. 'Is that not so?'

'In Stockholm a gentleman never contradicts a lady, Lady Essex,' he said, rising from the log to take her proffered goblet, smiling at her over its gilded rim.

'What else do they do in Stockholm?' she asked, a flirtatious note in her voice.

Anton laughed, his head tipped back to drink deeply of the wine. As he turned towards her, Rosamund had a clear view of him and she had to admit he was handsome indeed. Not quite a peacock—he was too plainly dressed for that, and he wore no jewels but a single pearl-drop in one ear. And not the same as Richard, who had a blond, ruddy, muscular Englishness. But undeniably, exotically, handsome.

He was on the tall side, and whipcord lean, no doubt from all that spinning on the ice. His hair was black as a raven's wing, falling around his face and over the high collar of his doublet in unruly waves. He impatiently pushed it back, revealing high, sharply carved cheekbones and dark, sparkling eyes.

Eyes that widened as they spied her standing there, staring at him like some addled peasant girl. He handed the lady his empty goblet and moved towards Rosamund, graceful and intent as a cat. Rosamund longed to run, to spin around and flee back into the woods, yet her feet seemed nailed into place. She could not dash off, could not even look away from him.

'Well, well,' he said, a smile touching the corner of his sensual lips. 'Who do we have here?'

Rosamund, feeling utterly flustered and foolish, was finally able to turn around and flee, Anton's startled laughter chasing her all the way back to the safety of her litter.

Chapter Two

'Very nearly there now, Lady Rosamund,' the captain of the guard said. 'Aldgate is just ahead.'

Rosamund slowly roused herself from the stupor she had fallen in to, a hazy, dream-like state formed of the cold, the tiredness—and thoughts of the mysterious Anton, that other-worldly man of dark beauty and inhuman grace spinning on the ice. Had she really seen him? Or had he been a vision?

Whatever it was, *she* had behaved like an utter ninny, running away like a frightened little rabbit—and for what? For fear? Aye, perhaps fear of falling into some sort of enchanted winter spell. She had made a mistake with Richard—she would not do that again.

'You are a very silly girl indeed,' she muttered. 'Queen Elizabeth will surely send you home as quick as can be.'

She parted the litter curtains, peering out into the grey day. While she'd dreamed and fretted, they had left the countryside behind entirely and entered a whole new world, the crowded, bustling, noisy world of London. As her little entourage passed through the gate, they joined a vast river-flow of humanity, thick knots of people hurrying on their business. Carts, coaches, horses, mules and humans on foot rushed over the frosty cobblestones, their shouts, cries and clatters all a tangled cacophony to her ears.

Rosamund had not been to London since she was a child. Her parents preferred the country, and on the few occasions when her father had to be at Court he came alone. She was educated in the ways of Queen Elizabeth's cosmopolitan Court, of course, in fashion, dancing, conversation and music. But like her parents she preferred the quiet of the country, the long days to read and think.

But after the solitary lanes and groves, with only the bird songs for company, this was astounding. Rosamund stared in utter fascination.

Their progress was slow through the narrow streets, the faint grey light turned even dimmer by the tall, close-packed, half-timbered buildings. Peaked rooflines nearly touched high above the streets, while at walkway-level shop windows were open and counters spread with fine wares: ribbons and gloves, gold and silver jewellery, beautiful leather-bound books that enticed her more than anything; their colour and shine flashed through the gloom and then were gone as she moved ever forward.

And the smell! Rosamund pressed the fur-lined edge of her cloak to her nose, her eyes watering as she tried to take a deep breath. The cold air helped; the latrine ditch along the middle of the street was almost frozen over, a noxious stew of frost, ice and waste. But there was still a miasma of rotting vegetables, horse manure and waste buckets dumped from the upper windows, overlaid with the sweetness of roasted meats and sugared nuts, cider and chimney smoke.

The previous year had been a bad plague-year, but it seemed not to have affected the London population at all to judge by the great crowds. Everyone was pushing and shoving their way past, hurrying on their business, slipping on the cobbles and the churned-up, frozen mud. They seemed too busy, or too cold, to harass the poor souls locked in the stocks.

A few ragged beggars pressed towards Rosamund's litter, but her guards shoved them back.

'Stand away, varlet!' her captain growled. 'This is one of the Queen's own ladies.'

The Queen's own lady—gawking like a milkmaid. Rosamund slumped back against her cushions, suddenly reminded of why she was here—not to stare at people and shops, but to take up duties at Court. Whitehall grew closer with every breath.

She took a small looking-glass from her embroidered travel-bag. The sight that met her gaze caused nothing but dismay. Her hair, the fine, silver-blonde strands that never wanted to be tidy, struggled from her caul. She had hastily shoved up the strands after her excursion in the woods, and it showed.

Her cheeks were bright pink with cold, her blue eyes purple-rimmed with too many restless nights. She looked like a wild forest-spirit, not a fine lady!

'My parents' hopes that I will find a spectacular match at Court are certainly in vain,' she muttered, tidying her hair the best she could. She put on her feathered, velvet cap over the caul and smoothed her gloves over her wrists.

Having made herself as tidy as possible, she peeked outside again. They had left the thickest of the city crowds behind and reached the palace of Whitehall at last.

Most of the vast complex was hidden from view,

tucked away behind walls and long, plain-fronted galleries. But Rosamund knew what lay beyond from her reading and her father's tales—large banquet-halls, palatial chambers, beautiful gardens of mazes, fountains and manicured flower-beds. All full of lushly dressed, staring, gossiping courtiers.

She drew in a deep breath, her stomach fluttering. She closed her eyes, trying to think of Richard, of anything but what awaited her behind those walls.

'My lady?' her guard said. 'We have arrived.'

She opened her eyes to find him waiting just outside the finally still litter, Jane just behind him. She nodded and held out her hand to let him assist her to alight.

For a moment, the ground seemed to rock beneath her boots; the flagstones were unsteady. The wind here was a bit colder at the foot of a staircase that led from the narrow lane in St James's Park up to the beginning of the long Privy Gallery. There were no crowds pressed close to warm the air, no close-packed buildings. Just the expanse of brick and stone, that looming staircase.

The stench too was much less, the smell of smoke and frost hanging behind her in the park. That had to be counted a blessing.

'Oh, my lady!' Jane fussed, brushing at Rosamund's cloak. 'You're all creased.'

'It does not signify, Jane,' Rosamund answered. 'We have been on a very long journey. No one expects us to be ready for a grand banquet.' She hoped. She really had no idea what to expect now that they were here. Ever since she'd glimpsed that man Anton spinning on the ice, she felt she had fallen into some new, strange life, one she did not understand at all.

She heard the hollow click of footsteps along flagstone, measured and unhurried, and she glanced up to

find a lady coming down the stairs. It could not be a
servant; her dark-green wool gown, set off by a small
yellow frill at the neck and yellow silk peeking out
from the slashed sleeves, was too fine. Grey-streaked
brown hair was smoothed up under a green cap, and her
pale, creased face was wary and watchful, that of
someone long at Court.

As she herself should be, Rosamund thought—wary
and watchful. She might be just a country mouse, but she
knew very well there were many pitfalls waiting at Court.

'Lady Rosamund Ramsay?' the woman said. 'I am
Blanche Parry, Her Grace's second gentlewoman of the
Privy Chamber. Welcome to Whitehall.'

Rosamund noticed then the polished cache of keys
at Mistress Parry's waist. She had heard tell that Blanche
Parry was truly the *first* gentlewoman, as Kat Ashley—
the official holder of the title—grew old and ill. Mistress
Ashley and the Parrys had been with the Queen since
she'd been a child; they knew all that went on at Court.
It would certainly never do to get into their ill graces.

Rosamund curtsied, hoping her tired legs would not
give out. 'How do you do, Mistress Parry? I am most
honoured to be here.'

A wry little smile touched Blanche Parry's pale lips.
'And so you should be—though I fear you may think
otherwise very soon. We will keep you very busy
indeed, Lady Rosamund, with the Christmas festivities
upon us. The Queen has ordered that there be every
trimming for the holiday this year.'

'I very much enjoy Christmas, Mistress Parry,'
Rosamund said. 'I look forward to serving Her Grace.'

'Very good. I have orders to take you to her right now.'

'Now?' Rosamund squeaked. She was to meet the
Queen *now*, in all her travel-rumpled state? She glanced

at Jane, who seemed just as dismayed. She had been planning for weeks which gown, which sleeves, which headdress Rosamund should wear to be presented to Queen Elizabeth.

Mistress Parry raised her eyebrows. 'As I said, Lady Rosamund, this is a very busy season of the year. Her Grace is most anxious that you should begin your duties right away.'

'Of—of course, Mistress Parry. Whatever Her Grace wishes.'

Mistress Parry nodded, and turned to climb the stairs again. 'If you will follow me, then? Your servants will be seen to.'

Rosamund gave Jane a reassuring nod before she hurried off after Mistress Parry. The gallery at this end was spare and silent, dark hangings on the walls muffling noise from both inside and out. A few people hurried past, but they were obviously intent on their own errands and paid her no mind.

They crossed over the road through the crenellated towers of the Holbein Gate, and were then in the palace proper. New, wide windows looked down onto the snow-dusted tiltyard. A shining blue-and-gold ceiling arched overhead, glowing warmly through the grey day, and a rich-woven carpet warmed the floor underfoot, muffling their steps.

Rosamund wasn't sure what she longed to look at first. The courtiers—clusters of people clad in bright satins and jewel-like velvets—stood near the window, talking in low, soft voices. Their words and laughter were like fine music, echoing off the panelled walls. They stared curiously at Rosamund as she passed, and she longed to stare in return.

But there were also myriad treasures on display.

There were the usual tapestries and paintings, portraits of the Queen and her family, as well as glowing Dutch still-lifes of flowers and fruits. But there were also strange curiosities collected by so many monarchs over the years and displayed in cabinets. A wind-up clock of an Ethiop riding a rhinoceros; busts of Caesar and Attila the Hun; crystals and cameos. A needlework map of England, worked by one of the Queen's many step-mothers. A painting of the family of Henry VIII, set in this very same gallery.

But Rosamund had no time to examine any of it. Mistress Parry led her onward, down another corridor. This one was lined with closed doors, quiet and dark after the sparkle of the gallery.

'Some of the Queen's ladies sleep here,' Mistress Parry said. 'The dormitory of the maids of honour is just down there.'

Rosamund glanced towards where her own lodgings would be, just before she was led onto yet another corridor. She had no idea how she would ever find her way about without getting endlessly lost! This space too was full of life and noise, more finely clad courtiers, guards in the Queen's red-and-gold livery, servants carrying packages and trays.

'And these are the Queen's own apartments,' Mistress Parry said, nodding to various people as they passed. 'If Her Grace sends you to someone with a message during the day, you will probably find them here in the Privy Chamber.'

Rosamund swept her gaze over the crowd, the chattering hoard who played cards at tables along the tapestry-lined walls, or just chatted, seemingly careless and idle. But their glances were bright and sharp, missing nothing.

'How will I know who is who?' she murmured.

Mistress Parry laughed. 'Oh, believe me, Lady Rosamund—you will learn who is who soon enough.'

A man emerged from the next chamber, tall, lean and dark, clad in a brilliant peacock-blue satin doublet. He glanced at no one from his burning-black eyes, yet everyone quickly cleared a path for him as he stalked away.

'And that is the first one you must know,' Mistress Parry said. 'The Earl of Leicester, as he has been since the autumn.'

'Really?' Rosamund glanced over her shoulder, but the dark figure had already vanished. So, *that* was the infamous Robert Dudley! The most powerful man at Court. 'He did not seem very content.'

Mistress Parry sadly shook her head. 'He is a fine gentleman indeed, Lady Rosamund, but there is much to trouble him of late.'

'Truly?' Rosamund said. She would have thought he would be over the strange death of his wife by now. But then, there were always 'troubles' on the horizon for those as lofty and ambitious as Robert Dudley. 'Such as…?'

'You will hear soon enough, I am sure,' Mistress Parry said sternly. 'Come along.'

Rosamund followed her from the crowded Privy Chamber, through a smaller room filled with fine musical instruments and then into a chamber obviously meant for dining. Fine carved tables and cushioned x-backed chairs were pushed to the dark linen-fold panelled walls along with plate-laden buffets. Rosamund glimpsed an enticing book-filled room, but she was led away from there through the sacred and silent Presence Chamber, into the Queen's own bedchamber.

And her cold nerves, forgotten in the curiosities of treasures and Lord Leicester, returned in an icy rush. She clutched tightly to the edge of her fur-lined cloak, praying she would not faint or be sick.

The bedchamber was not large, and it was rather dim, as there was only one window, with heavy red-velvet draperies drawn back from the mullioned glass. A fire blazed in the stone grate, crackling warmly and casting a red-orange glow over the space.

The bed dominated the chamber. It was a carved edifice of different woods set in complex inlaid patterns sat up on a dais, piled high with velvet-and-satin quilts and bolsters. The black velvet and cloth-of-gold hangings were looped back and bound with thick gold cords. A dressing table set near the window sparkled with fine Venetian glass bottles and pots, a locked lacquered-cabinet behind it.

There were only a few chairs and cushions scattered about, occupied by ladies in black, white, gold and green gowns. They all read or sewed quietly, but they looked up eagerly at Rosamund's appearance.

And beside the window, writing at a small desk, was a lady who could only be Queen Elizabeth herself. Now in her thirty-first year, the sixth year of her reign, she was unmistakable. Her red-gold hair, curled and pinned under a small red-velvet and pearl cap, gleamed like a sunset in the gloomy light. She looked much like her portraits, all pale skin and pointed chin, her mouth a small rosebud drawn down at the corners as she wrote. But paintings, cold and distant, could never capture the aura of sheer energy that hung all around her, like a bright, burning cloak. They could not depict the all-seeing light of her dark eyes.

The same dark eyes that smiled down from the

portrait of Anne Boleyn, which hung just to the right of the bed.

Queen Elizabeth glanced up, her quill growing still in her hand. 'This must be Lady Rosamund,' she said, her voice soft and deep, unmistakably authoritative. 'We have been expecting you.'

'Your Grace,' Rosamund said, curtsying deeply. Much to her relief, both her words and her salute were smooth and even, despite her suddenly dry throat. 'My parents send their most reverent greetings. We are all most honoured to serve you.'

Elizabeth nodded, rising slowly from her desk. She wore a gown and loose robe of crimson and gold, the fur-trimmed neck gathered close and pinned against the cold day with a pearl brooch She came to hold out her beringed hand, and Rosamund saw that her long, white fingers bore ink stains.

Rosamund quickly kissed the offered hand, and was drawn to her feet. Much to her shock, Elizabeth held onto her arm, drawing her close. She smelled of clean lavender soap, of the flowery pomander at her waist and sugary suckets; Rosamund was suddenly even more deeply aware of her own travel-stained state.

'We are very glad you have come to our Court, Lady Rosamund,' the Queen said, studying her closely. 'We have recently, sadly, lost some of our ladies, and the Christmas season is upon us. We hope you have come eager to help us celebrate.'

Celebrating had been the last thing on Rosamund's mind of late. But now, faced with the Queen's steady gaze, she surely would have agreed to anything.

'Of course, Your Grace,' she said. 'I always enjoy the Christmas festivities at Ramsay Castle.'

'I am glad to hear it,' the Queen said. 'My dear Kat

Ashley is not in good health, and she seems to live more and more in old memories of late. I want to remind her of the joyful holidays of her youth.'

'I hope to be of some service, Your Grace.'

'I am sure you shall.' The Queen finally released Rosamund's arm, returning to her desk. 'Tell me, Lady Rosamund, do you wish to marry? You are very pretty indeed, and young. Have you come to my Court to seek a handsome husband?'

Rosamund heard a quick, sharp intake of breath from one of the ladies, and the room suddenly seemed to go suddenly still and tense. She thought of Richard, of his handsome blue eyes, his futile promises. 'Nay, Your Grace,' she answered truthfully. 'I have not come here to seek a husband.'

'I am most gladdened to hear it,' Queen Elizabeth said, folding her graceful hands atop her papers. 'The married state has its uses, but I do not like to lose my ladies to its clutches. I must have their utmost loyalty and honesty, or there will be consequences—as my wilful cousin Katherine learned.'

Rosamund swallowed hard, remembering the gossip about Katherine Grey, which had even reached Ramsay Castle—married in secret to Lord Hertford, sent to the Tower to bear his child. Rosamund certainly did not want to end up like her!

'I wish only to serve Your Grace,' Rosamund said.

'And so you shall, starting this evening,' the Queen said. 'We are having a feast in honour of the Swedish delegation, and you shall be in our train.'

A feast? Already? Rosamund curtsied again. 'Of course, Your Grace.'

Elizabeth at last released Rosamund from the force of her dark gaze, turning back to her writing. 'Then you must rest until then. Mistress Percy, one of the other maids of honour, will show you to your quarters.'

A lady broke away from the group by the fireplace, a small, pretty, pert-looking brunette in white silk and a black-velvet sleeveless robe.

Rosamund curtsied one last time to the Queen and said, 'Thank you, Your Grace, for your great kindness.'

Elizabeth waved her away, and she followed the other girl back into the Presence Chamber.

'I am Anne Percy,' she said, linking arms with Rosamund as if they had known each other for months rather than minutes.

Rosamund had no sisters, nor even any close female friends; Ramsay Castle was too isolated for such things. She wasn't sure what to make of Mistress Percy's easy-going manner or her open smile, but it *was* nice to feel she was not quite alone at Court.

'And I am Rosamund Ramsay,' she answered, not certain what else to say.

Anne laughed, steering Rosamund around a group of young men who hovered near the doorway. One of them smiled and winked at Anne, but she pointedly turned her head away from him.

'I know,' Anne said as they emerged from the Queen's apartments into the corridor again. 'We have been talking of nothing but you for days!'

'Talking of *me*?' Rosamund said in astonishment. 'But I have never been to Court before. And, even if I had, I would look terribly dull next to all the exciting things that happen here.'

Anne gave an unladylike snort. 'Exciting? Oh, Lady Rosamund, surely you jest? Our days are long indeed, and always much of a sameness. We have been talking of you because we have not seen a new face among the ladies in months and months. We have been counting on you to bring us fresh tales of gossip!'

'Gossip?' Rosamund said, laughing. She thought of the long, sweet days at Ramsay Castle, hours whiled away in sewing, reading, playing the lute—devising foolish ways to meet Richard. 'I fear I have very little of that. No matter what you say, I would vow life in the country is far duller than here at Court. At least you do see people every day, even if they are always the same people.'

'True enough. At my brother's estate, I sometimes had to talk to the sheep just to hear my own voice!' Anne giggled, an infectiously merry sound that made Rosamund want to giggle too.

'Since I know so little of Court doings, *you* must tell me all *I* need to know,' Rosamund said. 'Maybe then the tales will seem fresh again.'

'Ah, now that I can do,' Anne said. 'A maid of honour's duties are few enough, as you will find. We walk with the Queen in the gardens, we go with her to church and stand in her train as she greets foreign envoys. We sew and read with her—and try to duck when she is in a fearsome mood and throws a shoe at us.'

'Nay?' Rosamund gasped.

Anne nodded solemnly. 'Ask Mary Howard where she got that dent in her forehead—and *she* is even the daughter of the Queen's great-uncle! But that is only on very bad days. Most of the time she just ignores us.'

'Then if our duties are so few what do we do with our time?'

'We watch, of course. And learn.' Anne paused in the curve of a bow window along the gallery. Below them was an elegant expanse of garden; neat, gravel walkways wound between square beds outlined in low box-hedges. The fountains were still, frozen over in the winter weather, the flowers and greenery slumbering under a light mantel of silvery frost and snow.

But there was no lack of colour and life. Yet more people flowed along the walkways, twining like a colorful snake in pairs and groups, their velvets and furs taking the place of the flowers.

Rosamund recognised Leicester's peacock-blue doublet, his black hair shining in the grey light. He stood among a cluster of other men, all more sombrely clad than he, and even from that distance Rosamund could still sense the anger etched on his handsome, swarthy face.

'We have no fewer than three important delegations with us for this Christmas season,' Anne said. 'And they all loathe each other. It provides us with much amusement, watching them vie for Her Grace's attention.' She lowered her voice to a confiding whisper. 'They will probably try to persuade you to plead their cause to the Queen.'

'Do you mean *bribes*?' Rosamund whispered back.

'Oh, aye.' Anne held out her wrist to display a fine pearl bracelet. 'But be very careful which faction you choose to have your dealings with, Lady Rosamund.'

'And what are my choices?'

'Well, over there you see the Austrians.' Anne gestured towards one end of the garden, where a cluster of men clad in plain black and gray hovered like a murder of crows. 'They are here to present the case for their candidate for the Queen's hand—Archduke Charles. Truly, they are like the new Spanish, since King Philip has given up at last and married his French princess. No one takes them seriously, except themselves. And *they* are very serious indeed.'

'How very dreary,' Rosamund said. 'Who else?'

'Over there we have the Scots,' Anne said, turning to another group. They did not wear primitive plaids, as Rosamund would have half-hoped, but very fashionable silks in tones of jewel-bright purple, green and gold. But then, they did serve a very fashionable queen indeed. Perhaps Queen Mary made them wear French styles.

'That is their leader, Sir James Melville, and his assistant, Secretary Maitland. And Maitland's cousin, Master Macintosh,' Anne continued. 'They are the tall ones there, with the red hair. They certainly seem more lighthearted than the Austrians. They dance and play cards every night, and Her Grace seems fond of them. But I would not be too open and honest around them.'

'Why is that? Why are they here? Surely they can have no marriages to propose?'

'On the contrary. The Queen of Scots is *most* concerned with her own marriage prospects.'

Rosamund stared down at the Scotsmen in the garden. 'She seeks an English match? After being married to the King of France?'

'Perhaps. But not the one Queen Elizabeth would have her make.'

'What do you mean?'

Anne leaned closer, her voice such a soft whisper Rosamund could hardly make it out. 'Queen Elizabeth desires Queen Mary to take Robert Dudley as her consort. They say that is why she made him an earl last autumn.'

'Nay!' Rosamund gasped. 'But I thought the Queen herself…?'

Anne nodded. 'So do we all. It is passing strange. I'm sure Melville thinks so as well, which is why he bides his time here rather than hurrying back to Queen Mary to press such an offer.'

'So, that is why the Earl stalks about like a thunder-cloud?'

'Indeed.'

'But then who is the third delegation? How do they fit into these schemes?'

Anne laughed delightedly; every hint of the serious-ness she'd showed when discussing the Austrians and the Scots vanished. 'Now, they are a very different matter, the Swedes.'

'The Swedes?'

'They are here to present again the suit of their own master, King Eric,' Anne said. 'It seems he is in great need of a powerful wife's assistance, with war looming with both Denmark and Russia, and possibly France, and his own brother scheming against him.'

'He doesn't sound like a very attractive marital prospect,' Rosamund said doubtfully.

'Oh, not at all! That is why he was already rejected a few years ago. I'm sure Her Grace has no intention of accepting him—or not much.'

'Then why does she keep his delegation here?'

'Why, see for yourself!' Anne pointed as a new group entered the garden through one of the stone archways. They were a handsome gathering indeed, tall and golden, well-muscled in their fine doublets and fur-lined short cloaks, laughing and as powerful as Norse gods entering Valhalla.

And, right in their midst, was the most handsome and intriguing of all—the mysterious Anton, he of the amazing feats on the ice.

He carried his skates slung over his shoulder, shining silver against the black velvet and leather of his doublet. A flat, black velvet cap covered his inky-dark hair, but his radiant smile gleamed in the grey day.

The striking red-haired lady from the pond held onto his arm, staring up at him with a rapt expression on her sharp-featured face, as if her very breath depended on his next word.

Rosamund feared she knew very well how that woman felt. Her own breath was tight in her throat, and her face felt warm despite the chill of the window glass.

Think of Richard, she urged herself, closing her eyes tightly. Yet even as she tried to remember Richard's summer kisses, the way his arms had felt around her as he pulled her close, all she could see was a man spinning across the winter ice.

'That is why the Queen keeps them here,' Anne said. 'They have proved a great ornament to the Court— almost worth the trouble.'

Rosamund opened her eyes. Anton was still there, whispering in the lady's ear as she covered her mouth with her gloved hand, no doubt hiding a peal of flirtatious laughter.

'Trouble?' she murmured. Oh, aye; she could see where he would be a great deal of trouble, especially to a Court full of bored ladies.

'The Swedes and the Austrians detest each other,' Anne said cheerfully. 'The Queen has had to strictly forbid duels. And I am sure the Scots are involved somehow, though I have not yet devised how.'

'Oh.' Rosamund nodded, rather confused. She certainly did have a great deal to learn about Court life! Translating Greek manuscripts was simple compared to the complexities of alliances.

'That dark one there—Anton Gustavson, his name is,' Anne said, gesturing to the handsome Anton. 'He is only half-Swedish, they say. His mother was English. He has come to England not only on behalf of King Eric but on his own errand. His grandfather has left him an estate in Suffolk, a most profitable manor, and he wants to claim it. But he is in dispute with a cousin over the property.'

Rosamund watched as Anton laughed with the lady, the two of them strolling the walkways as if they hadn't a care in the world. 'I can scarce imagine a man like that in dispute with anyone. Surely he could charm the very birds of the trees into his hand?'

Anne gave her a sharp glance. 'You have met Master Gustavson, then?'

Rosamund shook her head. 'That is merely what I observe from watching him now.'

'Oh, you must be wary of such observations! Here at Court, appearances are always deceiving. One never shows one's true nature; it is the only way to survive.'

'Indeed? And must I be wary of you, too, Mistress Percy?'

'Of course,' Anne said happily. 'My family, you see, is an old and wealthy one, but also stubbornly Catholic. I am here only on sufferance, because my aunt is friends with the Queen. But I will tell you this, Lady Rosamund—I am always an honest source of delicious gossip for my friends.'

Rosamund laughed. 'Tell me this, then, Mistress Honesty—who is that lady with Master Gustavson? Does he seek an English wife to go along with that new estate?'

Anne peered out of the window again. 'If he does, he has made a great mistake with that one. That is Lettice Devereaux, Countess of Essex—the Queen's cousin. Her husband the earl is away fighting the wild Irish, but it does not stop her making merry at Court.' She tugged at Rosamund's arm, drawing her away from the window and its enticing view. 'Come, let me show you our chamber. I will have much more gossip to share before the feast tonight.'

The feast in honour of those same quarrelling delegations, Rosamund remembered as she followed Anne along the corridor. It certainly should be a most interesting evening.

Perhaps if she wrote to Richard about it he would write to her in return? If he ever received the letter, that was. He was a country gentleman, not much interested in labyrinthine Court affairs, but he did enjoy a fine jest. It was one of the things she had liked about him. That was if she still wanted to hear from him, which she was not at all sure of.

Anne led Rosamund back to one of the quieter, narrower halls. It was dark here, as there were no windows, and the torches in their sconces were not yet lit. The painted cloths that hung along the walls swayed as they passed. Rosamund thought surely the intrigues of Court were already affecting her, for she imagined all the schemes that could be whispered of in such a spot.

'That is the Privy Council Chamber,' Anne whispered, indicating a half-open door. The room was empty, but Rosamund glimpsed a long table lined with straight-backed chairs. 'We maids *never* go in there.'

'Don't you ever wonder what happens there?' Rosamund whispered in return. 'What is said?'

'Of course! But Her Grace does not ask our opinion on matters of state. Though she does ask us for news of Court doings, which is much the same thing.'

She tugged on Rosamund's arm again, leading her into what could only be the chamber of the maids of honour. A long, narrow, rectangular space, it was lined with three beds on each side. They were certainly not as large and grand as the Queen's own sleeping space. The beds were made of dark, uncarved wood, but they were spread with warm, green velvet-and-wool quilts and hung with heavy, gold-embroidered green curtains. A large clothes chest and a washstand stood by each bed, and the rest of the room was filled with dressing tables and looking glasses.

It was a peaceful enough space now, but Rosamund could imagine the cacophony when six ladies were in residence.

Her maid Jane was at one of the beds on the far end, unpacking Rosamund's trunks; she clucked and fussed over the creased garments. The satins, velvets, brocades and furs her parents had provided were all piled up in a gleaming heap.

'Oh, wonderful!' Anne exclaimed. 'You are in the bed beside mine. We can whisper at night. It has been so quiet since Eleanor Mortimer left.'

'What happened to her?' Rosamund asked, picking up a sable muff that had fallen from the pile of finery.

'The usual thing, I fear. She became pregnant and had to leave Court in disgrace. She is quite fortunate she didn't end up in the Tower, like poor Katherine Grey!' Anne perched on the edge of her own bed, swinging her feet in their satin shoes. 'Did you mean it when you told the Queen you were not here to find a husband?'

'Of a certes,' Rosamund said, thinking again of Richard. Of the letters from him she had never received. One man to worry about at a time was enough.

'That is very good. You must keep saying that—and meaning it. Marriage without the Queen's permission brings such great trouble. Oh, Rosamund! You should wear that petticoat tonight, it is vastly pretty…'

Chapter Three

'She wants you, Anton,' Johan Ulfson said. He was laughing, yet his tone was tinged with unmistakable envy.

Anton watched Lady Essex stroll slowly away along the garden pathway, her dark-red hair a beacon in the winter day. She peeked back over her shoulder, then swept off with her friends, their laughter drifting back on the cold wind.

He had to laugh, too. The young countess was alluring indeed, with her sparkling eyes, teasing smiles and her claims of vast loneliness with her husband away in Ireland. He could even enjoy the flirtation, the distraction from the hard tasks he carried here at the English Queen's Court. But he saw it—and Lettice Deveraux—for what they were.

And now he could hardly see the countess's red hair and lush figure. A vision of silver and ivory, of wide blue eyes, kept overtaking his thoughts. Who was she, that beautiful winter-fairy? Why had she run away so fast, vanishing into the mist and snow before he could talk to her?

How could he ever find her again?

'You are blind when it comes to a pretty face,' he told Johan, but he could just as well be talking of himself. 'The countess has other game in her sights. I am merely a pawn for her.'

He inclined his head towards Lord Leicester, who stood across the garden amid a cluster of his supporters. Everyone at this Court seemed entirely unable to move singly; they had to rove about in packs, like the white wolves of Sweden.

Lady Essex might have her sights firmly on *him*, but Leicester had his on a far greater prize. It would be amusing to see which of them prevailed.

If Anton would be here to see the end-game at all. He might be settling into his own English estate, the birthright that should have been his mother's. Or he might be back in Stockholm, walking the perilous tightrope at the court of an increasingly erratic king and his rebellious, ambitious brother. Either way, he had to fulfill his mission now or face unpleasant consequences.

Lady Essex was a distraction, aye, but one he could easily manage. When she was away, he thought not of her. That winter-fairy, though...

Perhaps it was a good thing he did not know who she was, or where to find her. He sensed that she would be one distraction not so easily put away.

'Pawn or no, Anton, you should take what she offers,' Johan said. 'Our days are dull enough here without such amusements as we can find.'

'*Ja,*' Nils Vernerson added, his own stare sweeping over the occupants of the frost-fringed gardens. 'The Queen will never accept King Eric. She merely plays with us for her amusement.'

'Is it better to be the plaything of a queen?' Anton

said, laughing. 'Or a countess? If our fate this Christmas is only to provide entertainment for the ladies.'

'I can think of worse fates,' Johan muttered. 'Such as being sent to fight the Russians.'

'Better to fight wars of words with Queen Elizabeth,' said Nils, 'than battle Tsar Ivan and his barbaric hoards on the frozen steppes. I hope we are never recalled to Stockholm.'

'Better we do our duty to Sweden here, among the bored and lonely ladies of the Queen's train,' Anton said. 'They should help make our Christmas merry indeed.'

'If you ever solve your puzzle,' Johan said.

'And which puzzle is that?' said Anton. 'We live with so many of late.'

'*You* certainly do. But you have not yet said—do you prefer to serve the needs of the countess, or the Queen?'

'Or another of your endless parade of admirers,' Nils said as Mary Howard and two of her friends strolled past, giggling. Mary glanced at Anton, then looked quickly away, blushing.

'They are all enamoured after your great bouts of showing off on the ice,' Nils said, sounding disgruntled indeed.

'And now that the Thames is near frozen over he will have even more such opportunities,' Johan added.

'You can be sure all the ladies will find excuses to be in the Queen's Riverside Gallery just to watch,' Nils said. 'To blow kisses and toss flowers from the windows.'

Anton laughed, turning away from their teasing. He relished those stolen moments on the ice, speeding along with no thought except of the cold, the movement, the rare, wondrous rush of freedom. Could he help it if others too wanted to share in that freedom, in that feeling of flying above the cold, hard earth and all its complex cares?

'They merely want to learn how to skate,' he said.

'Skate, is it?' Nils answered. 'I have never heard it called *that*.'

Anton shook his head, twirling his skates over his shoulder as he strolled towards the palace. 'You should turn your attention to the feast tonight,' he called back. 'Her Grace deplores lateness.'

'So you have decided to be the *Queen's* amusement, then?' Nils said as he and Johan hurried to catch up.

Anton laughed. 'I haven't Lord Leicester's fortitude in such matters, I fear. I could not amuse her for long. Nor could I ever have Melville's and Maitland's devotion. To serve two queens, Scots and English, would be exhausting indeed. But we were sent here to perform a diplomatic task, *van*. If by making merry in Her Grace's Great Hall we may accomplish that, we must do it.'

He grinned at them, relishing the looks of bafflement on their faces. So much the better if he could always keep everyone guessing as to his true meaning, his true motives. 'Even if it is a great sacrifice indeed to drink the Queen's wine and talk with her pretty ladies.'

He turned from them, running up a flight of stone stairs towards the gallery. Usually crowded with the curious, the bored, and those hurrying on very important errands, at this hour the vast space was near empty. Everyone was tucked away in their own corners, carefully choosing their garments for the evening ahead.

Plotting their next move in the never-ending game of Court life.

He needed to do the same. He had heard that his cousin

had recently arrived at Whitehall to plot the next counter-move in the game of Briony Manor. Anton had not yet met with his opponent, but Briony was a ripe plum, indeed. Neither of them was prepared to let it go without a fight, no matter what their grandfather's will commanded.

But Anton could be a fierce opponent, too. Briony meant much more than a mere house, a mere parcel of land. He was ready to do battle for it—even if the battle was on a tiltyard of charm, flirtation and deception.

He turned towards the apartments given to the Swedish delegation, hidden amid the vast warrens of Whitehall's corridors. As he did, his attention was caught by a soft flurry of laughter. It was quiet, muffled, but bright as a golden ribbon, woven through the grey day and heavy thoughts.

'Shh!' he heard a lady whisper. 'It's this way, but we have to hurry.'

'Oh, Anne! I'm not sure…'

Curious, Anton peered around the corner to see two female figures clad in the silver and white of maids of honour tiptoe along a narrow, windowless passage. One was Anne Percy, a pretty, pert brunette who had caught Johan's devoted attention.

And the lady with her was his winter-fairy; her silvery-blonde hair shimmered in the shadows. For an instant he could hardly believe it. He had almost come to think her a dream, a woodland creature of snow and ice who did not really exist.

Yet there she was, giggling as she crept through the palace. She glanced back over her shoulder as Anton slid back into the concealment of the shadows, and he saw that it unmistakably *was* her. She had that fairy's pale, heart-shaped face with bright-blue eyes that fairly glowed.

For an instant, her shoulders stiffened and she went very still. Anton feared she'd spotted him, but then Anne Percy tugged on her arm and the two of them vanished around a corner.

He stared at the spot where she had been for a long moment. The air there seemed to shimmer, as if a star had danced down for only an instant then had shot away. Who was she?

His fanciful thoughts were interrupted by the clatter of Johan and Nils catching up with him at last.

'What are you staring at?' Nils asked.

Anton shook his head hard, trying to clear it of fairy dreams, of useless distractions. 'I thought I heard something,' he said.

''Twas probably one of your admirers lying in wait for you,' Johan laughed.

Anton smiled ruefully. If only that was so. But he was certain, from the way she had run away from him by the pond, that would never be. And that was a fortunate thing indeed. There was no room in his life for enchanting winter-fairies and their spells.

He found himself loath to ruin her happy sparkle with his dark, icy touch and uncertain future.

Chapter Four

❧

The Queen's feast was not held in her Great Hall, which was being cleaned and readied for the start of the Christmas festivities, but in a smaller chamber near her own apartments. Yet it felt no less grand. Shimmering tapestries, scenes of summer hunts and picnics, warmed the dark-panelled walls, and a fire blazed away in the grate. Its red-orange glow cast heat and flickering light over the low, gilt-laced ceiling and over the fine plates and goblets that lined the white damask-draped tables.

Two lutenists played a lively tune as Rosamund took her place on one of the cushioned benches below the Queen's, and liveried servants carried in the heavily laden platters and poured out ale and spiced wine.

Rosamund thought she must still be tired from the journey, from trying to absorb these new surroundings, for the scene seemed to be one vast, colourful whirl, like looking at the world through a shard of stained glass where everything was distorted. Laughter was loud; the clink of knives on silver was like thunder. The scent of wine, roasted meats, wood smoke and flowery perfumes was sharper.

She sat with the other maids in a group rather than scattered among the guests, all of them like a flock of winter wrens in their white-and-silver gowns. That was a relief to her, not having to converse yet with the sharp-eyed courtiers. Instead, she merely sipped at her wine and listened to Anne quarrel with Mary Howard.

Queen Elizabeth sat above the crowd on her dais, with the Austrian ambassador, Adam von Zwetko-vich, to one side and the head of the Swedish delegation to the other. Luckily, he was not the dark, skating man of the handsome smile, but a shorter, stockier blond man, who spent most of his time glaring at the Austrians. On his other side was the Scottish Sir James Melville.

But, if the dark Swede was not there, where was he? Rosamund sat with her back to the other table set in the U-formation, and she had to strongly resist the urge to glance behind her.

'Rosamund, you must try some of this,' Anne said, sliding a bit of spiced pork pie onto Rosamund's plate. 'It is quite delicious, and you have had nothing to eat since you arrived.'

''Tis not at all fashionable to be so slight,' Mary Howard sniffed, derisively eyeing Rosamund's narrow shoulders in her silver-satin sleeves. 'Perhaps they care not for fashion in the country, but here, Lady Rosa-mund, you will find it of utmost importance.'

'It is better than not being able to fit into one's bodice,' Anne retorted. 'Or mayhap such over-tight lacing is meant to catch Lord Fulkes's eye?'

'Even though he is betrothed to Lady Ponsonby,' said Catherine Knyvett, another of the maids.

Mary Howard tossed her head. 'I care not a fig for Lord Fulkes, *or* his betrothed. I merely wished to give

Lady Rosamund some friendly advice as she is so newly arrived at Court.'

'I hardly think she needs *your* advice,' Anne said. 'Most of the men in this room cannot keep their eyes off her already.'

'Anne, that is not true,' Rosamund murmured. She suddenly wished she could run and hide under her bed-clothes, away from all the quarrels.

'Rosamund, you are too modest,' Anne said. 'Look over there, you will see.'

Anne tugged on Rosamund's arm, forcing her to turn to face the rest of the chamber. She did not see what Anne meant; everyone appeared to be watching the Queen, gauging her mood, matching their laughter to hers. She was the star they all revolved around, and she looked it tonight in a shining gown of gold brocade and black velvet, her pale-red hair bound with a gold corona head-dress.

But one person did not watch the Queen. Instead he stared at her, Rosamund, with steady, dark intensity: Anton Gustavson. Aye, it was truly him.

He had been really beautiful in the cold, clear light of day, laughing as he'd flown so swiftly over the perilous ice, other-worldly in that aura of effortless happiness.

Here in the Queen's fine palace, lit by firelight and torches, he was no less handsome. His hair, so dark it was nearly black, was brushed back from his brow in a glossy cap and shone like a raven's wing. The flames flickered in shadows and light over the sharp, chiselled angles of his face, the high cheekbones and strong jaw.

But he no longer laughed. He was solemn as he watched her, the corners of his sensual lips turned down ever so slightly. He wore a doublet of dark-purple velvet inset with black satin that only emphasised that solemnity.

Rosamund's bodice suddenly felt as tight as Mary Howard's, pressing in on her until she could hardly take a breath. Something disquieting fluttered in her stomach. Her cheeks burned, as if she sat too close to the fire, yet she shivered.

What was wrong with her? What did he think when he looked at her so very seriously? Perhaps he remembered how ridiculous she had been, running away from him by the pond.

She forced herself to lift her chin, meeting his gaze steadily. Slowly those lips lifted in a smile, revealing a quick flash of surprisingly white teeth. It transformed the starkly elegant planes of his face, making him seem more the man of sunlight and ice.

Yet his dark-brown eyes, shielded by thick lashes longer than a man had a right to, were still unfathomable.

Rosamund found herself smiling back. She could no more keep herself from doing it than she could keep herself from breathing, his smile was so infectious. But she was also confused, flustered, and she turned away.

Servants cleared away the remains of the meat pies and the stewed vegetables and laid out fish and beef dishes in sweetened sauces, pouring out more wine. Rosamund nibbled at a bit of fricasséed rabbit, wondering if Anton Gustavson still watched her. Wondering what he thought of her, what was hidden behind those midnight eyes.

'Oh, why do I even care?' she muttered, ripping up a bit of fine white manchet-bread.

'What is it you care about, Rosamund?' Anne asked. 'Did one of the gentlemen catch your eye?'

Rosamund shook her head. She could hardly tell Anne how handsome and intriguing she found Anton

Gustavson. Anne was already an amusing companion, and she surely could offer some sage advice on the doings at Court, but Rosamund feared she would not refrain from teasing.

'I will tell you a secret, Anne,' she whispered. 'If you swear to keep it.'

'Oh, yes,' Anne breathed, wide-eyed. 'I am excellent at secret-keeping.'

'I have no interest in Court gentlemen,' Rosamund said, 'Because there is a gentleman at home I like.' Perhaps that would make Anne let her alone!

'A gentleman at home?' Anne squeaked.

'Shh!' Rosamund hissed. They could say no more as servants delivered yet more dishes.

'You must tell me more later,' Anne said.

Rosamund nodded. She didn't really want to talk about Richard, but surely better that than Master Gustavson. She poked her eating knife at a roasted pigeon in mint sauce. 'How is so much eaten every night?'

'Oh, this is naught!' Mary Howard said. 'Wait until the Christmas Eve banquet, Lady Rosamund. There will be dozens and dozens of dishes. And plum cake!'

'We never can eat all of it,' Anne said. 'Not even Mary!'

Mary ignored her. 'The dishes that are not used are given to the poor.'

As the talk among the maids turned to Court gossip—such as who stole unbroken meats from tables which they were not entitled to—sweet wafers stamped with falcons and Tudor roses were brought to the tables. The wine flowed on, making the chatter brighter and louder, and the laughter freer. Even Rosamund felt herself growing easier.

She almost forgot to wonder if Anton Gustavson still watched her. Almost. She peeked back at him once, only to find he was talking quietly with a lady in tawny-and-gold silk. The woman watched him very closely, her lips parted, as if his every word was vital to her.

Unaccountably disappointed, Rosamund swung back to face forward again. She certainly hoped that life at Court would never make *her* behave like that.

As the last of the sweets was cleared away, the Queen rose to her feet, her hands lifted as her jewelled rings flashed in the firelight. The loud conversation fell into silence.

'My dear friends,' she said. 'I thank you for joining me this eve to honour these guests to our Court. This has only been a small taste of the Christmas revels that await us in the days to come. But the evening is yet new, and I hope Master Vernerson will honour us with a dance.'

Nils Vernerson bowed in agreement, and everyone rose from their places to wait along the walls as servants pushed back the tables, benches and chairs and more musicians filed in to join the lutenists. Anton stood across the room, the attentive lady still at his elbow, but Rosamund turned away.

'I do hope you know the newest dances from Italy, Lady Rosamund,' said Mary Howard, all wide-eyed concern. 'A graceful turn on the dance floor is so very important to the Queen.'

'It is kind of you to worry about me, Mistress Howard,' Rosamund answered sweetly. 'But I did have a dancing master at my home, as well as lessons in the lute and the virginals. And a tutor for Latin, Spanish, Italian and French.'

Mary Howard's lips thinned. 'It is unfortunate your studies did not include Swedish. It is all the rage at Court this season.'

'As if she knows anything beyond *"ja"* and *"nej"*,'

Anne whispered to Rosamund. 'Mostly *ja*—in case she gets the chance to use it with Master Gustavson! It is very sad he has not even looked at her.'

Rosamund started to laugh, but quickly stifled her giggles and stood up straighter as she saw the Queen sweeping towards them on the arm of the Scottish Secretary Maitland.

'Mistress Percy,' the Queen said. 'Secretary Maitland has asked if you will be his partner in this galliard.'

'Of course, Your Grace,' Anne said, curtsying.

'And Lady Rosamund,' Queen Elizabeth said, turning her bright, dark gaze onto Rosamund. 'I hope you have come to my Court prepared to dance as well?'

'Yes, Your Grace,' Rosamund answered, echoing Anne with a curtsy. 'I very much enjoy dancing.'

'Then I hope you will be Master Macintosh's partner. He has already proven to be quite light on his feet.'

A tall, broad-shouldered man with a mane of red hair and a close-trimmed red beard bowed to her and held out his arm.

Rosamund let him lead her into the forming dance-set, feeling confident for the first time since setting foot in Whitehall. Her dance lessons in preparation for coming to Court had been the one bright spot amid the quarrels with her parents, the tears over leaving Richard. For those moments of spinning, leaping and turning, she had been lost in the music and the movement, leaving herself entirely behind.

Her instructor had told her she had a natural gift for the dance—unlike conversation with people she did not know well! That often left her sadly tongue-tied. But dancing seldom required talk, witty or otherwise.

The dance, though, had not yet begun, and could not until the Queen took her place to head the figures. Her

Grace was still strolling around the room, matching up couples who seemed reluctant to dance. Rosamund stood facing Master Macintosh, carefully smoothing her sleeves and trying to smile.

'Lady Rosamund Ramsay,' he said affably, as if he sensed her shyness. But there was something in his eyes she did not quite care for. 'Ramsay is a Scottish name too, I think?'

'Perhaps it was, many years ago,' Rosamund answered. 'My great-grandfather had an estate along the borders.' From which he had liked to conduct raids against his Scots neighbours, for which the Queen's grandfather had rewarded him with a more felicitous estate in the south and an earldom. But that did not seem a good thing to mention in polite converse with a Scotsman!

'Practically my countrywoman, then,' he said.

'I fear I have never seen Scotland. This is as far as I have ever been from home.'

'Ah, so you are new to Court. I was sure I would remember such a pretty face if we had met before.'

Rosamund laughed. 'You are very kind, Master Macintosh.'

'Nay, I only speak the truth. It's a Scots failing—we have little talent for courtly double-speak. You are quite the prettiest lady in this room, Lady Rosamund, and I must speak honestly.'

Rosamund laughed again, eyeing his fine saffron-and-black garments and the jewelled thistle pinned at the high collar of his doublet. The thistle, of course, signified his service to the Queen of Scots—a lady most gifted in 'courtly double-speak', from what Rosamund heard tell. 'You certainly would not be a disgrace to any court, Master Macintosh. Not even one as fine I hear as Queen Mary keeps at Edinburgh.'

He laughed too. 'Ah, now, Lady Rosamund, I see you learn flattery already. Queen Mary does indeed keep a merry Court, and we're all proud to serve her interests here.'

Interests such as matrimony? Rosamund noticed that Robert Dudley stood in the shadows with his friends, a dark, sombre figure despite his bright-scarlet doublet. He did not join the dance, though Rosamund had heard before that he was always Queen Elizabeth's favourite partner. He certainly did not look the eager prospective bridegroom, to either queen.

'Is she as beautiful as they say, your Queen Mary?' she asked.

Master Macintosh's gaze narrowed. 'Aye, she's bonny as they come.'

Rosamund glanced at Queen Elizabeth, who fairly glowed with an inner fire and energy, with a bright laughter as she swept towards the dance floor with Master Vernerson. 'As beautiful as Queen Elizabeth?'

'Ah, now, you will have to judge that for yourself, Lady Rosamund. They say beauty is in the eye of the beholder.'

'Will I have that chance? Is Queen Mary coming here on a state visit soon?'

'She has long been eager to meet her cousin Queen Elizabeth, but I know of no such plans at present. Perhaps Lord Leicester will let you study Queen Mary's portrait, which hangs in his apartments. Then you must tell me which you find fairer.'

Rosamund had no time to answer, for the musicians started up a lively galliard, and the Queen launched off the hopping patterns of the dance. Rosamund had no idea what she could have said anyway. She had no desire to be in the midst of complex doings of queens and their courtiers. She liked her quiet country-life.

Even being at Court for a mere few hours was making the world look strange, as if the old, comfortable, familiar patterns were cracking and peeling away slowly, bit by bit. She could see glimpses of new colours, new shapes, but they were not yet clear.

She took Macintosh's hand and turned around him in a quick, skipping step, spinning lightly before they circled the next couple. In her conversation with him, she had forgotten to look for Anton Gustavson, to see where he was in the chamber. But as she hopped about for the next figure of the dance she was suddenly face to face with him.

He did not dance, just stood alongside the dance floor, his arms crossed over his chest as he watched their merriment. A small, unreadable smile touched his lips, and his eyes were dark as onyx in the flickering half-light.

Rosamund found she longed to run up to him, to demand to know what he was thinking, what he saw when he looked out over their gathering. When he looked at *her*.

As if he guessed something of her thoughts, he gave her a low, courtly bow.

She spun away, back into the centre of the dance, as they all spun faster and faster. That sense she had of shifting, of breaking, only increased as the chamber melted into a blur around her, a whirl of colour and light. When she at last slowed, swaying dizzily in the final steps of the pattern, Anton had vanished.

As the music ended Rosamund curtsied to Master Macintosh's bow. 'Are you quite certain you have never been to Court before, Lady Rosamund?' he asked laughingly, taking her hand to lead her back to the other maids.

'Oh yes,' Rosamund answered. 'I am certain I would remember such a long journey!'

'You dance as if you had been here a decade,' he said. His voice lowered to a whisper. 'Better even than your queen, my lady, though you must never tell I said so!'

With one more bow, he departed, leaving Rosamund standing with Anne Percy.

'Did you enjoy your dance with the Scotsman, Rosamund?' Anne asked.

'Yes, indeed,' Rosamund said.

'That is good. I wouldn't be *too* friendly with him, though.'

'Why is that, Anne?'

'They say he has been meeting often of late with Lady Lennox, Margaret Stewart.'

'The Queen's cousin?'

'Aye, the very one.' Anne gestured with her fan towards a stout, pale-faced lady clad in heavy black satin. She stood near the fireplace, watching the merry proceedings with a rather sour look on her face. 'She cares not for the Queen's scheme to marry Leicester to Queen Mary, and it is said that some of the Scots party agree with her.'

Rosamund eyed the dour woman suspiciously. 'Whose marital cause would they advance instead?'

'Why, that of Lady Lennox's own son, Lord Darnley, of course. I don't see his Lordship here tonight. He must be off chasing the maidservants—or the manservants—as his mood strikes him,' Anne said.

'I vow I will never remember who is who here,' Rosamund muttered. 'Or who is against who!'

Anne laughed. 'Oh, you will remember soon enough! They will all make sure you do.'

They could say no more, for Queen Elizabeth was hurrying towards them, the Austrians and Swedes with her. They looked like nothing so much as an eager flotilla drifting in the wake of a magnificent flagship.

Rosamund and Anne curtsied, and as Rosamund rose to her feet she found Anton Gustavson watching her again. He no longer smiled, and yet she had the distinct sense he was still strangely amused.

By her? she wondered. By the whole glittering scene? Or by some secret jest none could share?

How she wished he was a book, a text of Latin or Greek she could translate, if she only worked diligently enough. Books always revealed their mysteries, given time. But she feared the depths of Anton Gustavson would be too much for her to plumb.

Then again, perhaps she was too hasty, she thought, studying his lean, handsome body sheathed in the fine velvet. She had not even yet spoken to him.

'You are a good dancer, Lady Rosamund,' the Queen said. 'I see your lessons were not in vain. It was Master Geoffrey who went to Ramsay Castle, was it not?'

'Yes, Your Grace,' Rosamund answered, tearing her gaze from Anton to the Queen. Elizabeth's stare was so steady, so bright, that Rosamund was quite sure she could read every tiny, hidden secret. 'I enjoy dancing very much, though I fear I have much to learn.'

'You are too modest, Lady Rosamund. Surely you have not so much to learn as some at Court.' The Queen turned suddenly to Anton. 'Master Gustavson here claims he cannot dance at all.'

'Not at all, Your Grace?' Rosamund remembered how he had looked on the ice, all fluid grace and power. 'I cannot believe that to be so.'

'Exactly, Lady Rosamund. It is quite unthinkable

for anyone *not* to dance at my Court, especially with the most festive of seasons upon us.'

Anton bowed. 'I fear I have never had the opportunity to learn, Your Grace. And I am a dismally clumsy oaf.'

Now, Rosamund knew *that* to be a falsehood! No one could possibly even have stood upright on the ice balanced on two thin, little blades, let alone spin about, if they'd been a 'clumsy oaf'.

'No one is entirely unable to learn to dance,' Elizabeth insisted. 'Perhaps they have not as much natural enjoyment of the exercise as I have, or as it seems Lady Rosamund has. But everyone can learn the steps and move in the correct direction in time to the music.'

Anton bowed. 'I fear I may prove the sad exception, Your Grace.'

The Queen's gaze narrowed, and she tapped one slender, white finger on her chin. 'Would you care to make a wager, Master Gustavson?'

He raised one dark brow, boldly meeting the Queen's challenging stare. 'What terms did Your Grace have in mind?'

'Only this—I wager that anyone can dance, even a Swede, given the proper teacher. To prove it, you must try and a dance a volta for us on Twelfth Night. That will give you time for a goodly number of lessons, I think.'

'But I fear I know of no teachers, Your Grace,' Anton said, that musical northern accent of his thick with laughter. *Why*, Rosamund realised, *he is actually enjoying this!* He was enjoying the wager with the Queen, the challenge of it.

Rosamund envied that boldness.

'There you are wrong, Master Gustavson.' Queen

Elizabeth spun round to Rosamund. 'Lady Rosamund here has shown herself to be a most able dancer, and she has a patient and calm demeanour, which is quite rare here at Court. So, my lady, I give you your first task at my Court—teach Master Gustavson to dance.'

Rosamund went cold with sudden surprise. Teach him to dance, when in truth she barely knew the steps herself? She was quite certain she would not be able to focus on pavanes and complicated voltas when she had to stand close to Anton Gustavson, feel his hands at her waist, see his smile up-close. She was quite confused just looking at him—how would she ever speak? Her task for the Queen would surely end in disaster.

'Your Grace,' she finally dared to say, 'I am sure there are far more skilled dancers who could—'

'Nonsense,' the Queen interrupted. 'You will do the job admirably, Lady Rosamund. You shall have your first lesson after church on Christmas morning. The Waterside Gallery will be quiet then, I think. What say you, Master Gustavson?'

'I say, Your Grace, that I wish to please you in all things,' he answered with a bow.

'And you are also never one to back away from a challenge, eh?' the Queen said, her dark eyes sparkling with some mischief known only to her.

'Your Grace is indeed wise,' Anton answered.

'Then the terms are these—if I win, and you can indeed dance, you must pay me six shillings as well as a boon to be decided later to Lady Rosamund.'

'And if I win, Your Grace?'

Elizabeth laughed. 'I am sure we will find a suitable prize for you among our coffers, Master Gustavson. Now come, Ambassador von Zwetkovich, I crave another dance.'

The Queen swept away once again, and Anne followed her to dance with Johan Ulfson. She tossed back a glance at Rosamund that promised a plethora of questions later.

Rosamund turned to Anton in the sudden quiet of their little corner. It felt as if they were enclosed in their own cloud, an instant of murky, blurry silence that shut out the bustle of the rest of the room.

'I believe, Master Gustavson, that you are a sham,' Rosamund hissed.

'My lady!' He pressed one hand to his heart, his eyes wide with feigned hurt, but Rosamund was sure she heard laughter lurking in his voice. 'You do wound me. What have I done to cause such accusations?'

'I saw you skating on that pond. You are no *clumsy oaf.*'

'Skating and dancing are two different things.'

'Not so very different, I should think. They both require balance, grace and coordination.'

'Are you a skater yourself?'

'Nay. It is not so cold here as in your homeland, except this winter. I seldom have the chance of a frozen pond or river.'

'Then you cannot know if they are the same, *ja*?' A servant passed by with a tray of wine goblets, and Anton claimed two. He handed one to Rosamund, his long fingers sliding warmly against hers as he slowly withdrew them.

Rosamund shivered at the friction of skin against skin, feeling foolish at her girlish reaction. It was not as if she had never touched a man before. She and Richard had touched behind the hedgerows last summer. But somehow even the brush of Anton Gustavson's hand made her utterly flustered.

'I am sure they are not dissimilar. If you can skate, you can dance,' she said, taking a sip of wine to cover her confusion.

'And vice versa? Very well, then, Lady Rosamund, I propose a wager of my own.'

Rosamund studied him suspiciously over the silver rim of her goblet. 'What sort of wager, Master Gustavson?'

'They say your Thames is near frozen through,' he answered. 'For every dancing lesson you give me, I shall give you a skating lesson. Then we will see if they are the same or no.'

Rosamund remembered with a pang the way he had flown over the ice. What would it be like to feel so very free, to drift like that, above all earthly bonds? She was quite tempted. But… 'I could never do what you did. I would fall right over!'

He laughed, a deep, warm sound that rubbed against her like fine silk-velvet. She longed to hear it again, to revel in that happy sound over and over. 'You need not go into a spin, Lady Rosamund, merely stay upright and move forward.'

That alone sounded difficult enough. 'On two thin little blades attached to my shoes.'

'I vow it is not as hard as it sounds.'

'And neither is dancing.'

'Then shall we prove it to ourselves? Just a small, harmless wager, my lady.'

Rosamund frowned. She thought he surely did not have a 'harmless' bone in his handsome body! 'I don't have any money of my own yet.'

'Nay, you have something far more precious.'

'And what is that?'

'A lock of your hair.'

'My hair?' Her hand flew up to touch her hair

which was carefully looped and pinned under a narrow silver headdress and sheer veil. Her maid Jane had shoved in extra pins to hold the fine, slick strands tight, but Rosamund could feel them already slipping. 'Whatever for?'

Anton watched intently as her fingers moved along one loose strand. 'I think it must be made of moonbeams. It makes me think of nights in my homeland, of the way silver moonlight sparkles on the snow.'

'Why, Master Gustavson,' Rosamund breathed. 'I think you have missed your calling. You are no diplomat or skater, you are a poet.'

He laughed and that flash of seriousness dissipated like winter fog. 'No more than I am a dancer, I fear, my lady. 'Tis a great pity, for it seems both poetry and dancing are highly prized here in London.'

'Are they not in Stockholm?'

He shook his head. 'Warfare is prized in Stockholm, and not much else of late.'

'It *is* a pity, then. For I fear poetry would be more likely to win the Queen's hand for your king.'

'I think you are correct, Lady Rosamund. But I must still do my duty here.'

'Ah, yes. We all must do our duty,' Rosamund said ruefully, remembering her parents' words.

Anton smiled at her. 'But life is not all duty, my lady. We must have some merriment as well.'

'True. Especially now at Christmas.'

'Then we have a wager?'

Rosamund laughed. Perhaps it was the wine, the music, the fatigue from her journey and the late hour, but she suddenly felt deliciously reckless. 'Very well. If you cannot dance and I cannot skate, I will give you a lock of my hair.'

'And if it is the opposite? What prize do you claim for yourself?'

He leaned close to her, so close she could see the etched-glass lines of his face, the faint shadow of beard along his jaw. She could smell the summery lime of his cologne, the clean, warm winter-frost scent of him. *A kiss*, she almost blurted out, staring at the faint smile on his lips.

What would he kiss like? Quick, eager—almost overly eager, like Richard? Or slow, lazy, exploring every angle, every sensation? What would he taste like?

She gulped and took a step back, her gaze falling to his hand curled lightly around the goblet. On his smallest finger was a ring, a small ruby set in intricate gold filigree. 'That is a pretty bauble,' she said hoarsely, gesturing to the ring. 'Would you wager it?'

He held his hand up, staring at the ring as if he had forgotten it was there. 'If you wish it.'

Rosamund nodded. 'Then done. I will meet you in the Waterside Gallery on Christmas morning for a dance lesson.'

'And as soon as the Thames is frozen through we will go skating.'

'Until then, Master Gustavson.' Rosamund quickly curtsied, and hurried away to join the other maids where they had gathered near the door. It was nearly the Queen's hour to retire, and they had to accompany her.

Only once she was entirely across the room from Anton did she draw in a deep breath. She felt as if she had suddenly been dropped back to earth after spinning about in the sky, all unmoored and uncertain. Her head whirled.

'What were you and Master Gustavson talking of for so long?' Anne whispered.

'Dancing, of course,' Rosamund answered.

'If I had him to myself like that,' Anne said, 'I am

certain I could think of better things than *dancing* to
talk of! Do you think you will be able to win the
Queen's wager?'

Rosamund shrugged, still feeling quite dazed. She
feared she was quite unable to think at all any more.

Svordom! What had led him to promise her his
mother's ring?

Anton curled his hand into a fist around the heavy
goblet, the embossed silver pressing into the calluses
along his palm as he watched her walk away. It
seemed as if all the light in the chamber collected
onto her, a silvery glow that carried her above the
noisy fray.

He knew all too well what had made him agree to a
ridiculous wager that didn't even make sense, to offer
her that ring. It was her, Rosamund Ramsay, alone. That
look in her large blue eyes.

She had not been at Court long enough to learn to
conceal her feelings entirely. She had tried, but every
once in a while they had flashed through those expres-
sive eyes—glimpses of fear, nervousness, excitement,
bravery, laughter—uncertainty.

He had lived so long among people who had worn
masks all their lives. The concealment became a part of
them, so that even *they* had no idea what they truly
were, what they truly felt. Even he had his own masks,
a supply of them for every occasion. They were better
than any armour.

Yet when he looked at Rosamund Ramsay he felt the
heavy weight of that concealment pressing down on
him. He could not be free of it, but he could enjoy her
freedom until she, too, learned to don masks. It would
not be long, not here, and he felt unaccountably melan-

choly at the thought of those eyes, that lovely smile, turning brittle and false.

Aye, he would enjoy her company while he could. His own task drew near, and he could not falter now. He unwound his fist, staring down at the ruby. It glowed blood-red in the torchlight, reminding him of his promises and dreams.

'Making wagers with the Queen?' Johan said, coming up to Anton to interrupt his dark thoughts. 'Is that wise, from all we have heard of her?'

Anton laughed, watching Queen Elizabeth as she talked with her chief advisor, Lord Burghley. Burghley was not terribly old, yet his face was lined with care, his hair and beard streaked with grey. Serving the English Queen could be a frustrating business, as they had learned to their own peril. She kept them cooling their heels at Court, dancing attendance on her as she vacillated at King Eric's proposal. Anton was certain she had no intention of marrying the king, or possibly anyone at all, but they could not depart until they had an official answer. Meanwhile, they danced and dined, and warily circled the Austrians and the Scots.

As for Anton's own matter, she gave no answer at all.

Maddening indeed. Battle was simple; the answer was won by the sword. Court politics were more slippery, more changeable, and far more time-consuming. But he was a patient man, a determined one. He could wait—for now.

At least there was Rosamund Ramsay to make the long days more palatable.

'I would not worry, Johan,' Anton said, tossing back the last of the wine. 'This wager is strictly for Her Grace's holiday amusement.'

'What is it, then? Are you to play the Christmas fool, the Lord of Misrule?'

Anton laughed. 'Something like it. I am to learn to dance.'

Chapter Five

Christmas Eve, December 24

'Holly and ivy, box and bay, put in the house for Christmas Day! Fa la la la…'

Rosamund smiled at hearing the notes of the familiar song, the tune always sung as the house was bedecked for Christmas. The Queen's gentlewomen of the Privy and Presence chambers, along with the maids of honour, had been assigned to festoon the Great Hall and the corridors for that night's feast. Tables were set up along the privy gallery, covered with holly, ivy, mistletoe, evergreen boughs, ribbons and spangles. Under the watchful eye of Mistress Eglionby, Mistress of the Maids, they were to turn them into bits of holiday artistry.

Rosamund sat there with Anne Percy, twisting together loops of ivy as they watched Mary Howard and Mary Radcliffe lay out long swags to measure them. The Marys sang as they worked, sometimes pausing to leap about with ribbons like two morris dancers.

Rosamund laughed at their antics. For the first time

in many days, she forgot her homesickness and uncertainty. She only thought of how much she loved this time of year, these twelve days when the gloom of winter was left behind, buried in music, wine and satin bows. She might be far from home, but the Queen kept a lively holiday. She should enjoy it as much as possible.

Rosamund reached for two bent hoops and tied them into a sphere for a kissing bough. She chose the darkest, greenest loops of holly and ivy from the table, twining them around and tying them with the red ribbons.

'Are you making a kissing bough, Rosamund?' Anne said teasingly. She tied together her own greenery into wreaths for the fireplace mantels.

Rosamund smiled. 'My maid Jane says if you stand beneath it and close your eyes you will have a vision of your future husband.'

'And if he comes up and kisses you whilst you stand there with your eyes closed, so much the better!' Anne said.

'That would help settle the question, I think.'

'But you need not resort to such tricks, I'm sure,' Anne whispered. 'What of your sweetheart at home?'

Rosamund frowned as she stared down at her half-finished bough; last Christmas, Richard had indeed kissed her under one very like it. That was when she had begun to think he cared for her, and she for him. But that seemed so long ago now, as if it had happened to someone else. 'He is not my sweetheart.'

'But you do wish him to be?'

Rosamund remembered Richard's kiss that Christmas Eve. 'That can't be.'

'Do your parents disapprove so much, then?'

Rosamund nodded, reaching for the green, red and white Tudor roses made of paper to add to her bough.

'They say his family is not our equal, even though their estate neighbours ours.'

'Is that their only objection?'

'Nay. They also say I would not be content with him. That his nature would not suit mine.' Rosamund felt a pang as she remembered those words of her father. She had cried and pleaded, sure her parents would give way as they always did. Her father had seemed sad as he'd refused her, but implacable. 'When you find the one you can truly love,' he said, 'you will know what your mother and I mean.'

'But you love him?' Anne asked softly.

Rosamund shrugged.

Anne sighed sadly. 'Our families should not have such say over our own hearts.'

'Is your family so very strict?' Rosamund asked.

'Nay. My parents died when I was a small child.'

'Oh, Anne!' Rosamund cried. Her own parents might be maddening, but before the business with Richard they had been affectionate with her, their only child, and she with them. 'I am so sorry.'

'I scarcely remember them,' Anne said, tying off her length of ribbon. 'I grew up with my grandmother, who is so deaf she hardly ever knew what I was up to. It wasn't so bad, and then my aunt came along and found me this position here at Court. They want me to marry, but only their own choice. Much like your own parents, I dare say!'

'Who is their choice?'

Anne shrugged. 'I don't know yet. Someone old and crabbed and toothless, I'm sure. Some crony of my aunt's husband. Perhaps he will at least be rich.'

'Oh, Anne, no!'

'It does not signify. We should concentrate on *your*

romance. There must be a way we can smuggle a message to him. Oh, here, put mistletoe in your bough! It is the most important element, otherwise the magic won't work.'

Rosamund laughed, taking the thick bunch of glossy mistletoe from Anne and threading it through the centre of the bough. Surely there was some kind of magic floating about in the winter air. She felt lighter already with Christmas here.

Yet, strangely, it was not Richard's blond visage she saw as she gazed at the mistletoe but a pair of dark eyes. A lean, powerful body sheathed in close-fitting velvet and leather flying across the glistening ice.

'Holly and ivy, box and bay,' she whispered, 'put in the house for Christmas Day.'

There was a sudden commotion at the end of the gallery, a burst of activity as a group of men rushed inside, bringing in the cold of the day. Among them was the handsome young man who had winked at Anne the day before—and been soundly ignored.

And there was also Anton Gustavson, his skates slung over his shoulder, black waves of hair escaping from his fine velvet cap. They were full of loud laughter, noisy joviality.

The ladies all giggled, blushing prettily at the sight of them.

As Rosamund feared she did too. She felt her cheeks go warm, despite the sudden rush of cold wind. She ducked her head over her work, but there in the pearly mistletoe berries she still saw Anton's brown eyes, his teasing smile.

'Mistress Anne!' one of the men said. Rosamund peeked up to find it was the winker. He was even more good-looking up close, with long, waving golden-brown hair and emerald-green eyes. He smiled at Anne flirtatiously, but Rosamund thought she saw a strange tension at the edges of his mouth, a quickly veiled flash in his eyes. Perhaps she was not the only one harbouring secret romances. 'What do you do there?'

Anne would not look at him; instead she stared down at her hands as they fussed with the ribbons. 'Some of us must work, Lord Langley, and not go frolicking off ice-skating all day.'

'Oh aye, it looks arduous work indeed,' Lord Langley answered, merrily undeterred. He sat down at the end of the table, fiddling with a bit of ivy. On his index finger flashed a gold signet-ring embossed with the phoenix crest of the Knighton family.

Rosamund gasped. Anne's admirer was the Earl of Langley. And not old and crabbed at all.

She glanced at Anton, quite against her will; she didn't want to look at him, to remember their wager and her own foolish thoughts of kissing boughs and ice-skating. But she still felt compelled to look, to see what he was doing.

He stood by one of the windows, lounging casually against its carved frame as he watched his other companions laughing with the Marys. An amused half-smile curved his lips.

Rosamund's clasp tightened on her bough, and she had a sudden vision of standing with him beneath the green sphere, of gazing up at him, at those lips, longing to know what they would feel like on hers. She imagined touching his shoulders, heated, powerful muscles under fine velvet, sliding her hands down his chest as his lips lowered to hers…

And then his smile widened, as if he knew her very thoughts. Rosamund caught her breath and stared back down at the table, her cheeks flaming even hotter.

'We were not merely skating, Mistress Anne,' Anton said. 'We were sent by the Queen to search for the finest Yule log to be found.'

'And did you discover one?' Anne asked tartly, snatching the ivy from Lord Langley's hand.

He laughed, undeterred as he reached for a ribbon instead. 'Not as yet, but we are going out again this afternoon. Nothing but the very best will do for the Queen's Christmas—or that of her ladies.'

'You had best hurry, then, as Christmas Day is tomorrow.'

'Never fear, Mistress Anne,' Lord Langley said. 'I always succeed when I am determined on something.'

'Always?' said Anne. 'Oh, my lord, I do fear there is a first time for everything—even disappointment.'

Lord Langley's green eyes narrowed, but Anton laughed, strolling closer to the table. He leaned over Rosamund's shoulder, reaching out to pick up a sprig of holly.

Rosamund swallowed hard as his sleeve brushed the side of her neck, soft and alluring, warm and vital, yet snow-chilled at the same time.

'Ah, Lord Langley,' Anton said. 'I fear working with this holly has made the ladies just as prickly today. Perhaps we should retire before we get scratched.'

Lord Langley laughed too. 'Have they such thin skins in Sweden, Master Gustavson? We here have heavier armour against the ladies' barbs.'

'Is there armour heavy enough for such?' Anton asked.

Rosamund took the holly from his hand, careful not to let her fingers brush his. The ruby ring gleamed, reminding her of their wager. 'They say if the holly leaves are rounded the lady shall rule the house for the year. If barbed, the lord.'

'And which is this?' Anton took back the holly, running his thumb over the glossy green leaf. 'What does it signify if half the leaf is smooth, half barbed?'

'The impossible.' Lord Langley laughed. 'For each house can have only one ruler.'

'And in the Queen's house every leaf is smooth,' Anne said. 'Now, make yourselves of use and help us hang the greenery in the Great Hall.'

Anton tucked the holly into the loops of Rosamund's upswept hair, the edge of his hand brushing her cheek. 'There, Lady Rosamund,' he whispered. 'Now you are ready for the holiday.'

Rosamund gently touched the sprig, but did not draw it away. It rested there in her hair, a reminder. 'Best you beware my prickles, then, Master Gustavson. They may not be as obvious as this leaf, but they are there.'

'I am warned. But I am not a man to be frightened off by nettles, Lady Rosamund—not even thickets of them.' He laid his skates on the table, taking up a long swag of ivy and ribbon as he held out his hand to her. 'Will you show me where your decorations are to go? I should hate to ruin your decking of the halls.'

After a moment's hesitation, Rosamund nodded and took his hand, letting him help her rise. In her other hand she took up her kissing bough, and they followed the others from the gallery as a song rose up.

'So now is come our joyful feast, let every man be jolly!' they sang as they processed to the Great Hall, bearing their new decorations. 'Each room with ivy leaves is dressed, and every post with holly.'

Rosamund couldn't help being carried along by the song, by the happy anticipation of the season. She smiled up at Anton, surprised to find that he too sang along.

'Though some churls at our mirth repine, round your

foreheads garlands twine, drown sorrow in a cup of wine and let us all be merry!'

'You know our English songs, Master Gustavson?' she asked as they came to the vast stone fireplace. He let go of her hand to fetch a stool, and Rosamund suddenly felt strangely bereft, cold, without him.

She flexed her fingers, watching as he set the stool beneath the mantel. No fire blazed in the grate today, and they could stand close.

'My mother was English,' he said, climbing up on the stool. Rosamund handed him the end of the swag, which he attached to the elaborately carved wood. 'She taught everyone in our house her favourite old songs.'

'What else do you do at Christmas in Sweden?' she asked curiously. She followed along as he fastened the swag to the mantel, tying off the bows.

'Much the same as you do here, I suppose,' he said. 'Feasting, pageants and plays, gifting. And we have St Lucy's Day.'

'St Lucy's Day?'

'Aye, 'tis a very old tradition in Sweden, as St Lucy is one of our protectors. Every December we honour her with a procession led by a lady who portrays Lucy herself, who led Roman refugees into the catacombs with candles and then supplied them with food, until she was martyred for her efforts. The lady elected wears a white gown with red ribbons and a crown of candles on her head, and she distributes sweets and delicacies as everyone sings songs to St Lucy.'

Rosamund laughed, fascinated. 'It sounds delightful. We have no saints here now, though.'

'None in Sweden, either, except Lucy. And you would certainly be one of the ladies chosen to be St Lucy, Lady Rosamund.'

'Would I? I am sure my parents would say I am the least saint-like of females!'

Anton chuckled. 'You do seem rather stubborn, Lady Rosamund.'

'Oh, thank you very much!' Rosamund teased. 'Is another Swedish custom insulting ladies at Christmas time?'

'Not at all. Stubbornness is a trait that serves all of us well at a royal court.'

'True enough. I may not have been here long, but I do see that.'

'But you would surely be St Lucy because of your beauty. Lucy is always a lady with fair hair, blue eyes and the ability to convey sweetness and generosity. Those two attributes are surely not negated even by copious doses of stubbornness.'

Rosamund could feel that cursed blush creeping up again, making her face and throat hot in a way no one else's compliments could. He thought her beautiful? 'Perhaps, then, that is one tradition we could borrow from Sweden.'

'And so you should.' Anton stepped off the stool, examining their handiwork. 'Does it please you?'

'Does what please me?' she asked, still dazed. Pleased by him? She very much feared she might be. He was so different from Richard.

'The decorations.'

'Oh—aye. It looks most festive.'

'*Ganska nyttig.* Shall we find a place for that, then?'

He reached for the kissing bough Rosamund still held, half-forgotten. 'It is a silly thing,' she protested, stepping back. 'The Queen would surely not want it in her hall.'

'Why is that?' Anton persisted, moving closer until he could take the sphere of greenery from her hand. As he examined the mistletoe, the fluttering ribbons, a slow smile spread over his face. 'A kissing bough!'

Rosamund snatched it back. 'I told you it was silly.'

'My mother said when she was a girl she made kissing boughs at Christmas to divine who her future husband might be.'

'Well, that is not why I made it. I merely thought it looked pretty.'

Anton stepped even closer, leaning down to whisper in her ear. His cool breath stirred the curls at her temple, making her shiver. 'She also said if you kiss someone beneath it at midnight on Christmas Eve they will be your true love for the rest of the year.'

Rosamund closed her eyes, trying to ignore the way his voice whispered over her skin. 'I had best not hang it up, then. True love seems to wreak enough havoc here at Court.'

Anton laughed, taking the bough from her hand. 'Nay, it is much too pretty to hide. We will hang it over there, behind that tapestry. Only those who truly need it can find it there.'

Before she could protest, he carried it off. A tapestry depicting a bright scene of wine-making was looped up, revealing the gap between it and the panelled wall. Anton leaped up to attach the ribbon loop to a ripple in the carving.

The bough swayed there, all verdant-green and enticing. Anton unhooked the tapestry, letting it fall back into place before the little hidey-hole.

'There now, Lady Rosamund,' he said with a smile. 'Only we two know it is there.'

Their secret. Rosamund longed to run away as she had when she'd first seen him by the frozen pond. Yet she could not. It was as if she was bound to him, tied by loops of ivy and red ribbon. Caught by the dark glow of his eyes.

She touched the tip of her tongue to her dry lips, watching as his gaze narrowed on that tiny gesture.

'Is the Thames yet frozen through?' she queried softly.

'Very nearly,' he said roughly. 'They talk of a frost fair in the days to come.'

'A frost fair? There has not been one of those in many years, not since my mother was a child, I think.' Rosamund twined her hands in her velvet skirts, feeling suddenly bold. 'Then will you be able to teach me to skate, do you think?'

'You seem a quick enough learner to me, Lady Rosamund. And will I be able to dance at Twelfth Night?'

'That remains to be seen. Our first dancing lesson is not until tomorrow.'

'I very much look forward to it.'

Rosamund curtsied and hurried away. She too found she looked forward to their lessons. Lessons of *all* sorts.

Z'wounds! She had been so comfortable in her cozy life at Ramsay Castle. Now she felt so unsure of everything. She felt as if she balanced on the edge of some vast, unknown precipice, between her old self and a new self she did not yet see. Just one push would send her one way or the other.

Or she could jump. But that was probably for bolder souls than herself, much as she wished to.

She rushed out of the hall, turning towards the staircase that led back to the maids' apartment. But she went still as her foot touched the first step.

Anne stood in the darkness of the landing just above, deep in conversation with Lord Langley. Their voices were low and intense, as if they quarrelled. He reached for her hand, but she stepped back, shaking her head. Then she fled up the stairs, her footsteps clattering away.

Lord Langley swung round to come back down, and Rosamund shrank back against the wall, hoping he would not see her there in the dim light. He did not seem able to see anything. His handsome face, so alight with merriment earlier, was solemn, taut with anger.

'Bloody stubborn woman,' he muttered as he strode past her.

Rosamund lingered there for a moment, unsure what to do. Her own romantic life was so very confused, she was quite sure she could be of no help in anyone else's. But Anne was her friend, or as close as she had here at Court.

Feeling like she dove between Scylla and Charybdis, Rosamund climbed the stairs and made her way to the maids' dormitory.

Unlike last night, when the laughter and chatter had gone on for hours, the chamber was silent. All the other ladies were still decking the halls, and Anne lay alone on her bed, her back to the door.

She was very still, making no sound of tears or sighs. Rosamund tiptoed closer. 'Anne?' she said softly. 'Is something amiss?'

Anne rolled over to face her. Her eyes were dry but reddened, her hair escaping in dark curls from her head-dress. 'Oh, Rosamund,' she said. 'Come, sit beside me.'

Rosamund perched on the edge of the bed, reaching into the embroidered pouch at her waist for a handker-chief in case it was needed.

'Tell me more about your sweetheart at home,' Anne said, sitting up against the bolsters. 'Is he very handsome?'

'Oh!' Rosamund said, startled by the request. She

forced herself to remember Richard, the way he had smiled at her. A smile with no hidden depths and facets, unlike Anton Gustavson's.

'Aye,' she said slowly.

'Is he fair or dark? Tall?'

'Fair, and only middling tall.'

'But a fine kisser, I would wager.'

Rosamund laughed. 'Fine enough, I think.' Though she had little to compare him to.

'And he loves you. He wants to marry you and always has.'

Rosamund hesitated at that. 'He said he did, when last I saw him.' But then he had vanished, leaving her alone to argue their cause with her parents. The servants had said he had even quit the neighbourhood entirely in the autumn.

'You are fortunate, then,' Anne sighed.

'Does Lord Langley not want…?'

'I do not want to speak of him,' Anne interrupted. 'Not now. I would much rather hear of your love, Rosamund.'

Rosamund lay back with a sigh, staring up at the embroidered underside of the hangings as if she could read her answers in the looping flowers and vines. 'I have not heard from him in an age. I am not sure now I want to hear from him at all.'

'I would wager he has written to you but your parents intercepted the letters,' Anne said. 'That happened with my friend Penelope Leland when she wanted to marry Lord Pershing.'

'Truly?' Rosamund frowned. She had not thought of such a thing. 'How can I be sure?'

'Aye. We must find a way to contact him,' Anne said, her voice full of new excitement at coming up with a scheme. 'Once he knows where you are, he will surely come running to your side.'

Rosamund was not so certain. Her infatuation with Richard seemed to belong to someone else, a young girl with no knowledge of herself or of the world. But if it helped to distract Anne, and herself, she was willing to attempt it.

Perhaps then she would cease to drown in a pair of winter-dark eyes.

'Round your foreheads garlands twine, drown sorrow in a cup of wine, and let all be merry!'

Rosamund laughed helplessly as the entire Great Hall rang with song. It was quite obvious that the whole company had already drowned their sorrows copiously as the Christmas Eve banquet progressed. The long tables were littered with the remains of supper, with goblets that were emptied, and the musicians' songs were louder, faster than they'd been early in the evening.

The decorations of the hall, lit now by a blazing fire and dozens of torches, fairly shimmered with rich reds, greens and golds, making the vast space a festive bower. Laughter was as loud as the song, and glances grew longer and bolder, ever more flirtatious, as the night went on.

Not everyone was happy, though, Rosamund noticed. The Austrians seemed rather ill at ease, though they tried gamely to enter into the spirit of the holiday. A few of the more Puritanical of the clergymen hovered at the edges of the bright throng, looking on with pinched expressions.

Surely they would be happier if everyone passed the holiday in solemn prayer, Rosamund thought, not frisking about with song and greenery, which echoed of the old days of popery. But Queen Elizabeth seemed not to notice at all; she sat on her dais, clapping in time to the song.

On the wall behind her was a large mural, an early

Christmas gift from her minister, Walsingham. It was an allegory of the Tudor succession, centred on an enthroned Henry VIII, right here in the Great Hall of Whitehall, with a young Edward VI kneeling beside him. To his left was Queen Mary, with her Spanish husband King Phillip with Mars the god of war, all dark blacks, browns and muted yellows. To his right was Queen Elizabeth, with Peace trampling on a sword of discord, trailed by Plenty, spilling out her cornucopia. They gleamed in bright whites, silvers and golds.

Just as the Queen herself did tonight, presiding over her own feast of plenty and joy. She wore a gown of white satin, trimmed in white fur and sewn with pearls and tiny sapphire beads. She looked on the holiday she had wrought with a contented smile.

The others on the dais with her did not look so very sanguine. The Queen's cousin Lady Lennox, Margaret Stewart, sat to the Queen's left with her son, Lord Darnley, her ample frame once again swathed in black. He was handsome enough, Rosamund had to admit, with his pale-gold, poetic looks set off by his own fine black-velvet garments. But he looked most discontented, almost sulky, as if there was somewhere he would rather be. Chasing the servants into his bed, as Anne had said?

Next to them sat Lord Sussex and his wife, sworn enemies of Leicester, and thus united with Lady Lennox in their cause. On the Queen's other side was Lord Burghley and his serene wife Mildred, and the Queen's cousin, Lord Hunsdon, and his wife. The marital delegations were at their own tables tonight, just below the royal dais.

Rosamund peeked at Anton over the edge of her goblet, remembering the kissing bough that hung behind the tapestry, known only to the two of them. She remembered the warmth of his hand as it had touched hers, the brilliant light of his smile.

He smiled now as he listened to the song, his long fingers tapping out the time on the table. His ruby ring caught the light, gleaming like the holly berries. He saw her looking over and his smile widened.

Rosamund smiled back. She could not help herself. Despite her nervousness, her uncertainty of life at Court and what she should do, every time she looked at Anton Gustavson she felt lighter, freer.

There was still her family, her home, her duties—still Richard out there somewhere, as Anne had reminded her. But when Anton smiled at her for just an instant she forgot all of that. He made her want to laugh at the wondrous surprise of life, the delightful mysteries of men.

But she only forgot for an instant. She turned away from him, and found Anne watching her quizzically. Rosamund just shrugged at her. She remembered Anne's red eyes all over Lord Langley and some mysterious romance gone sour. Rosamund wanted none of that for herself, or for her friend. Not now. Not when it was Christmas.

The large double doors of the hall burst open in a flurry of drums. Acrobats tumbled through, a blur of bright-coloured silks and spangles, tinkling bells and rattles. They somersaulted down the aisles between the tables, leaping up to flip backwards through the air.

As everyone applauded their antics, another figure appeared in the doorway, a broad-shouldered man swathed in a multi-coloured cloak and hood. His face was covered by a white leather Venetian mask painted in red-and-green swirls.

He rattled a staff of bells as the acrobats tumbled around him.

The Queen rose to her feet. 'What do you do here at our Court?' she demanded.

'I am the Lord of Misrule! I am the high and mighty Prince of Purpoole, Archduke of Stapulia, Duke of High and Nether Holborn, Knight of the Most Heroical Order of the Helmet and sovereign of the same,' the cloaked man announced, his voice amplified and distorted behind the mask. 'For this holiday season, I declare all kingdoms my dominion—the realm of merriment.'

The Queen laughed. 'The realm of chaos, I would vow! Very well, my Lord of Misrule—let your reign begin. But pay heed that it will only last until Twelfth Night.'

The Lord of Misrule bowed, and his tumbling minions dashed amongst the tables to claim partners for the dance. Anne, the Marys, Catherine Knyvett, even Mistress Eglionby, were all borne away into a wild, disorganised galliard.

Rosamund watched, astonished, as the Lord of Misrule himself came to her side, holding out his gloved hand to her. She stared up into that eerily masked face, searching for some clue to his identity, yet there was none at all. Even his eyes were shadowed, set deep behind that painted visage.

'Will you dance with me, my lady?' he asked, shaking those bells.

Rosamund slowly nodded, taking his gloved hand and letting him lead her to the centre of the dance. The steps were familiar, but the patterns disorganised, constantly shifting and reforming. The dancers lurched into each other and reeled away, laughing.

The Lord of Misrule twirled Rosamund around in an ever-growing circle, faster and faster, until the whole room spun in a wild blur. His hands held tightly to hers, in a grip that was almost painful, but she was pressed in on all sides by the other dancers and could not escape.

Her breath felt tight in her lungs, constricted by her tight bodice, and her heart pounded until she could scarcely hear the music. The brilliant lights of the banquet dimmed and she suddenly felt like a wild bird beating her wings against confining bars.

At last she was able to free her hands from her unseen partner and break away from the close patterns of the dance. Once out of the hot press of the crowd, she wasn't sure where to go. She just needed to breathe again.

She lifted the heavy hem of her skirt, dashing across the room past the knots of courtiers who did not dance. They were too busy with their own wine-soaked laughter to pay her any heed; even the Queen was occupied with watching the dance. Rosamund ducked behind one of the tapestries, wedging herself into the small, safe space between the heavy cloth and the wood-panelled wall.

She leaned back against the solid support of that wall, closing her eyes. The music and laughter was muffled, as if heard from under water, distorted by the thud of her heartbeat in her ears. Everything had changed so fast, the evening going from merry holiday-making to surreal strangeness in only a moment. Who *was* that man? He was indeed a Lord of Misrule.

She pressed her hand to her white silk bodice that was stiff with silver embroidery, willing her heart to slow, her breath to flow easily.

Suddenly, there was a rush of warm air, the scent of smoke, pine boughs and clean soap, as the tapestry was brushed aside. Rosamund gasped as she opened her eyes, afraid that the masked man had followed her into her sanctuary. She even went up on her toes in her velvet shoes, prepared to flee.

But it was not the Lord of Misrule who slid behind the tapestry with her. It was Anton. She had only a glimpse of his tall, lean figure, the dark-star gleam of his eyes, before the cloth dropped behind him. They were enclosed in their own little shadowed world.

Rosamund found she was not frightened, though. She felt no urge to run from him. Instead, she could at last breathe easily.

She was no longer alone.

'Rosamund?' he said quietly. 'Are you unwell?'

'I…' She swayed closer to him, drawn by the clean scent of him, by his warm, silent strength. 'I could not breathe out there.'

'I, too, mislike crowds,' he said. 'But we are safe here.'

His arms came around her, drawing her close, and she *did* feel safe. She rested her forehead against his velvet-covered chest, closing her eyes as she listened to his strong, steady heartbeat. It echoed her own heart, binding them together there in the dark.

She slid her arms around his waist, feeling the supple strength of him bonding to her. The chaotic dance outside vanished, and she had only this one moment in the eye of the storm.

She felt him kiss the top of her head, and she tilted her face up to his. His lips lightly touched her brow, her temple, the edge of her cheekbone, leaving tiny droplets of flame wherever he touched. Her breath caught again, and she shivered with the sudden force of her weakness, her desire for more of those kisses, more of *him*.

At last his lips touched hers with glancing, alluring

kisses—once, twice. And again, a slightly deeper caress, a taste that made her moan for more. That small sound against his lips made him groan, and he dragged her even closer until their bodies were pressed tight together. Every curve and angle fit perfectly, as if they were meant to be just so.

She strained up on tiptoe, her lips parting beneath his. His tongue, light and skilled, touched the tip of hers before deepening the kiss, binding her to him even closer.

Rosamund twined her arms around his neck, her fingers driving into the softness of his hair, holding him to her as if she feared he would escape her. But he made no move to leave her. Their kiss turned desperate, heated, blurry, full of a primitive need she did not even know was in her. Her whole body felt heavy and hot, narrowed to the one perfect moment of their kiss.

He pressed her back to the wall, lifting her up until her layers of skirts fell away and she wrapped her stockinged legs around his hips. He rocked into the curve of her body, his velvet breeches abrading her bare thighs above her garters. The friction was delicious, and she moaned against his open mouth, wanting more of that feeling, that wondrous oblivion.

His lips trailed wetly from hers, along her jaw and the arch of her throat as she leaned her head back on the wall, leaving herself open to him. His tongue swirled lightly in the hollow of her throat, just where her pulse pounded, before he nudged aside her sheer-silk partlet to kiss the slope of her breasts.

'Oh!' she gasped. She rocked her hips into his, clasping his hair even tighter as his teeth nipped at her sensitive skin and his tongue soothed the tiny sting. His erection was heavy, taut as iron against her through layers of velvet and leather.

She opened her eyes, staring up at the kissing bough as it swayed above her head. It had worked its enchantment on her indeed, weaving a sensual spell that made her sure she would do anything, anything at all, to feel more of this. Of him.

She closed her eyes again, bending her head to kiss his tumbled hair. He rested his forehead against the wall beside her, his breath ragged in her ear. Slowly, slowly, she slid her feet back to the floor, feeling the earth solid beneath her again. She heard the music outside their haven, louder, more discordant than ever, the pounding thunder of dancing feet.

She tried to ease away from Anton. She was so close to him she could not think at all, could not stop all her senses from reeling crazily. But his hands tightened on her waist, holding her against him as their breath slowed.

'Nay,' he gasped, his accent heavy. 'Don't move. Not yet.'

Rosamund nodded, leaning against his shoulder. His entire body was rigid, perfectly still, as if he struggled to find his control.

''Twas the kissing bough,' she whispered.

He laughed tightly. 'Perhaps your Puritans are right in trying to ban them from the halls, then.'

It felt as if their wild kiss had released something inside Rosamund, some bold imp she had not even realised was a part of her. 'But where would be the merriness in that?'

'You are a most enticing winter-fairy, Lady Rosamund Ramsay,' he said, kissing her cheek quickly. 'But will the bough erase all memory of this madness tomorrow?'

Rosamund did not know. She half-hoped so; this had been a true moment of madness, one that made her understand the poet's sonnets after all. Passion was an unstoppable force, one that clouded all sense. But it would be a great pity to lose the sensation of his caress.

'We must all to church in the morning with the Queen,' she answered. 'And reflect on our mistakes.'

'I fear I would need more time than one Christmas morning for *that*,' he said wryly.

'Are your mistakes so many, then?'

'Oh, my winter fairy, they are myriad.'

And she had just added them, and to her own. She edged away from him, suddenly cold and very tired as she smoothed her gown and hair and straightened her partlet. What would tomorrow bring? She had no idea. It was as if Misrule had indeed taken control of the world, a world she had once thought so comfortable and ordered.

'I must go back to my duties before I'm missed,' she said.

He nodded, the movement a small flurry in the darkness. He swept aside the edge of the tapestry, and Rosamund eased past him back into the light and noise of the hall. The Lord of Misrule and his acrobats had vanished, but the dancing still went on. Queen Elizabeth sat at her dais, talking with a lady who stood just beside her.

Rosamund blinked in the sudden change from shadow to light. She could see only that the lady who talked with the Queen was tall and reed-thin, clad in purple velvet and black silk that went with her black hair drawn back tight from her pale, oval face. She was almost like a raven among bright-plumed peacocks.

Then Rosamund was startled to recognise her. She was Celia Sutton, the widow of Richard's elder brother. She had seldom been seen in the neighbourhood since the death of her husband, though she and Rosamund had once been friends of a sort. Yet here she suddenly was at Court, still clad in mourning for a husband who had died in the spring, leaving Richard heir to the estate. Whatever did she do here now?

'Celia!' Rosamund murmured aloud.

'Ah, Master Gustavson,' Queen Elizabeth called, gesturing to Anton. 'There you are. Your cousin, Mistress Sutton, has arrived at our Court just in time for Christmas. I am sure she is most eager to greet you.'

Rosamund's gaze flew to Anton. Celia was his cousin—the same one who disputed his English inheritance?

His jaw was tight, his eyes utterly opaque as he looked at the Queen and at Celia. She watched him too, her lips drawn close.

'My cousin Anton,' she said slowly. 'So, we meet at last.' Her gaze slid past Anton to Rosamund, and she finally smiled. 'Rosamund! You *are* here. We could scarcely credit that your parents would part with you.'

'Only to serve the Queen,' Rosamund said. 'How do you fare, Celia?'

'Well enough, now that I have come to petition for justice—' Celia answered.

'We will not talk of such solemn matters as petitions, not at Christmas,' Queen Elizabeth interrupted with a wave of her feathered fan. 'We will speak of this later, privily, Master Gustavson and Mistress Sutton. In the meantime, I hope the two of you might find time to converse in a civil manner. There is such resemblance between you. Family should not quarrel so, as I well know.'

Anton bowed. 'As Your Grace commands,' he said affably. Yet Rosamund heard tension laced within his polite words. What was his connection with Celia? What were his feelings as he stood there before all the Court?

'Very good,' the Queen said. 'Come! It is time we retired for the evening, I think.'

As she stepped from the dais on Lord Burghley's arm, Rosamund and the other maids falling into their place behind her, the doors to the hall flew open once again. But it was not the Lord of Misrule, it was Lord Leicester who stood there, his dark, curling hair mussed, his green-satin doublet torn and streaked with dust and his eyes full of flashing anger.

'My Lord Leicester,' the Queen said. 'How quickly you transform yourself!'

He gave her a low bow, his shoulders still held stiff, his fist opening and closing, as if he longed for a sword. 'Indeed I do not, Your Grace. I have worn this garb all evening, though not by my will.'

A small frown creased the Queen's white brow. 'What do you mean? Were you not the Lord of Misrule here, not an hour ago?'

'I was to be, by Your Grace's order,' Leicester answered. 'But some churl locked me in the stables, as I made sure all was in readiness for the hunt tomorrow. I have only just escaped. When I do discover the villain…'

The Queen's hand tightened on her fan, a flush spreading over her cheeks. 'Then who was in our hall?'

'Come, Your Grace!' Burghley suddenly urged, gesturing for the Queen's guard to surround her in a tight phalanx and escorting her quickly from the hall. 'We must get you securely to your chamber immediately, where you can be safe.'

Leicester snatched up a sword from one of the tables,

brandishing it in the air. 'We will find this varlet, Your Grace, I vow to you!'

'Robin, no!' the Queen gasped, reaching out her hand to him as she was swept from the room. Rosamund hurried after them with the other ladies, suddenly cold with fear as she remembered the strange Lord of Misrule, that painfully tight clasp of his hands on hers.

Even the Queen seemed uncharacteristically flustered, glancing back at Leicester as she was pushed through the door, the room in disarray and confusion behind her.

Whatever would happen next? The whole Court seemed to have gone utterly mad.

Chapter Six

Christmas Day, December 25

Anton stared down at the garden from the window of the sitting room of the Swedish apartments. It was quite early yet; the walkways and flowerbeds were shrouded in curls of frosty morning fog blending with the smoke from the chimneys to form a thick, silver veil. No one was yet abroad except for one lady who strolled the paths.

Celia Sutton. She walked along slowly swathed in a black cloak, the hood thrown back to reveal her smooth, dark hair. Her head was bent, her hands clasped tightly together as if in deep spiritual contemplation on this Christmas Day—or, more likely, plotting her next move in their battle over Briony Manor.

He had never met her before, this cousin of his, the daughter of his mother's brother, yet he felt he knew her. They had exchanged letters for months, ever since their grandfather's will had been read and Briony had been revealed as Anton's. Letters that were full of a palpable anger he knew could not be assuaged while they remained strangers to each other.

The opportunity to travel to England with the marital delegation had been a most welcome one. King Eric had no chance of marrying Queen Elizabeth, everyone knew but him that after his last failed mission when the Queen had been new-crowned. If even the king's charming brother Duke John had not been able to finish the deal back then, none could. But it was perfect for Anton's personal business of claiming Briony Manor and making a new home there, a new start where he could right old wrongs.

And meeting his cousin, the only family he now possessed.

His lost family despised him as a stranger. He'd seen it in her eyes last night, those dark eyes so like his own and those of his mother. It would not be easy forging new links here in England. But he could not go back to Sweden.

Anton frowned as he watched Celia wend her way around hedges and fountains, her black cloak like a raven's wings in the cold mist. He thought of his home in Sweden, the ancient, chilly stone castle on the shores of a frozen lake, solitary and hard. Ruled over by an even colder father.

Roald Gustavson was a man of most uncertain temper, of no human emotion or feeling. Fortunately for Anton and his mother, he'd usually been away from home over the years, leaving them to their own devices. Anton's days had been spent studying with his tutors, skating on the lake and hunting in the forest that lurked behind the castle.

At night, his mother had told him tales of her English home, enticing stories of green woods and lanes, of people of learning and music; old stories of knights and

quests; new stories of her own childhood visits to
Briony Manor. Briony sounded like a magical place as
the land of distant as Arthur and his knights. But his
mother had insisted it was a real place, and one he
would see some day. One day it would be his reality too,
and the cold castle a memory.

And, when he was older and she'd been dying, she'd
told him secrets too—secrets that had made him more
determined to come to England, to Briony Manor. To
find a new beginning.

His path had not been easy. It had been forged in
battle against the Russians, in long days at the court of
a king going mad. A knife's edge of a court, where
there'd been none of the colour and merriment that surrounded the English queen's.

Much as he'd hated the place, he'd had to see to his
father's castle too. After his father's death, before he'd
gone off to battle, Anton had put his father's own
cousin as steward of the place. Now he cared not if he
ever saw it again.

Briony Manor was to be his new home. And, much
as he hated to disoblige a lady, Celia Sutton would not
stop him. She had dower property from her late
husband; Briony was all he had now.

He watched as his newfound cousin turned back
towards the palace, and he remembered how she had
looked last night as she'd talked to the Queen: determined—just as determined as he was. There'd been no
eager family reunion there!

And Rosamund Ramsay knew Celia. Were they
friends, then? Co-conspirators of some sort?

If that was so, they were not very good at it, as
Rosamund had obviously been surprised by Celia's appearance at Court. But that did not preclude them from

being confidantes. And that meant he had to be very careful around Rosamund and not be drawn in by the warm, welcoming glow of her sky-blue eyes, the eager passion of her kiss.

Ah, yes—that kiss. Anton scowled as he remembered last night, the two of them wrapped around each other in the heated, secret darkness. The sudden rush of desire had taken him by surprise, but it had been no less potent for being unexpected. Indeed, it had been building between them like a spark grown to a roaring flame since he'd first glimpsed her by that pond.

The taste of her soft lips, the way her body felt pressed to his, the smell of her rose perfume—it was intoxicating, wondrous. He wanted more and yet more of her, wanted everything she could give. Her body, her smiles, her laughter—her secrets.

But she would surely demand the same of him in return, and that he could not give. Not when she knew Celia Sutton and when she was a loyal servant of Queen Elizabeth. His secrets were buried too deep, and they could cost him everything he wanted if he grew incautious. He had learned from his mother's mistake, and put the demands of his head above his heart. He had come here to find a sort of justice for his mother, to retrieve her estate and start a new life. He could not abandon that mission.

That left the question—what *could* he do about Rosamund Ramsay? He could not avoid her; there was the Queen's silly wager. The Court was too small, too intimate, to maintain distance from her for long.

There was yet one more consideration too—the mystery of the Lord of Misrule, the masked figure who had taken Leicester's place then disappeared. The plot was a strange one, and thick with the miasma of some sinister intent. The Queen was well guarded, but what of Rosamund? The villain had danced with her, after all, and she had seemed frightened of him. It made anger stir deep in Anton's heart, a burning desire to protect her from anything that could ever frighten her.

He folded his arms across his chest, frowning as he stared out at the empty garden. He had to be cautious, to be watchful. He could protect Rosamund from the Lord of Misrule and see what she knew of Celia's doings.

Without letting a lower part of his anatomy rule his brain again.

'I am no shivering coward, Cecil!' Queen Elizabeth cried. 'I will not let some misguided mischief ruin my Christmas.'

As Rosamund looked on, astonished, the Queen slammed her fist down on her dressing table, rattling Venetian-glass bottles and pots, upending her own jewel case. Pearl ropes and ruby brooches spilled out onto the floor, and maidservants scrambled to scoop them up.

William Cecil, Lord Burghley, leaned on his walking stick, a look of long-suffering patience on his bearded face.

Rosamund stared at the scene—the Queen clad in her fur-trimmed bedrobe with her hair half-down as her ladies scrambled to ready her for the day, the bedchamber strewn with the results of her temper, tossed shoes, spilled pearl-powder, terrified faces.

She feared her own face might be one of them. Anne had told her the Queen had fits of pique at least once or twice a day, but they soon passed and she calmly turned to her business. The trick was to stay out of her way, as one would shelter from a rainstorm until the thunderclouds drifted away. So Rosamund stood half-hidden behind the looped-up bed curtains, clutching at a stack of prayer books as she watched the scene.

She doubted she could ever be as sanguine as Lord Burghley. No doubt he had witnessed such storms many times before and knew ways to persuade the Queen to do things for her own good. Today he tried to urge her to curtail the elaborate Christmas festivities in order to see to her safety. To stay guarded in her privy rooms until the mysterious Lord of Misrule was captured and questioned.

It would surely not be long, not with a furious Lord Leicester and his men tearing the palace apart. But the Queen would hear none of it.

'Your Grace,' Burghley said. 'None could ever accuse you of being a shivering coward. But it would not be wise to go among crowds when there is some plot at work.'

'Plot!' Elizabeth snorted. 'It was hardly a *plot*, just some holiday mischief against Leicester, who could certainly stand to be taken down a peg or two, anyway.'

'I cannot disagree with Your Grace about that,' Burghley said wryly. 'Yet we cannot know if it was solely a prank against Robert Dudley, or if deeper forces are at work. The fact that some villain was able to infiltrate your feast is most alarming. With the Spanish, the French and the Queen of Scots all in communication…'

'Do not speak to me of the Queen of Scots!' Elizabeth shouted. A maidservant who had cautiously begun to pin up her red hair hastily backed away. 'I am sick of the sound of her name. First Lady Lennox constantly beseeching me to let her useless son go to Edinburgh, and now you. Can I not enjoy my Christmas at least without *her* intervening?'

'I fear we cannot stop her from "intervening",' Burghley said. 'She is a constant threat, Your Grace, just over the border as she is and with France at her back. Her ambition has long been well-known.'

'If she would do as I say and marry Lord Leicester, her ambition would be curtailed,' the Queen muttered, reaching for a scent bottle. The smell of violets filled the chamber as she dabbed at it distractedly.

'Do you really think she will do that?' Burghley said.

Elizabeth shrugged. 'Not with Leicester distracted by some silly prank.'

'And what if it is not some silly prank, Your Grace?'

The Queen sighed. 'Very well. Add more guards to the chapel and the corridors. But that is all I agree to!'

'It would be best for you to stay here in your apartments.'

'Nay!' Elizabeth shook her head fiercely, dislodging the pins that had just been eased into her hair. 'It is Christmas Day, probably dear Mistress Ashley's last, and I want her to enjoy it without worry. Time enough for doom and gloom later.'

'Very well, Your Grace.' Burghly bowed and departed, leaving the ladies to hover indecisively.

Until the Queen again pounded on her table, tumbling the jewels back to the floor. 'Why are you all standing about so slack-jawed? We must to church! And those sleeves will *not* do, fetch the gold ones.'

At last she was dressed in her fine green-and-gold garments, her hair bound up in a gold-net caul and jewelled band, her fur-lined cloak draped over her shoulders. She held out her beringed hand for her prayer book, which Rosamund hastened to give her.

'Thank you, Lady Rosamund,' the Queen said. 'Will you walk with me to the chapel?'

'Of course, Your Grace,' Rosamund said, surprised. Her allotted place was at the end of the procession with the other maids. But she could hardly protest with the Queen. She stayed by Elizabeth's side as they left the bedchamber and made their slow way through the Presence and Privy Chambers and along the gallery, where other courtiers joined the retinue.

'You danced with our unknown Lord of Misrule last night, did you not?' the Queen asked quietly, smiling and nodding at the crowds who made their obeisances to her.

'Yes, Your Grace,' Rosamund answered. She had been woken far too early that morning by Burghley to be questioned about it, too. She had no more to add, and was afraid of what might happen if they thought she did know more.

'You have no idea who he was?'

'None, Your Grace,' she said, giving the same answer she'd given Burghley—the only answer she had. 'He was masked, and I have not been at Court long enough to recognise anyone by their mannerisms.'

'It was probably not a courtier anyway,' the Queen said with a sigh. 'If you see anything else, anything at all, you will tell me immediately.'

'Of course, Your Grace.'

'In the meantime, I believe you know our newest arrival at Court, Mistress Celia Sutton?'

'Her family lives very near mine at Ramsay Castle, Your Grace. I do know her a little.'

'She has brought us a petition, one of dozens to be considered this holiday. Perhaps you will speak with her about it and tell me your thoughts.'

'Certainly, if Your Grace wishes it,' Rosamund said slowly. She had no idea what sort of petition Celia could be bringing to the Queen, or what she, Rosamund, could think of it. But if she helped the Queen then perhaps in turn the Queen could help her—and Richard.

If that was what she still wanted…

Rosamund remembered well the night before, kissing Anton Gustavson behind the tapestry. Nay, not just kissing, wrapping her bare legs around his hips, feeling his mouth on her breast, the hot, heady plunge down into desperate desire. A wild recklessness that was unlike her but could not be denied. She had wanted Anton, wanted him madly, beyond all reason.

She wanted him still.

She had been awake all night, pretending to sleep as she'd listened to the whispers of the other maids. In reality, she thought of nothing but him, of his kiss, the way his hands had felt as they'd slid against her naked skin. Of all the things she wished he would do to her— naughty, wicked, delicious things she had never dared think of before. That she had never wished of Richard. And that was what really worried her. She had come here to serve the Queen, to prove herself to her family again, not get them into even more trouble.

Nay, she had to be very, very careful.

Her cheeks felt hot again as they turned onto yet another corridor, and she cursed her pale skin as she clutched at her prayer book until its leather edges bit into her hand. She was a most disloyal lover. Surely it was very wrong of her to think such things of the dark, dashing Swede, a man she had just met, when she had vowed to defy her parents for Richard?

Perhaps it was the romantic intrigues of Court invading her thoughts and emotions, turning her from herself, from her plans for the future. Aye, that was it. She needed to talk to Celia, to hear news of home.

Rosamund filed into the chapel, taking her seat on the bench behind the Queen's high-backed chair with the other maids. Even in the chapel—a long, vast space of soaring, ribbed ceilings, and marble columns draped with royal standards—there were gossiping whispers, but they were hushed. A breath of wind blew along the aisles between the cushioned benches.

Rosamund folded her hands atop the prayer book in her lap, staring up at the window high above the altar to the east of the chapel. But the reds and blues of the Crucifixion and Resurrection scenes were muted in the grey day and gave little scope for contemplation or distraction.

Plus the nape of her neck prickled, as if someone watched her most intently. She rubbed at the tingling spot, peeking surreptitiously over her shoulder.

Anton grinned at her from his place in one of the galleries. Rosamund instinctively wanted to laugh in return, but she pressed her lips tightly, returning her stare to her hands.

She had been so busy with her own feelings about their kiss, about what it meant, but now she wondered what *he* thought. What he felt. Was he, too, moved by what had happened between them? Or was it a mere diversion to him, one of many? She remembered all the ladies who followed him about, and feared she was becoming one of them.

Just another reason to stay away from him. If she could.

She peeked at him again, to find that he still watched her. One of his dark brows arched, as if in question. But she had no answers, either for him or herself.

She faced forward again as Master Buckenridge, one of the Queen's chaplains, climbed into the pulpit. 'On this blessed day of the Nativity,' he began, 'we must always reflect on the Lord's many gifts to us for the year ahead…'

'What then doth make the element so bright? The heavens are come down upon earth to live!'

The Yule log was borne into the Great Hall, carried on the shoulders of a dozen strong men. Anton and Lord Langley had indeed found a grand one, Rosamund thought, applauding with the rest of the company. As long and thick as a ceiling beam, the great, oak log was adorned with greenery and garlands tied up with ribbons. It would be lowered into the great fireplace, where it would burn until the end of the holiday on Twelfth Night.

And, as it burst into light, who knew what would happen?

Rosamund smiled as she watched the log being paraded around the hall, its streamers waving merrily. She remembered Christmases at Ramsay Castle; her father and his men had gone out to proudly carry back the largest, thickest Yule log from their own forest. Her mother had laughingly protested that it was too big even to come through the door. And the entire household would sing as the embers from last year's Christmas had set it alight.

Suddenly, she was engulfed by a cold wave of homesickness, of sadness that she was not there with her family to share their holiday. She felt terribly alone in the very midst of the noisy crowd, adrift.

Rosamund eased away from the others as they pressed towards the log until she could slip out of the doors and into the comparatively quiet corridor. There was no one there to see her as she hurried towards the Waterside Gallery. No one to see the sheen of tears in her eyes.

She furiously scrubbed at those tears, brushing them away as she dashed up a narrow staircase. She was a fool to cry, to miss something she'd never really had in the first place. Once, she had imagined her parents had truly cared for her and her happiness. She had envied their long marriage, their contented home, and had imagined she could have the same. It would never have been with Richard, though; she saw that now.

'It is only the holiday,' she muttered to herself as she tiptoed into the gallery. 'Everyone turns melancholy and sentimental at Christmas.'

She stopped by one of the high windows, leaning on the narrow sill as she peered outside. No one was in the gallery today; they were all in the Great Hall to watch the Yule log being brought in, and she had the echoing space to herself.

The gallery was narrow but very long, running along the Thames to afford a view of the life of the river, the boats and barges that constantly passed by. But now the great river was frozen over, a silver-blue expanse that sparkled under the weak sunlight. Only a small rivulet of slushy water ran along the centre.

Soon it would be frozen, through, solid enough to walk or ride on. Assuredly solid enough to skate on.

Rosamund wondered what it felt like, gliding along as if on glass, twirling through the cold air, her hand anchored in Anton's as he pulled her along. She knew his body now, the lean, flexible strength of it. He knew the ice; could he keep her safe on it too? Teach her his secrets?

'Rosamund?' she heard him say, as if her visions made him real. 'Is something amiss?'

She glanced over her shoulder to see him standing at the end of the gallery. He wore black as usual, fine velvet with an almost blue sheen set off with pewter-grey satin trim that made his dark hair gleam.

'Nay,' she said. 'It was just too warm in the hall. I needed some fresh air.'

'Very wise,' he said, walking slowly towards her. His movements had a powerful, cat-like grace, reminding her of her ice dreams. 'We should save our breath for dancing.'

Rosamund laughed. 'And you will need it. The volta is most challenging.'

He smiled at her, leaning against the window sill at her side. 'Do you think I am not equal to it?'

She took a deep, unsteady breath, remembering the strength of his hands as he'd grasped her waist, lifting her against him as she'd wound her legs around his hips. 'I think you have a fair chance of succeeding.'

'Only fair? You have not a high estimation of my skills, then.'

On the contrary, Rosamund thought wryly. His 'skills' were of a high calibre indeed. 'I am sure you will be able to dance by Twelfth Night. But when can we skate on the Thames?'

He peered out of the window, his dark eyes narrowed as he gauged the view of the river. 'Not long now, I think. But I should hate to try it too soon and run into danger. Not when you have not tried skating before.'

It is too soon; Rosamund remembered her father saying this about Richard. *You do not know him well enough to know your own mind. He is not the one for you.* She sensed, deep down, that Anton was not as Richard was, was not shallow. He was like the river under the ice, all hidden currents that promised escape and wondrous beauty such as she had never known. That was what made him so very dangerous.

'You look sad, Rosamund,' Anton said, turning his intent gaze onto her. 'You *are* unwell.'

She shook her head. 'I am not ill. I was just thinking of my family, my home. Christmas is a very merry time there.'

'And this is your first holiday away from them?'

'Nay. Sometimes, when I was a very small child, really before I can remember, my parents would come to Court. My father served the Queen's father and her brother. But in the last few years we have always been together. My father takes special pride in his Yule log, and my mother would always have me help her make wreaths and garlands to put all over the house. And, on Christmas night, all the neighbours come to a feast in our hall, and it is…'

Rosamund paused, the homesickness upon her again. 'But I will not be there tonight.'

Anton leaned closer to her, his shoulder brushing hers. Rosamund blinked up at him, startled to read understanding in his eyes. Sympathy. 'It is a difficult thing, to feel far from home. From where one belongs.'

'Aye,' she said. 'But your home is much farther than mine, I fear. You must think I am ridiculous, to be so sad when I am here at Court, surrounded by my own countrymen and all this festivity.'

'I do not miss Sweden,' he answered. 'But if I had a family like yours I would long for them, too.'

'A family like mine?'

''Tis obvious that you love them, Rosamund, as they must love you. I've often wondered what it would feel like to have a home such as that. A place to truly belong, not just possess. A place where there are well-loved traditions, shared hopes, comfortable days.' He smiled at her. 'And feasts for the neighbours.'

'I…' Rosamund stared at him in astonishment. He described so exactly her own secret hopes, the dreams she had come to feel were impossible in an uncertain world such as theirs. 'That sounds wondrous indeed. Yet I fear it is an impossible dream.'

'Is it truly? And here I thought your England was a land of dreams. Of families like yours.'

'But what of your own family?'

His lips tightened. 'My family is dead, I fear. Yet my mother, she left me tales of her homeland here. Of, as you say, impossible dreams.'

Rosamund watched him, suddenly deeply curious. What was his family like—his home, his past? Where did he truly come from? What other dreams did he hold? She so wanted to know more of him, to know everything. To see what else they shared. 'What tales did she tell you, Anton?'

But the moment of quiet, intense intimacy was gone, vanished like a rare snowflake drifting towards earth. He gave her a careless smile.

'Far too many to tell now,' he said. 'Don't we have a great deal of work to do if I am to dance a volta on Twelfth Night?'

Rosamund sensed he would share no more glimpses of his soul now, and she should guard hers better. 'Quite right. Come, we will begin our lessons, then.'

'Just as you say, my lady,' he said, giving her an elaborate bow as he offered his hand with a flourish. 'I am yours to command.'

Rosamund laughed. She doubted he was anyone's to command at all, despite the fact that he was here on an errand for his king. But she would play along for the hour. She took his hand, leading him to the centre of the gallery.

As his fingers closed over hers, she had to remind herself that they were here to dance. To win—or, rather, lose—a wager, not to hide behind tapestries and kisses. To fall deep, deep into that blissful forgetfulness of passion. To leave behind the Court, the Queen, all she owed her family, all the careful balancing that life at Whitehall was. She wanted him, and that could not be. Not here, not now.

'Now,' she said sternly, as much to herself as him. 'We begin with a basic galliard. Imagine the music like this— one, *two*, one, *two*, three. Right, left, right, left, and jump, landing with one leg ahead of the other. Like so.'

She demonstrated, and he followed her smoothly, landing in a vigorous leap.

'Very good,' Rosamund said, laughing. 'Are you certain you do not know how to dance?'

'Nay. You are merely a fine teacher, Lady Rosamund.'

'We shall see, for now we come to the difficult part. We take two bars of music now to move into the volta position.' Rosamund drew in a deep breath, trying to brace herself for the next steps.

Her parents considered the volta a scandalous Italian sort of dance, and had only allowed her to learn it when Master Geoffrey had insisted it was essential at Court, the Queen's favourite dance. But Master Geoffrey was an older, mincing, exacting man who tended to have loud, ridiculous tantrums when frustrated by her slowness. She had a feeling that dancing the volta with Anton would be a rather different experience.

'Now, let go of my hand and face me, like so,' she said, trying to be stern and tutor-like.

'And what do I do now?' he said, smiling down at her as they stood close.

Rosamund swallowed hard. 'You—you place one hand on my waist, like this.' She took his right hand in hers, laying his fingers just where her stiff, satin bodice curved in. 'And your other hand goes on my back, above my...'

'Your—what?'

'*Here.*' She put his hand above her bottom, her whole

body feeling taut and brittle, as if she might snap as soon as he moved his body against hers.

His smile flickered as if he, too, felt that crackling tension. 'And what do you do?'

Stand and stare like a simpleton, mayhap? Rosamund could hardly remember. 'I put my hand here, on your shoulder. Now, you face me thus, and I face to the side. We turn with a forward step, both with the same foot at the same time. One, two…'

But Anton got ahead of her, stepping forward before she did. His leg tangled in her skirts and she tilted off-balance, falling towards the floor.

'Oh!' she gasped, clutching at his shoulders. His balance from skating on the ice stood him in good stead, though, for he caught her swiftly in his arms, swinging her upright before she could drag both of them down.

'You see why I do not dance?' he muttered hoarsely, his gaze on her parted lips as he held her above him, suspended above time. 'Disaster always ensues.'

Rosamund shook her head. 'You give up too easily, Master Gustavson.'

'Me? I never give up. Not when something is of importance.'

'Then we should begin again,' she whispered, her mouth dry.

He nodded, slowly lowering her to her feet until they once again had themselves in position.

'After—after the step, which we take *together*,' she said, 'We turn with another step. Hop onto the outside foot—' she tapped at his foot with her toe '—and lift the inside foot ahead. See?'

They made the step and hop with no incident, and Anton grinned at her. 'Like thus? Perhaps this dancing business is not so very difficult.'

'Do not get *too* confident, Master Gustavson,' she warned. 'For now is the difficult part.'

'I am ready, Madame Tutor.'

'After the hop, there is a longer step on the second beat, close to the ground, thus. And that is when I bend my knees to spring upward.'

'What must I do?'

'You lift me up as I jump, like…' He suddenly swung her into the air as if she was a feather, his hands tight at her waist. Rosamund laughed in surprise. 'Aye, like that! Now, turn.'

He spun her around, both of them laughing giddily. The bright glass windows whirled around her, sparkling as diamonds. 'Not so fast!' she cried. 'We would knock over all the other dancers.'

He lowered her slowly to her feet, still holding her close. 'Then how do we turn properly?'

'We, well, it is a three-quarter turn at each measure. When the crowd cries out "volta!" we do it again. Then we return to the galliard position.'

'That does not sound so jolly,' Anton said, twirling her up into the air again. 'Is not our version much better?'

Rosamund laughed helplessly, laughed until her sides ached and tears prickled at her eyes. She couldn't remember ever laughing so much, or ever being with anyone who made her feel as Anton Gustavson did— as if she was carefree again, as if the world was all laughter and dancing.

'Our version is merrier,' she cried. 'But I do not think it would win the Queen's wager!'

He lowered her to her feet again, yet the gallery still spun around her. She clung to his shoulders, aching with laughter, her breath tight in her lungs. This, surely, was how all those ladies who got into trouble with the

Queen for their amorous affairs felt right before they plunged down into ruin? It was intoxicating—and worrying.

'Why does it feel as if we have already won?' he whispered against her hair.

Rosamund stared up at him, startled by his words. He, too, looked startled; for a mere instant, it was as if his courtly mask had dropped. She saw surprise and a naked longing in his eyes that matched her own. And briefly a flash of loneliness, assuaged by their laughter.

Then it was gone; the armoured visor dropped back into place. He stepped back from her, giving her a quick, small bow.

They were separate again, as if the frozen Thames lay between them. And it felt even colder after the bright sun of their shared laughter.

'Excuse me, Lady Rosamund,' he said roughly, his accent heavy. 'I fear I have an appointment I have forgotten. Perhaps we can have another lesson tomorrow.'

Rosamund nodded. 'After the Queen's hunt.'

He bowed again and walked away, leaving her alone in the middle of the empty gallery. Rosamund was not sure what to do; the silence seemed to echo around her, the air suddenly chilled. She rubbed at her arms, wondering what had just happened.

Everything had been turned tip-over-tail ever since she'd arrived at Court. She hardly seemed to know herself any longer, and she did not know how to set it aright again. She seemed to be infected with the pervasive air of flirtation and romance all around at Whitehall, that danger and amorous passion all mixed up into one intoxicating brew.

Perhaps if she went home to Ramsay Castle? Yet, even as she thought it, Rosamund knew that would not be the cure. Even if she did go back, and everything there was just the same, *she* would be different. She was not the same as she had been before she'd come to Court and seen the wider world. Before she'd met Anton.

She left the gallery, walking down the stairs and turning back towards the long walk to the Privy Chambers and the Great Hall. She needed to be around people, to find some distraction.

But even in the crowded hall, where the Yule log at last smouldered in the vast stone grate, she found no respite from her restless thoughts. Anton stood near the fireplace, but he was not alone. Lettice Devereaux, Lady Essex, stood beside him; the two of them had their heads bent together in quiet conversation, her hand on his sleeve. The pretty countess's dark-red hair, laced with fine pearls, gleamed in the firelight.

So that was his urgent 'appointment', Rosamund thought, feeling some hot emotion like temper rise in her throat, choking and bitter. She suddenly wished she was the Queen, so she could throw her shoe at his too-handsome, too-infuriating head! She had been all in a quandary over him, while he'd merely had one of his many flirtations to see to.

First Richard had vanished, never writing to her, and now this. 'A pox on all men,' she muttered.

'I see you have at last settled into the ways of Court,' she heard Anne Percy say in a most smug tone.

Rosamund glanced over her shoulder to see her friend standing close behind her. Anne smiled at her. 'We must all be in either a passion or a pique over someone,' she said. 'It is not Court life otherwise.'

Rosamund had to laugh. 'I don't wish to be in either.'

Anne shrugged. 'You cannot escape it, I fear.

There is only one cure, though I'm afraid it is only a temporary one.'

'What is it?'

'Shopping, of course. Catherine Knyvett tells me that Master Brown's mercer's shop in Lombard Street has some new silks from France. The Queen is with her Privy Council now and does not need us until this evening, we should go purchase a length or two before all the other ladies snatch them away. There is no better distraction from thoughts of dim-witted men than looking at silks.'

Rosamund nodded. She needed more than anything to cease thinking of men—one in particular. It had all gone much too far. 'Yes, let's. A temporary cure is surely better than none at all.'

'Here comes I, old Father Christmas!' proclaimed the player on the Great Hall's temporary stage, striding about in his green-velvet robes and long, white beard to much laughter from the audience. 'Christmas comes but once a year, but when it does it brings good cheer. Roast beef and plum pudding, and plenty of good English beer! Last Christmastide I turned the spit, I burnt my finger and can't find of it!'

The gathering burst into more helpless laughter as Father Christmas hopped and flailed around, but Anton found he could pay no attention to the stage antics. He could not look away from Rosamund's face.

He stood along one of the panelled walls, hidden in the shadows, while the rest of the company sat on tiered benches rising behind the Queen's tall-backed chair. The maids were on either side of her in their shining white-satin gowns, and Anton had a perfect view of Rosamund as she watched the mummers' play.

Her cheeks, usually winter-pale, glowed bright pink as she laughed. Every trace of the wariness that often lurked in her eyes was gone as she joined with the others in the holiday fun.

He could not turn away; he was utterly enraptured by her. Despite the way he had made himself leave her that afternoon, had made himself remember why he was in England—why there was no room for such a lady in his life—he had not been able to cut her from his emotions. From his thoughts, his heated imaginings.

She pressed her hand to her lips, her eyes shining with mirth, and he remembered too well what those lips felt like against his. How she tasted more intoxicating than any wine, sweet and tempting. How their bodies felt pressed together in the darkness. And how he wanted so much more, wanted to taste her breast against his lips, feel her naked skin, wanted to drive himself into her and feel that they were one.

Would nothing ever erase that raw need he knew whenever she was near? For one more smile from her, he would forget all he worked for here—and that could never be. He had promises to keep, to himself as much as his family, and he could not be lured from them by Rosamund Ramsay's kisses, by the softness of her white skin—as hard as it would be to resist! Perhaps harder than anything he had done before.

But his passion put Rosamund into danger, made her place at Court threatened. He could not do that to her.

'I'll show you the very best activity that's shown on the common stage,' said Father Christmas, sweeping his long sleeves to and fro. 'If you don't believe me what I say, step in, King George, and clear the way!'

A knight in clanking, shining armour leaped onto the

stage, and for a moment a ripple of silent unease spread across the room as everyone remembered the strange Lord of Misrule at the Christmas Eve banquet. Leicester and his men gathered closer to the Queen, and Anton reached for the dagger sheathed at his waist. If that villain dared return, he would not again touch Rosamund!

But the knight threw back his helmet's visor, revealing the pretty face of Anne Percy. She bowed elaborately amid much applause and relieved laughter, the elaborate plumes of her helmet flourishing.

Anton noticed Lord Langley scowling as he watched the stage, watched Anne Percy swagger back and forth, brandishing her sword. For an instant, he almost looked as if he would snatch her off the stage, but then he just swung around, pushing his way out of the mirthful crowd.

Anton shook his head ruefully. So, he was not the only one infatuation had wreaked havoc with here at the English Court! Cupid played at Christmas too. Langley and Anne were bold indeed, and surely braver than Anton when it came to matters of the heart at Court.

'I am King George, this notable knight!' Mistress Percy proclaimed, waving her sword high. 'I shed my blood for England's right. England's right and glory for to maintain! If any should challenge me, I stand ready.'

As she swung the sword in a wide arc, another knight, clad in matte-black armour and a black-plumed helmet, leaped onstage.

'I am that gallant soldier, Bullslasher is my name,' he announced, his voice deep and muffled behind the visor. 'Sword and buckle by my side, I mean to win the game! First I draw my sword—then thy precious blood.'

Anne Percy laughed. 'Don't thou be so hot, Bullslasher! Don't thou see in the room another man thou has got to fight?'

'Nay—a battle betwixt thee and me, to see which on the ground dead first shall be. Mind the lists and guard the blows—mind thy head and thy sword.'

Their swords met in a great clash; for a moment Anton—and, it appeared, everyone else—forgot it was a mere mock Christmas battle. The two players fought fiercely, first one then the other driven back to the very edge of the stage. The laughter in the hall faded, replaced by a taut tension, a breathless silence as the battle ground furiously on.

At last, King George was the one pushed back, falling to the stage as her sword skittered away. Bull-slasher's blade pressed to her armoured breast, but she was undaunted, heaving up to push his helmet away.

Lord Langley's face was revealed, streaked with sweat, set in anger.

'You!' Anne cried. 'What have you done with Master Smithson? How dare you…?'

Queen Elizabeth rose abruptly to her feet, her emerald-green skirts swaying. 'Enough,' she said loudly. 'We are bored with this scene, bring back Father Christmas. Lord Leicester, perhaps you would escort the gallant King George from the hall so he can change his garb?'

In only a moment, Leicester had herded Anne Percy from the stage and Lord Langley had vanished, leaving a rather bewildered Father Christmas to resume the play with a doctor but no wounded King George. He managed it, though, helped by the Queen's loud laughter, and soon the rest of the company was laughing and clapping again.

Anton looked to Rosamund. She still sat in her place behind the Queen, but her rosy laughter had faded; her brow had creased with puzzlement. Her gaze suddenly met his, and she did not turn away. She just watched him, and the rest of the room faded into a dark silence.

The bright, shimmering cord that was *her*, that was the ephemeral bond between them, tightened around his heart. Suddenly he knew too well how Lord Langley felt—but fighting against desire only made it flame hotter.

Rosamund whispered something to Mary Radcliffe, who sat beside her, before hurrying out of the hall. Anton followed, needing to make sure she was well and safe. He would not let her see him; if they spoke, if she came close, he wouldn't be able to stop himself from kissing her. And more—much more.

She hurried up the stairs toward the maids' apartment, her gown a white beacon in the night. At the top she glanced back down, and he thought she glimpsed him there, that she would call out.

But she just shook her head, running back along the corridor out of sight. He stood there until he heard her door shut, a click in the distance. Even then he could not quite turn away, could not leave her.

He sat on the bottom step, resting his elbows on his knees as he listened to the laughter from the hall. His plans had been so carefully laid out when he'd left Sweden for England; he'd known just what he wanted, what he had to do. Now it all seemed in complete disarray, like a pair of dice tossed up in the air and yet to land. What danger awaited when they came to earth?

'Good eve to you, cousin,' he heard a soft voice say.

He glanced up, cursing his distraction, to find Celia Sutton standing across the corridor as still as a marble sculpture. He rose to his feet, watching her warily.

If Rosamund Ramsay was a bright winter-fairy, Celia was a night bird, all glossy black hair and black-satin gown, her jewels onyx and dull diamonds. Her pale, pointed face was framed by a high, fur-trimmed collar. She, too, gazed at him with wariness in her eyes.

'I see you also needed a respite from false merriment,' she said.

'Is it false?' he said. Another burst of loud laughter drifted out of the hall. 'The pleasures of the holiday seem real enough here.'

'Of course it is false—as everything is here at Court.' She took a step towards him, her gown whispering over the stone floor. 'I will give you warning, cousin—I don't know how it is in Sweden, but here one must always beware the promises of princes. Of *all* men. For they are as hollow and changeable as Christmas cheer. And I will say this too—an English wife will not help you to Briony Manor, even a daughter of an earl.'

There was a chilly bleakness to her words, a flat hollowness in her eyes that made him half-raise his hand towards her. She was his family, after all, his own mother's niece, despite their rivalry, despite the fact that they were strangers to each other. Despite her warnings.

But she'd already turned away, vanishing down the corridor like a black wraith. He was alone again. Alone with the secrets of his own heart, and the yearnings that could prove his undoing at last.

Chapter Seven

St Stephen's Day, December 26

'Make way for the Queen! Make way for the Queen!'

The guards in the lead of the royal procession cried out as they made their slow way down the Strand, through Cheapside and towards London Bridge. Eventually they would make it to Greenwich Great Park for their hunt, but the Queen seemed in no hurry at all. From atop her prancing white horse, she waved and smiled at the crowds as they cheered for her and tossed bouquets of winter greenery.

Everyone seemed so happy they did not notice the extra number of guards, the way they suspiciously scanned the throngs of people, nor did they notice Leicester and his sword close by Elizabeth's side. The bitter winter and all it entailed was lost in the excitement of seeing their queen.

Rosamund also studied the scene from atop her own horse, trying to keep the prancing, restive little mare from edging out of line. These were the same narrow, dirty, crowded streets she'd traversed on her way to Whitehall, yet they were transformed. The cobbles were scrubbed clean, covered by a new layer of snow and frost in the night that made the greys and browns of the city shimmer. Wreaths and swags of Christmas greenery draped from windows, where more people strained for a glimpse of their queen.

And the Queen rewarded them. Clad in a riding costume of red and dark-brown velvet, a tall-crowned, plumed hat on her head, she waved and laughed.

'Good people, pray do not remove your hats!' she called out. 'It is much too cold.'

But still they did remove their hats, brandishing them in the air as she passed by. A merry, excited gathering indeed.

Rosamund remembered her father's story of the Queen's first entrance to London after her accession to the throne. He had been there, witnessing the pageants and plays, the yards and yards of white satin and cloth-of-gold, the fountains running with wine; the ecstatic jubilation after years of fear and oppression under Queen Mary and her Spanish husband, the hope centred around the young, red-haired princess.

It seemed none of that had faded in six years. The crowds happily gathered in the bitter cold just to wave at Queen Elizabeth.

'Is it like this every year?' Rosamund asked Anne, who rode beside her.

'Oh, yes,' Anne said. 'Londoners wait all year for the St Stephen's Day hunt, or for the Queen to leave on her summer progress. It takes hours to depart the city then, with all the baggage carts.'

Rosamund laughed, picturing the endless train of

carts it would take to transport the contents of Whitehall, both humans and furnishings. 'I can imagine.'

'But you needn't worry about that, Rosamund! You
will be married and settled in your own home before we
go on progress again.'

Rosamund smiled, but in her heart she doubted that
prospect. Ramsay Castle, Richard—it all seemed
terribly far away, further with every day amid the sparkling distractions of Court. Richard's face faded in her
mind, like a painting left too long in the sun—and other,
more vivid images replaced it. Had her father been
right? Yes, indeed, he had. For Anton was different from
Richard, from anyone else she had ever known, and her
feelings for him were richer and deeper than any she
had ever known.

She shook her head. She could not think of all that
now, with her horse frisking about and crowds pressing
on all sides. She had to keep her place in the procession
and not fall behind.

On London Bridge, that vast edifice lined on either
side with looming structures of houses and shops, they
stopped to listen to a children's chorus sing a Christmas
tune for the Queen.

'Blessed be that maid Marie, born was he of her body!
Very God ere time began, born in the time of Son of
Man.' Their sweet, young voices rang out in the cold, clear
air, like holiday angels soaring over the earth. Their little
round faces, scrubbed clean for this important moment,
reflected nervousness, joy, terror and sheer pleasure.

Rosamund had to smile as she watched them, for she
knew how they felt. It reflected her own emotions ever
since she'd come to Whitehall and begun learning new,
frightening things about herself: that she was not
entirely the quiet, shy girl her family thought her; that

she needed a man who could bring out those depths in her, could understand them. And someone whose own depths she could spend a lifetime discovering for herself.

She had grown up, and found her woman's heart.

She glanced back over her shoulder to where the Swedish party rode. Anton was in their midst, once again clad in black wool and leather riding-clothes. He almost looked like a centaur on his glossy black horse, a powerful warrior set to thunder into battle. His face was drawn in serious, thoughtful lines, his shoulders held taut under his short cloak, as if he planned his war strategy.

How endlessly interesting he was, she thought as she studied him. He was constantly revealing new facets, new contrasts of light and shadow. He could laugh and jest as if he hadn't a care in the world, could tease and flirt and play the courtier, the lover of ladies. Yet she could see the flash of granite-hard determination beneath the laughter. He hid secrets there, she was sure of it.

What was his life like in Sweden? What did he really hope to gain here in England—a disputed estate? Or something more?

Rosamund wished she knew how to find out. Wished she had had more years at Court to learn subterfuge and intrigue.

Anton caught her watching him and grinned at her. Once again that secret solemnity vanished, like a cloud burned away by the sun. She smiled back, facing ahead as the song ended and a girl stepped forward to give a bouquet of herbs to the Queen.

Rosamund's gaze caught the heads displayed over the entrance to the bridge, a gruesome contrast to the music, the happy cheers. Their empty eye-sockets proclaimed silently that all was not entirely merry in the

Queen's realm, even now at Christmas. Everyone had their secrets, and some led to pikes on the bridge.

They moved forward again, their long train snaking along the bridge and out of London proper. The congestion of narrow streets flowed to large estates along the river, and then to farms and fields. There were people to cheer even there, but they were fewer, and progress was quicker. Then they were on the road to Greenwich.

The tightly packed procession fanned out, still following the Queen and Lord Leicester, but more fluid. Conspirators and couples found each other, hoping for a quiet word before the rush of the hunt.

Anton drew up next to Rosamund just as Anne discreetly pulled away, falling back to ride with Catherine Knyvett. Rosamund smiled at him tentatively, not sure what to expect after he'd left their dance lesson so abruptly the day before.

'Good day to you, Master Gustavson,' she said.

'And to you, Lady Rosamund,' he answered. 'How do you fare this morning?'

'Quite well, thank you. Fortunately for me, it was Mary Howard who dropped the Queen's necklace and bore her temper today, so I escaped!'

She nearly clapped her hand to her mouth for joking about the Queen's temper in public, but Anton laughed. 'May you fare so well every day at Court.'

Rosamund smiled ruefully. 'We must all take our turn, I fear.'

'But you have had no more encounters with masked villains?' he asked in concern.

'Nay, thankfully.' Rosamund shivered, as much from remembering the Lord of Misrule and his tight grasp on her hands as from the sudden, sharp breeze. 'I have seen nothing at all suspicious, though I'm afraid I am not as observant as I should be here at Court.'

'We must all be vigilant,' Anton said. 'Her Grace does not seem worried, though.'

He gestured towards the head of the procession, where the Queen appeared to be teasing Lord Leicester about something. She leaned from her saddle towards him, laughing as he smiled reluctantly.

'Lord Burghley urged her to curtail the Christmas festivities,' Rosamund said. 'But she refused.'

'Hmm,' Anton muttered. 'She is probably wise. People who plot in the shadows thrive on fear and disruption.'

'So, to combat evil we must laugh and make merry?' Rosamund said. 'La, but I can do that!'

Anton laughed. 'I hope that will always be so, Lady Rosamund. The winter day looks brighter when you smile.'

Rosamund bit her lip, absurdly pleased at his compliment. 'I will smile even more when I win our wager. Should we have a dance lesson tomorrow?'

'I have a better idea,' he said. 'We should go skating.'

'Skating?' she said, startled. 'Already?' She had known that by the terms of their wager she would have to strap on skating blades eventually and launch herself out onto the ice. But not just yet.

'There is no better time,' he answered cheerfully. 'A few of us are going to the pond tomorrow, if you would care to join us once your duties to the Queen are finished?'

A few of us? Rosamund remembered the first time she'd seen him at that pond, when Lady Essex had held onto his arm. And then there was the lady in the gardens, and Lady Essex again yesterday, after he'd left their lesson so abruptly. Would *all* those ladies be there?

'Your friend Mistress Percy is to be one of the party, I believe,' he said, as if he read her doubts. 'It will be a fine respite from the Court. And I promise to be a very careful skating-teacher. I will not let you fall.'

The thought of escaping from the palace for a while, even if it was just a few hours, was very tempting. She missed quiet time to think, to just *be*, and this hunting excursion just whetted her appetite for more.

Not that she would be doing much thinking around Anton! When she was near him, all rationality seemed to fly away. She was just like all those passion-addled courtiers who ended in the Tower, and she surely did not want to be one of them. But there was not much trouble to get into in a large group, surely?

'Very well,' she said. 'The Queen always meets with her Privy Council in the afternoon and will not need us.'

'*Ganska myttig.*' They fell into a companionable silence for a moment as they rode along the country lane. The grime and noise of the city was left far behind, and there was only the rustle of hooves on the frosty earth, their own laughter and talk. Their harmony with each other.

'I am sorry, Lady Rosamund, for my sudden departure from our lesson,' Anton said slowly. 'You must think me ill-mannered indeed.'

Rosamund smiled at him. 'Perhaps manners are different in Stockholm?'

He smiled back wryly. 'We Swedes are rougher, I suppose, but I hope we are not so ungallant.'

'I don't think anyone could accuse you of lack of gallantry, Master Gustavson,' she said. Except perhaps Celia Sutton. But Rosamund had not been able to discover the exact nature of their family quarrel yet. It was yet another of Anton's facets, one of the things that drew her to him to the exclusion of all else.

The gates of Greenwich Palace stood open for them as they turned down a new lane. In the distance, the palace's red-brick towers stood against the pearl-grey sky, but they rode instead towards the waiting Great Park. The undulating hills and slopes, no doubt beautifully green in the summer, were brown and black, streaked with white veins of snow. The bare trees stood like bleak skeletons, frosted with ice at the tips. This would be the last hunt for a while.

But Rosamund did not mind the bare landscape at all. The rush of the cold, fresh wind against her face, the clean, country smells and wide, open spaces felt wondrous after long days indoors. She had not realised just how very much she missed it all, the freedom of the open fields. The horse pranced beneath her, as restless as she was to run.

Rosamund held tight to the reins, keeping the mare in check as they all came to a halt outside the head game-keeper's cottage. The Queen's stewards had to greet her before the St Stephen's Day fox and the Queen's hounds could be set free and they could all take off in pursuit.

She glanced at Anton, who grinned at her again. In his expression, eager and excited, she saw some of her own exhilaration at the day. He was a wild creature, set free from his Court confines at last.

Then the fox was released, streaking away across the field in a russet blur, and the Queen and Leicester shot off after him. Everyone else galloped behind them, fanning out in pursuit to cover the extensive fields and woods. The horses thundered along, as thrilled as their riders to be set free at last.

Rosamund laughed as she urged her mount faster, the wind rushing through her hair, past her ears, in a high, whistling whine. 'I'll race you!' she shouted to Anton.

He also laughed, his horse gaining on hers. They leaped over a shallow ravine, and Rosamund felt as if she was flying. They skittered around a corner through a stand of trees, tumbling down a slope.

The hounds set up a howl in the distance, and the riders turned to follow the beckoning sound. Rosamund tightened her thighs, swinging her horse around, with Anton close behind her. Her horse galloped deeper into the woods, leaping lightly over fallen logs and ditches, veering around corners and off the pathway into the trees, excited by the chance to run. Rosamund laughed, just as excited. She felt free! Free of the stuffy rooms of the palace, of her worries and cares.

Perhaps a bit too excited, for suddenly up ahead of her was a low-hanging branch. She ducked her head, but she was just an instant too slow. The branch snagged at her hat, snatching it from her head. Laughing helplessly, she reined up her horse, leaning over its neck as her stomach ached from the laughter, from the pure wonderment of the chase.

Anton clattered to a halt beside her. His own hat was gone, his black hair rumpled over his brow. 'Rosamund! Are you hurt?'

She shook her head, quite unable to draw breath to speak. 'Only my dignity, I fear.'

He swung down from his saddle, reaching up to grasp her waist and lift her down beside him. She leaned against his shoulder, gasping for breath. His heart pounded in her ear, and he smelled delicious, of leather, soap, snow and honest sweat.

She wrapped her arms around his shoulders, holding him tight. How he seemed a part of this day, of the freedom and excitement. Of the wide outdoors and the wild, winter beauty.

'I am quite sure the Queen never loses her hat,' Rosamund murmured.

'The Queen would be fortunate to be half the rider you are, Rosamund,' he answered. 'You led me on a grand chase.'

She tilted back her head, staring up at him. His high cheekbones were stained a dull red with exercise and emotion, his eyes as black as midnight. A few tendrils of hair clung to his brow.

She had never seen anything so beautiful in her life.

'What will you do now that you have caught me?' she whispered.

In answer, he kissed her, his mouth taking hers hungrily as they clung together. His hands at her waist dragged her closer, until they were pressed together. She went up on tiptoe, wanting more, wanting to feel every inch of his body against hers.

His lips opened, welcoming the press of his tongue to hers, the wet, humid heat of desire that blotted out all else. The day wasn't cold now—it sizzled with a need so deep, so elemental, she could no longer deny it even to herself.

She twined her gloved fingers into his hair, holding him to her, half-fearing he would try to escape her. But he made no move to leave her; his kiss deepened even more, his lips slanting across hers.

Through the haze of her need, she felt one of his hands slide to her bodice, freeing the top button of her riding doublet, then the next and the next. As the cold wind bit through her thin chemise to touch her bare skin, Rosamund felt a shock shiver all through her. It was not frightening or surprising, though. It was just thrilling.

Their kiss seemed to *fit*, as if they had always been

thus, had known each other's mouths and bodies for years and years. He knew just where to press, to feather lightly, to touch just where it would make her world spin.

She moaned against his lips. He drew back at the sound, as if he thought she protested, but Rosamund pulled him back to her, back into their kiss. She didn't want him to leave, didn't want to lose that glorious moment, the way he made her feel. The wondrous, hot forgetfulness.

His fingers fell away from her bodice, but she seized them, carrying them back to finish what they had begun. It was as if her small gesture freed something in him too. He groaned, his kiss deepening; their tongues entwined as his arms tightened around her and he tumbled them both back down to the ground.

Her thighs fell apart and his body cradled between them, hard against her heavy skirts. He leaned his hands on either side of her, their kiss rough and wild, born of the desire that had been simmering like embers from the very first moment they'd met. It burst into flame now, threatening to completely consume her.

Her hands slid down to his backside, taut in his tight leather riding-breeches, and pressed him even closer, wrapping her thighs around his hips as her skirts billowed around them.

'*Alskling,*' he muttered, his voice tight, as if he was in pain. His mouth moved from hers, kissing her jaw and the curve of her neck as she tilted her head back against the soft ground. He impatiently spread the fabric of her riding doublet, revealing her breasts, which were barely concealed in her thin chemise, pressed high over the edge of her light stays.

The cold wind rushed over her, but not for long. His

hot kiss fell on the slope of her breast, making her gasp as his body covered hers.

'Anton,' she whispered, revelling in the delicious sensation of his caress. When Richard had tried such a thing with her, it had frightened her. Now, with Anton, she wanted more and more…

A scream suddenly rent the air. For a shocked instant, Rosamund feared it was her scream, that the wild excitement was breaking free. But Anton rolled off her, his body tense and alert as he peered through the trees.

Rosamund slowly sat up, drawing the gaping edges of her doublet together, hardly daring to breathe. Her heart pounded in her ears, an erratic pattern veering from sexual desire to sudden fear in only a second.

Another cry rang out, and then a clamour of loud, confused voices. The baying of the hounds carried over it all, a discordant madrigal.

Anton leaped lightly to his feet, reaching out to help her stand. Her boot caught on her skirt hem as she lurched to her feet, and he caught her against him, holding her protectively close. His body was taut as he listened as if, like some graceful, powerful forest creature, he could sense danger tightening all around.

Rosamund curled her hands in the open vee of his shirt, holding on as she too listened. She tried to decipher where the cacophony came from, but it seemed both very distant and impossibly close.

'What is it?' she whispered.

'Shh,' he murmured. He hastily buttoned her doublet and then smoothed his own clothes before taking her hand, leading her back to the horses. 'Stay very close to me,' he said as he lifted her into the saddle. 'I have to get you to the palace, behind sturdy walls.'

Rosamund nodded, enveloped in a haze of confusion. Everything felt unreal, as if she was caught in a bad dream where all was disjointed, out of place. The woods, so peaceful and private only a moment ago, were dark and menacing.

And the man she had kissed so ardently, so overcome with need for him that she'd forgotten all else, was now a cold-eyed stranger. Suddenly she recalled all too well how very little she really knew of him. She had once liked Richard too—how could she trust what she thought of a man, what she felt? Yet still those feelings were there. The attraction, the trust. The danger.

He swung up onto his own mount, flicking the reins into motion. 'Remember,' he said to her, looking at her through those black eyes that saw all and gave nothing away, 'Stay close to me, Rosamund. I promise I will keep you safe.'

Her throat felt dry, aching, but she merely nodded. She urged her horse onto the path behind his, listening to the distant hubbub. The wind whispered through her loose hair, tangling it around her shoulders, and she remembered her lost hat and caul, the hairpins scattered as she and Anton had tumbled to the ground. But it did not seem very timely to mention it.

They emerged from the shelter of the trees to find the rest of the party gathered a short distance away at the edge of the woods. It first appeared that it was merely the capture, the end of the day's hunt, but then Rosamund noticed the pale fear on the ladies' faces, the fury on the men's. The horses pranced restively in a close pack, as if they sensed the confusion.

Anton reached out to grasp her mare's bridle, holding her close as they moved cautiously closer, coming to a halt just beyond the tangled edge of the crowd.

For a moment, Rosamund could see nothing; the

knot of people and horses was too dense. But then it parted, and she saw the Queen and Lord Leicester, their horses drawn up beneath one of the bare winter trees. Leicester held his dagger unsheathed, bellowing something in furious tones, but Queen Elizabeth just stared straight ahead, white-faced.

Rosamund followed her stare—and gasped. Hanging from one of the lower branches was a poppet, with bright-red hair and a fine, white silk gown, streaked with what looked like blood. It was topped with a gold paper-crown, and pinned to the bodice was a sign proclaiming, 'thus to all usurpers'.

Leicester suddenly rose up in his stirrups, slashing out with his dagger to cut the horrible thing down. It tumbled to the frosty ground, landing in a white and red jumble. The hounds crept nearer to it, baying, but even they would not touch the thing. Surely it reeked too much of evil, of traitorous intentions.

A contingent of more guards came galloping over the crest of the hill. As they surrounded the Queen, Anne Percy edged her horse closer to Rosamund's.

'Rosamund!' she cried. 'Are you all right? You look as if you will be ill.'

Rosamund shook her head, sweeping her hair back off her shoulder. 'I just fell behind,' she said. 'I fear my riding skills are poor. And then at last I caught up, only to find—this.' She shivered, staring at the crumpled doll.

Anne nodded grimly. 'The Queen has many enemies, indeed. It is easy to forget that on a fine day like this, but there is always danger for princes. Always black thoughts lurking behind smiles.'

And danger for those near to the princes, too? Rosamund looked back to find Anton again with his

Swedish cohorts, who were listening as they whispered together intently. But he watched her closely, as if he could see her thoughts and feelings. Her suspicions.

Rosamund shivered again; the day was unbearably cold. Anne was right. It was all too easy to forget the realities of the world on a day like this. The fresh air, the wild ride—Anton and his touch, his kiss. It made her forget *everything* and want only him. Only those precious moments when he lifted her above the world.

But that was all an illusion. This was the world, with danger, secrets and hidden agendas all around.

Lord Langley drew near to them, his handsome face also solemn, watchful. Even Anne did not pull away from him today, but leaned infinitesimally towards him, as if she knew not what she did.

'Who has done this?' she asked him quietly.

'No one yet knows,' he answered tightly. 'Greenwich has only a small staff now, and they will be questioned, but it is doubtful they saw anything. The Queen will stay here until her safe transport back to Whitehall can be arranged.'

'It has been a strange Christmas,' Anne said.

'Strange indeed,' Lord Langley said, with a humourless little smile. He pushed the tangled length of his golden-brown hair back from his brow, reminding Rosamund of her own dishevelment—and how she had got that way.

Her enchanted-forest interlude with Anton seemed impossibly distant now.

'Come, ladies, let me see you to the palace,' Lord Langley said. 'A fire is being laid in one of the chambers for you.'

'You seem quite knowledgeable about our sudden

change of arrangements,' Anne said, falling into step beside him as they turned towards the palace. The Queen, surrounded by her guards, had already disappeared through its doors.

'Ah, Anne,' he answered sadly. 'To know all is my constant task.'

The events of the hunt did not seem to greatly affect the maids, Rosamund thought as she lay in her bed at Whitehall late that night. Catherine Knyvett and the Marys were practising their dancing along the aisle between the two rows of beds, galloping and leaping in their chemises as they laughed and shouted.

Rosamund held her book tightly, sliding down against the pillows. How could they possibly dance after all that had happened? Her own mind was still spinning, filled with whirling images of Anton, shouts and screams, hanging dolls. And then the long afternoon in a half-bare chamber at Greenwich until they could be taken back to Whitehall by sleigh along the frozen river.

Queen Elizabeth had been silent as they'd waited, calm and serene. Rosamund could not even fathom her thoughts, her plans. The machinery was turning in the dark background of the Court to find the culprits.

Supper, too, had been quiet on their return to Whitehall, a quick repast in the Queen's privy apartments, but Elizabeth had vowed that the rest of Christmas would go on with no alterations. Feasts, dancing, plays—and foolish wagers—would go on.

'Rosamund?' Anne said softly. 'Are you asleep, or just hiding over there?'

Rosamund tugged down the bedclothes she had piled

around herself, to find Anne watching her from her own bed. 'I'm reading,' she said.

'A great talent you have, then, for reading upside down.'

'What?' Rosamund stared down at her book, only to find that Boethius was indeed the wrong way round. 'Oh, bother. 'Tis true I haven't read a word since I opened it.'

'Better than listening to their shrieking,' Anne said, inclining her head towards the wild dancers.

'How can they be so carefree after what happened?'

'I suppose that is their way of forgetting. Such things occur all too often at Court. My uncle says it is all the foreigners who gather here.'

'The foreigners?'

'Aye. The foreign monarchs must send their delegations, even though many of them secretly think Mary of Scots is the *true* Queen of England. I suppose it is just surprising we don't see more such incidents.'

Rosamund frowned, thinking of Master Macintosh, the glowering Austrians. Of Anton, and all she knew of him—and did not know. 'Perhaps.'

'But if we thought too much of such things we would be frightened all the time,' Anne said. 'Better to get on with our business and forget it. However we can.'

Rosamund sighed. 'I'm sure you are right, Anne. But, still, must they forget by dancing so very *badly*?'

Anne laughed. 'Speaking of dancing,' she whispered, 'How do your lessons progress with the beauteous Master Gustavson?'

'Well enough,' Rosamund said cautiously. 'He has a great deal of natural grace, though perhaps some difficulty remembering the correct progression of the steps.'

'Which will require many more lessons, of course.'

Rosamund had to giggle. 'Mayhap.'

'Oh, Rosamund. Tell me—where were you really when you disappeared from the hunt? For I find it hard to believe you are any kind of poor horsewoman.'

Rosamund feared she could hide nothing from Anne. She surely had a long way to go before she became a true Court lady, jaded with plotting.

She slid down lower in the bed, whispering back, 'I was talking with Master Gustavson.'

'Talking?'

'Yes!' And a bit more—but secret-keeping had to start somewhere.

'Hmm. No wonder you were so flushed. And no wonder you have a little mark just there below your neck.'

Rosamund glanced down, drawing away the wide neckline of her chemise. 'Blast!' she muttered, yanking that neckline higher.

'Not that I blame you one bit. He is a luscious-looking gentleman indeed, all the ladies here are mad for him. But what of your old sweetheart? Do you no longer care for him?'

Rosamund was not sure she had ever cared for Richard, not really. There had only been her girlish dreams, which she had pinned onto him. 'Oh, Anne. I simply don't know. I thought I did once. But I haven't for a long time. Am I a faithless harlot, to be so easily distracted?'

Anne laughed. 'If you are a faithless harlot for a bit of flirting, Rosamund, then so are we all. It's easy to be distracted here at Court, especially if our lovers do not keep faith with *us*. But what think you, really, of Master Gustavson? Is he just a distraction for you?'

If he was, then he was a truly potent one. Rosamund could not think of anyone else when he was around. All the glimpses he gave her of his inner self, of a yearning for a home and place that matched her own, only increased his attraction. What did it mean?

Before she could answer, the door to their chamber burst open. Elderly Lord Pomfrey appeared there, clad in a nightcap tied over his unruly grey hair—and nothing else. His shrivelled, purplish member flapped about as he strode angrily down the aisle.

Rosamund sat straight up, staring in utter startlement as the dancing maids shrieked and dove into their beds.

'You cursed chits have kept me awake for the last time, I vow!' Lord Pomfrey thundered. 'You shout and frisk about all the night long, and it will end here! No more of your riots, I say. No more!'

As he continued his ranting and shouting—stopped only when a most indignant Mistress Eglionby appeared—Rosamund fell back onto her pillows, laughing helplessly. Anne was entirely right—one never knew what would happen at Court.

Chapter Eight

⚜

St John the Evangelist's Day, December 27

The cold air snapped at Rosamund's cheeks, whipping her cloak around her as she wondered if this was such a very good idea. The palace was warm, with plenty of fireplaces to huddle next to, and letters waiting to be written, mending to be done. Surely if she was sensible at all she would be back there?

But at the palace she would have to listen to the Marys gossiping and sniping. And there would be no Anton to look at.

She tucked her hands deeper into her fur muff, watching him as he built a fire with Master Ulfson and Lord Langley. He was a sight to see indeed, his close-fitting dark-brown doublet stretched taut over his lean shoulders as he stacked the wood. He had taken off his cap, and his hair gleamed like a raven's wing. He laughed at some jest of Lord Langley's, his smile as bright as any summer sun. It warmed Rosamund right down to the tips of her toes.

She was very glad indeed that she had ventured out today. Any danger, any doubt, seemed so far away.

That decides it, Rosamund thought cheerfully. *I am a faithless hussy!*

She had to face the fact that whatever had happened with Richard did mean what she'd once thought. That—horrors!—perhaps her parents had been right, that she would know the right person for her, the right situation, when she found it.

But her parents were not here now, and she was starting to enjoy the sensation of being a flirtatious Court lady, at least for a short time. At least for today, with Anton.

She went and sat next to Anne and Catherine Knyvett, where they perched on a fallen log covered by an old blanket. At their feet was a hamper, filled with purloined delicacies from the Queen's kitchen, which Anne was sorting through.

'Oh, marzipan!' she said. 'And cold beefpies, manchet bread. Even wine. Very well done, Catherine.'

Catherine laughed nervously. 'I did feel so terrible filching them. But no one seemed to notice, so I suppose all is well.'

'They are all too busy preparing for tomorrow night's feast to even notice one or two little things missing,' Anne said. 'And, even if they did, the Queen is too busy consulting with her Privy Council to listen to their complaints. Here, Rosamund, have something to drink. Wine will soon warm us.'

'Thank you,' Rosamund said, taking the pottery goblet from Anne. As she sipped at the rich, ruby-red liquid, she went back to studying Anton. The men had finished building the bonfire by the frozen pond, and it crackled and snapped merrily as they watched in smug self-satisfaction.

'Humph,' Anne scoffed. 'They act as if they were the first men to discover fire.'

Rosamund laughed. 'Better than letting us shiver here.'

'Quite right, Lady Rosamund,' Lord Langley said, turning to them with a grin. His gaze lingered on Anne, who did not look at him. 'What would you do without our fire-making skills?'

A reluctant little smile touched Anne's lips. 'Perhaps that is the *only* useful skill you possess, Lord Langley.'

'*Touché*, Mistress Percy,' Anton said. 'A palpable hit from the lady, Lord Langley. It seems we must work much harder to impress your fine English females.'

He sat down beside Rosamund on the log, unlooping his leather skate-straps from over his shoulder. Rosamund did not move away but stayed where she was, pressed to his side, feeling his body next to hers. They seemed wrapped in their own warm cocoon in the cold air, bound by invisible cords of memory and heady desire.

She remembered their kisses in the Greenwich woods, remembered falling heedlessly to the ground, their bodies entwined. She could hardly breathe.

He seemed to remember, too, staring down at her, at her parted lips.

'I doubt anything at all would impress such hard hearts,' Lord Langley said.

'Oh, we are not so immune as all that,' Rosamund said, glancing away from Anton. But even as she watched the red-gold ripple of the fire the spell held, and she was entirely aware of him beside her; their shoulders were touching. Through the thick wool and fur, her bare skin tingled. She worried for a moment they would cause gossip, but the Queen could not see them.

'We are impressed by diamonds and pearls,' Catherine said.

'And fine French silks!' said Anne.

'Furs are rather nice, too,' added Rosamund. 'Especially a nice sable on a day like today. And books! Lots of books.'

'I dare say we could also be impressed by great feats of strength,' said Catherine. 'It is a great pity there are no tourneys in winter.'

'We shall just have to make do with what we have, then,' Anton said, all mock-sadness. 'As, alas, we have no pearls, silks or tourneys to fight in. I challenge you to a race on the ice, then, Langley.'

Lord Langley laughed, pulling out his own skates from his saddlebags. 'Very well, Master Gustavson, I accept your challenge! If the ladies can provide a suitable prize, that is.'

'You shall have our undying admiration,' Rosamund said before Anne could venture something quarrelsome. 'And a share of our picnic.'

'A prize worth fighting for indeed,' Anton said. He bent to strap one of the skates to his boot, tying the leather thongs tight over his instep and calf until the thin, shining blade seemed a part of him.

'Will you gift me with your favour, Lady Rosamund?' he asked as he strapped on the other skate, raising his head to smile at her.

Rosamund smiled back, as she always did when he looked at her that way. His merriment was infectious; it chased away the doubts and fears that plagued her in the night. Until she was alone again, and it all came back.

But not now. Now, she just wanted to feel happy and young again, as she had not done in so long.

'I have never gifted a favour for a skating contest,' she said. 'Or for anything else, either, except country fairs.'

'Is that not what life is about, my lady?' he said. 'New experiences, new—sensations?'

Rosamund shivered, remembering all the new sensations he had shown her already. 'I am beginning to think so.'

She snapped one of the ribbons from her sleeve, a shining bit of creamy silk, and knotted it around his upper arm. It showed there, pale against the brown fabric, and for just a moment Rosamund felt some satisfaction at the mark. He wore *her* favour, fought for her, even if it was just here at this quiet pond with friends watching.

'And a kiss for good luck?' he said teasingly.

She laughed, shaking her head. 'When you have claimed victory, Sir Knight.'

'Ah, so you are right, Lord Langley—your English ladies *are* hard of heart,' Anton said. 'But I shall defeat all foes for you, my lady, and claim my prize ere long.'

He stood up from her side, launching himself onto the frozen pond in one long, smooth glide. As he waited for Lord Langley to finish putting on his skates, he looped around in long, lazy-seeming patterns, backward and forward again. He left smooth scores in the ice, unbroken lines and circles that showed the precision and grace of his movements.

Yet his hands were clasped behind his back, and he whistled a little madrigal as if it was all nothing.

When Lord Langley was ready, they stood side by side on the ice, poised to break into motion.

'Mistress Percy,' Johan Ulfson said as he and the three ladies gathered at the edge of the pond. 'Perhaps you would do the starter's honours? And help to keep count—three laps around the pond.'

Anne drew a handkerchief from inside her sleeve, waving it aloft. 'Gentlemen,' she cried. 'On your marks—one, two, three—go!'

The handkerchief fluttered to the ground and the men shot away. Lord Langley was good, powerful and fast, but not quite with the same easy, leonine grace as Anton. Lord Langley tried to push ahead with sheer, mute speed, but Anton bent lower to the ice, his feet a blur as his steps lengthened.

He truly seemed one with the ice, encircled by the same elegant, easy power, the same single-mindedness of purpose he showed on horseback or in dancing. The rest of the world seemed to vanish for him, and he was entirely, intently focused.

That was how he kissed, too, Rosamund thought as her cheeks turned warm. How he would make love to a woman—as if she was his entire focus, his whole world.

At the end of the pond, they twirled round and circled back. Anton did not even seem out of breath, nor at all distracted from his task, his goal. The onlookers, including Rosamund, cheered as the racers dashed past, and Lord Langley looked up to wave. But Anton appeared not to even hear them.

Three laps was the agreed length of the race, and Rosamund watched, transfixed, as Anton circled around again. He bent closer to the ice, hands behind his back as he flew along faster than she would have thought humanly possible.

Lord Langley, though quite fast when starting out, expended his energy and fell behind. By the time they finished their final loop, and slid past Anne's fallen handkerchief for the last time, he was at least two steps behind Anton. He stumbled off the ice to fall onto the log, laughing and winded.

'I am defeated!' he declared. 'I cede all victory in ice-skating to the barbaric Northman for evermore.'

Anton grinned. He still stood on the ice, balanced lightly on his blades, but he leaned his hands on his knees. His shoulders lifted with the force of his expelled breath. 'You only cede in skating, Langley?'

'Aye. I challenge you to a horse-race next. We Englishmen are renowned for our horsemanship!'

'I would not be so quick to brag, Lord Langley,' Catherine said. 'Did you not see Master Gustavson at the hunt yesterday? It seems the Swedes do not neglect their equestrian education either.'

'And yet they *do* seem to neglect their dancing,' Lord Langley said. 'What say you, Lady Rosamund? How goes your tutelage?'

'Quite well,' Rosamund answered. 'I think he will surprise you on Twelfth Night, if he will apply himself to his lessons.'

'That will be no hardship, I think,' Anton said. 'Given the sternness of my teacher.'

''Tis true,' Rosamund said, pouring out a goblet of wine and finding a serviette in the hamper. 'I am a very stern teacher, indeed.'

As the others turned to the food and the fire, she went to the edge of the pond, watching as Anton removed his skates. When he finished, she held out the wine and cloth to him.

'They are poor spoils for the victorious hero, I fear,' she said.

Anton laughed, wiping at his damp brow. His dark hair clung to his temples, and a faint flush stained his high cheekbones, but those were the only signs of his athletic effort. He looked as if he had just finished a stroll in the garden.

'I would prefer that kiss for my prize,' he murmured.

Rosamund shook her head. 'Patience is another virtue heroes must possess, I fear.'

'And kisses are not so easily won?'

'Hercules, a hero if there ever was one, had *twelve* labours, did he not?'

'You will not make me clean a stable next, will you?'

She laughed. 'That remains to be seen!'

He laughed too, and took a long swallow of the wine. She watched the movement of his throat muscles, fascinated. 'Come, Lady Rosamund, walk with me for a while.'

'Should you not sit and rest?' she asked, glancing over at Lord Langley, who lounged on the fallen log as Catherine fed him marzipan.

'Nay—he will be sorry when his muscles ache tonight,' Anton said. 'It's better to keep moving until the body is cooler.'

Rosamund shivered as another gust of wind swept around her. 'That should not take long.'

Anton left the empty goblet and his skates near the fire, taking her arm as they walked out of the clearing. They went through the narrow, wooded path where Rosamund had walked on her journey into London on that day she'd first seen Anton. Then the bare trees and tangled pathways had seemed somehow ominous, lonely, her heart full of trepidation.

Today, with him by her side, they were beautiful, a Christmas marvel of glass-like icicles and glittering frost. She did not even fear masked Lords of Misrule and dark warnings, not when she was with Anton. She had never met anyone she trusted more to keep her safe; he was so steady, so firm of purpose. So determined.

'I remember when I first saw you,' he said. 'You

suddenly appeared there by that very pond, like a ghost or a fairy. I thought you an illusion at first.'

'And I you,' she admitted. 'I didn't know people could perform such feats on the ice. I am sorry I ran away so quickly.'

'Ah, yes. When you vanished, I was *convinced* you were an illusion!' he said. 'That I imagined a winter-fairy. No human woman could be so very beautiful.'

Rosamund's breath caught in her throat at his words, at the force of them. Anton thought her beautiful! Other men had said so—Richard, men of the Court. Yet they had seemed empty words, polite conventions that they said to every lady. Perhaps that was all it was with Anton, too—but his tone, his gentle smile, had the soft ring of sincerity. And the lure of all she had ever really wanted, despite the danger of reaching out to grasp it.

She had never thought herself beautiful at all, despite the gift of her fashionable pale hair. Next to vibrant women like Anne Percy, Lady Essex, and even Celia Sutton's dark mystery, she was a milk-faced mouse. But with Anton, she felt transformed, like a rosebud under the summer sun. Or a winter-fairy in the ice.

Would she shrink back inward again, when he was gone, back to Sweden?

'Perhaps I never should have spoken to you, then,' she said. 'I like the idea of being a beautiful winter-fairy.'

'*Nej,*' he answered. He suddenly faced her, taking both her hands in his. Holding them tightly, he pressed them to his chest. His heart thrummed against her gloved hands, flowing through her whole body, meeting her own heartbeat, joining their life forces as one.

'A warm, human woman with a kind heart is far better than a cold fairy,' he said. 'You have been a gift in these English days, Rosamund, one I could never have expected.'

'And so have you,' she said, leaning into his body, into the hot protection of his strength. She rested her forehead on his chest, sliding her arms around to wrap all about him, as if by holding tightly she could keep him from flying away. 'I was so sad, so frightened when I came to Court. But that is all gone when I'm with you.'

'*Alskling,*' he whispered, and lowered his head to kiss her.

Their kiss was slow, gentle, as if they had all the time they wanted. As if there were long hours to come to know one another, not the mere stolen moments they really had together.

He framed her face between his hands, softly pressing tastes to her lips as if she was the finest of wines, the most delectable of delicacies. Rosamund revelled in his tenderness, in being close to him. She wanted to memorise every moment, every sensation, store them up for that time when their moments ran out. She flattened her palms against his chest, the fine fabric of his doublet rubbing against her soft skin. She stared, fascinated, at the pulse throbbing at his throat, feeling the rise and fall of his breath under her touch.

Rosamund slid her hands up to curl over his shoulders, holding on tightly as the earth seemed to tilt under her. She felt so giddy, dizzy, with wild anticipation. She went up on tiptoe, leaning against him as he deepened their kiss. His tongue pressed hungrily, roughly, between her lips, suddenly greedy as if he, too, felt that knife-edge of need.

She wanted everything—*all* of him! And she wanted to give him everything of herself. Their tongues mated, clashing, unable to find enough of each other.

But then he drew slowly back from their kiss, from the fireworks building up between them, before they could explode in an uncontrollable conflagration. He rested his forehead against hers, his breath heavy, as if he was in pain.

Rosamund closed her eyes tightly, clinging to Anton as if he would vanish from her, as he well could very soon. He was from Sweden, and surely his errand here would end soon enough. He could gain his English estate, but, even then, persuading her parents as to the prudence of the match would be difficult—as would persuading the Queen, who so hated for her ladies to marry.

And, also, he had not talked to her of any tender feelings, any real intentions. Any plans or hopes for the future. She was a foolish romantic indeed. A romantic who put her love before all else.

Yet this moment, alone with him in the cold winter silence, felt right. Right in a way her hurried meetings with Richard never had been. The deep, dark passion was so very different, the urge to be with him, to know him. She had to absorb every tiny sensation of the now, of how he smelled, how his body felt under her touch. The wind swirled around them as if to bind them together.

This moment might be all she had. She had to make it count, make it a memory she could hold onto for the years ahead.

She tilted back her head to stare up at him. His face was etched in shadows, his smile as bittersweet as the feelings in her own heart. She smoothed back the wind-tossed waves of his black hair from his brow, framing his face in her hands. His skin was warm through the thin leather of her gloves, and with her fingertips she traced the line of his high cheekbones, his nose, the chiselled edge of his jaw. A muscle tensed under her caress.

She wanted to memorise every detail. 'Some day, when I am an old woman huddled by my fire,' she murmured, 'I will remember this moment. I'll remember a young, strong, handsome man who held me in his arms like this. I'll remember everything he made me feel, and made me know about myself.'

He reached up to take her hands in his, holding them tightly. 'What do you feel?' he said roughly, his accent heavy. Usually his English was nearly impeccable, she thought wonderingly, but in moments of emotion the edge of his words turned lilting, musical.

'I feel alive,' she said. 'When I'm with you, Anton, I feel all warm and tingling with life. As if I could fly higher and higher like a bird, above these trees, above Whitehall and London and everything. Fly until I find my own place, where there is safety and happiness always.'

'Oh, *alskling*,' he said, pressing her open palm to his cheek as he smiled sadly. 'There is no place with happiness always.'

'There is when you find your true home, your real place,' she insisted. 'I have always believed that. It is just not easy to find, I fear.'

'And what should one do when it *is* found?'

'Hold onto it with all your might, of course. Fight for it. Never let it go.'

In answer, he kissed her again, pulling her up on tiptoe as their bodies pressed together. Their kiss was swift, hard, a deep caress that tasted of promise. Of hope.

'Rosamund,' he murmured, hugging her close. 'We will meet tomorrow, yes? I think we have much to speak of.'

And more kisses to share? Rosamund could only hope. Feeling absurdly happy, she nodded. 'Tomorrow.'

* * *

Rosamund paused at the top of the stairs leading to the maids' apartment, peering down over the carved balustrade before she turned down the corridor after Anne and Catherine, who had already disappeared. Anton still stood down in the foyer with Lord Langley, laughing over some jest.

How she did love it when he laughed! When he looked so young and happy. It made the whole room seem to blaze with the light of a thousand torches, and warmed her own heart more than any fire could.

If only it could be thus all the time.

He glanced up to find her watching him, and his smile widened. Rosamund waved, laughing, and ducked away.

Perhaps it would not last long, she thought, but surely it would be glorious while it did. She saw now what drove people like Katherine Grey and her secret husband to dive headfirst into foolish passion—it was a force impossible to resist. It was like a sonnet, brought to vivid, unruly life. She did not want to put her reputation, her family's opinion of her, in danger again. But she could not seem to help herself.

She drew off her gloves, holding them carefully as she remembered how she'd touched Anton's face. How she'd felt the heat of him through the leather. Then she laughed at her silliness. Soon she would be pilfering his cap-feather or eating-knife, making a treasure of them!

'Lady Rosamund,' she heard someone say, startling her from her giddy romantic fantasies.

She looked up to find Celia Sutton emerging from one of the chambers. She still wore her mourning colours, a black-velvet surcoat trimmed in dark fur over a violet and black gown. She smiled, yet it seemed tense, unsure, as if she did not often use it.

'Mistress Sutton,' Rosamund answered. At home, they had sometimes called each other Rosamund and Celia when they'd met, but now that felt too strange. 'How do you do this day?'

'As well as one can be, in this crowded, cold city,' Celia answered. 'I look forward to the day I can return to the country, as I'm sure you do too. You must miss Ramsay Castle.'

'Of course,' Rosamund answered. 'But Court has its own attractions, I'm finding.'

Celia's smile stretched tauter. 'Like the Court gentlemen, perhaps?'

'They are handsome, I believe. And fashionable.'

'And clever? Unlike our men of the countryside.'

Rosamund remembered Celia's late husband, Richard's elder brother, who had seemed to be a man who'd enjoyed hunting and hawking and not much else. His conversation at local weddings and banquets had always revolved around how many stags he'd killed on his last outing, how many pheasants bagged, or the new hounds in his kennel. A good-looking man, but a dull one.

Everyone had been secretly surprised when he'd married Celia, the granddaughter of Sir Walter Leonard, a landowner of old and distinguished family from another county. It seemed an uneven match, especially once they met Celia and found she was a dark beauty, well-educated for a lady and very elegant.

It had proved to be a match that did not last long, as the husband had died in a hunting accident a few months later, leaving Richard heir to the family's lands. But it seemed Celia still mourned her husband.

And, Rosamund suddenly remembered, Sir Walter Leonard must also be Anton's grandfather. How strange to think the two of them related. They were so very different—both mysterious, yes, but there was a light edge to Anton that was missing in Celia.

'Court is not *better* than the country,' Rosamund said. 'Merely different. I am finding the experience— educational.'

'Will you stay here, then, and continue that education?'

'I will stay as long as Her Grace requires me. Or until I am needed at home.'

'Home?' Celia said quietly, and Rosamund remembered why she was here at Whitehall—the dispute over the estate.

She also remembered that the Queen had asked her to speak with Celia about the matter.

'I am surprised you travelled all this way in the winter,' Rosamund said. 'Especially when you are still in mourning.'

'I had not the time to have new Court clothes made,' Celia answered. 'But I did not mind the journey. It was a chance to be quiet with my thoughts, away from my husband's parents.'

Rosamund knew the feeling, the inexpressible ache to be alone, to be able to think clearly again. Her own journey to London had taught her so much. 'And will you stay here long?'

'As long as it takes for my petition to be addressed,' Celia said. 'Do you know if the Queen has yet read it?'

'I fear I don't know. She never talks to her ladies of state matters. But she has been quite distracted of late.'

'Oh, yes.' A tiny, humourless smile just touched the corner of Celia's lips. 'The Lord of Misrule and the hanging poppet. What will happen next this Christmas, one wonders?'

'Nothing at all, I hope,' Rosamund said sharply. Only fine things could happen this Christmas; if only there was not that edge of worry constantly hanging over her, over the whole Court.

'Well, what can one expect with a Court full of Scotsmen? Not to mention Austrians—and Swedes. They all have their own scores to settle, their own interests to serve.'

'Just as you have yours?'

'And you yours, Lady Rosamund.' Celia's dark eyes, so like Anton's, narrowed. 'You seem to enjoy my foreign cousin's company.'

Rosamund frowned, slapping her gloves against her palm. 'He is quite charming. I am sure if you came to know him…'

Celia cut her off with a wave. 'I do not *wish* to know him. My grandfather sought to cause a great family mischief in leaving him Briony Manor, but I will soon see things set right. Even if I have to fight here at Court, on my own, to do so.'

'Oh, Celia, he *is* your family. Perhaps you need not be on your own here! If you would talk to him, perhaps an accord could be reached.' Families should surely always be united, whether they were Anton's or her own?

Celia shook her head. 'Lady Rosamund, you cannot understand. You have always had the protection of your family. But I have always been on my own, have always had to fight for my very place in the world. My own father sold me in marriage, and he is now dead. My husband's family cares naught for me now that I am a widow and they owe me my dower rights. My brother-in-law has not even been seen in months—he is probably spending the last of my dowry!

'I will not now throw myself on the uncertain mercies of some foreign cousin. I am not so foolish as that.'

Rosamund knew not what to say. After the sweet delight of her afternoon with Anton, to be faced with Celia's bitterness was saddening. It reminded her too much of the clouds hanging over her own life.

But surely now, at Christmas, anything was possible.

'I am sorry, Celia,' she said gently. 'Yet surely there is time for matters to come aright?'

'Only if the Queen grants me my estate,' Celia answered. 'You will tell me if she mentions the matter?'

'Yes, though I doubt she will to me.'

'Because she keeps her ladies free of serious matters—or because you think my cousin so *charming*?'

Before Rosamund could answer, Celia turned and hurried away down the corridor, her dark garments blending into the late-afternoon shadows. But she left that palpable air of sadness behind her. A sadness that infected everything, and reminded Rosamund of the true danger of her life at Court, her feelings for Anton.

It was only when Rosamund was changing her clothes for the evening's pageant that she remembered something. When they'd met in that corridor, Celia had been emerging from the Scottish delegation's rooms. What business could she have there?

Chapter Nine

Holy Innocents' Day, December 28

The leather tennis-ball smacked against the black-painted walls of the Queen's court, rebounding like a clap of thunder as Anton and Lord Langley raced to defeat each other in their game. Langley was ahead at the moment, but Anton was intent on gaining the winning point by hitting the ball through the opening in the dedans penthouse high above their heads. It was hot work, and neither of them ever seemed to get far enough ahead.

But Anton relished the burn of his muscles, the sweat that dampened his brow. It gave him something to focus on besides Rosamund, something to take the knife-edge from his hunger for her. He gave a fierce swing of his racket, smacking the leather ball back to Lord Langley. Langley dove for it, but missed, falling onto the court floor with a curse. Anton finally hit the ball through the opening, gaining his winning point.

Anton swiped his damp shirt-sleeve over his face, calling out, 'Do you concede then, Lord Langley?'

Langley rolled to his feet, laughing. 'I concede—for now! But this can't go on, Gustavson. First skating, now tennis. I shall have to best you at *something* soon.'

'Such as? It is too cold for a tourney, and everyone is told to stay at the palace for the rest of Christmas.'

'Thus no horse races, fortunately for you,' Langley said. They went to the end of the tennis court, where pages waited with linen towels and warm, velvet jackets to keep away the cold chill from damp skin. 'I am sure I could best you there. For don't you Swedes just skate everywhere?'

Anton laughed, roughly running the towel over his hair. 'Skates are of little use in battle, I fear, so we are sometimes forced to the primitive transport of horseback.'

'Not so very primitive as all that, I hope. Equestrian feats do seem to impress the ladies.'

'As much as they are impressed by a lofty title?'

Langley grinned wryly. 'Alas, that is only too true. I could have a hunchback and a squint, and there would still be ladies to flatter and fawn.' He accepted a goblet of ale from one of the pages, drinking deeply before he added, 'And then there are ladies who are impressed by nothing at all.'

'Sadly, that only makes us want them more, does it not?'

'I see you learn the ways of courtly romance, Master Gustavson.'

'Your English ways, you mean?' Anton drank his own ale, but there was no forgetfulness in its heady, spiced blend. He still saw Rosamund's blue eyes in his mind, felt the touch of her hand on his skin. Her sweetness—the innocent, heedless force of her passion—they were addictive, and he feared he came to need

them more and more as the days went on. He could not
stay away from her.

The more he saw her, the greater her charms. The
more he wanted to know. And that craving was dangerous. It distracted him from his work here, from the
careful plans he had held so long. It made him dare to
think things he never could have before. If he gained
possession of Briony Manor, if he was able to settle in
England, his mother's homeland, if he could take an
English wife...

It was too many 'if's, and Anton preferred to work
in certainties. In what *was*, and how he had to work to
achieve his goals. Rosamund did not seem like a logical
goal. There were too many dreams of her own that she
harboured in her heart; he could see that when he looked
in her eyes.

His cousin Celia accused him of seeking an English
wife to aid his petition for Briony Manor. But she was
wrong. Rosamund was one of the Queen's ladies, and
the Queen did not easily relinquish those in her household to marriage. Such a wife could only harm him in
his errand.

And it would not do her any good, either, even if
Rosamund would have him, which he did not think she
would. He could never do anything to harm her, his
beautiful winter-fairy, even as he fantasised about
making love to her. Of seeing her pale, perfect body in
his bed, her hair spread over his pillows as she held out
her arms to him, smiled at him in welcome.

'*Svordom,*' he muttered, and tossed back the rest of
his ale.

'Our English ways of romance can be labyrinthine
indeed,' Lord Langley said. 'English ladies insist on
being properly wooed, but each of them seems to have

a different notion of what that means. What works for one repels another.'

Anton thought of Langley's efforts to impress Anne Percy, and laughed. 'I thought the ladies claimed to be impressed by pearls and silks.'

'Ah, that is another thing you must learn about our English females,' Langley said. 'What they desire changes day by day. And, also, they sometimes lie, just to confound us. Are the Swedish ladies so contrary? Or is it merely here, because we are ruled by a queen?'

'Nay, the Swedish ladies are every bit as demanding,' Anton answered. 'Perhaps they are affected by what they hear of the English, and insist on poetry and gifts. But matters of marriage are much simpler—it is arranged willy-nilly, and everyone does as they must, poetry or no.'

'So it often is here as well,' Langley muttered.

'Have you a betrothed, then? Someone chosen by your family?'

Langley shook his head. 'Not as yet, though my mother has taken to writing insistent letters every fortnight, suggesting this lady or that. She and her friends have played matchmaker for years, ever since I attained my majority. But I have not yet found the one who meets my family's requirements *and* my own inclination.'

Anton knew how he felt. His duty and his inclinations were decidedly at odds. 'The two are seldom reconciled.'

'How is it that you are not married, Gustavson?' Langley asked. 'You seem to have collected enough female attention here in London. Surely there is some lady in Sweden?'

'I have been too occupied of late with my own family

matters to think of marrying. Perhaps once I have settled into a proper home, a place that needs a chatelaine…' And could that chatelaine be Rosamund? She would grace any house. But the Queen, and her family, would have to let her go first, and he feared they never would. He would not put her in danger by spiriting her away from them.

'Fortunately for us, we don't have to marry every lady who catches our eye,' Langley said, laughing.

'True. But there are some who would insist on it!'

Langley sighed. 'You are correct. But come, enough of this solemn talk! I fear we will never solve the mysteries of women today. Let us go out and see how the frost-fair preparations progress.'

Anton nodded, glad of the distraction. But even then his thoughts were of how much Rosamund would surely enjoy the delights of the frost fair…

'Tidings I bring for you to tell, what in wild forest me befell, when I in with a wild beast fell, with a boar so fierce…'

Rosamund smiled as she passed by the chamber where the chapel choir rehearsed, pausing for a moment to listen to the old tune of the boar's head.

Since tonight's traditional Feast of Fools had been changed to a mere banquet, with the mummer's antics cancelled, everyone had to work just a bit harder to make things festive. Everyone looked forward to the feast of Bringing in the Boar two night's hence.

She did not linger long, though. She had been sent across the palace to fetch some books for the Queen, and still had a distance to go. She didn't mind the errand. It was difficult to sit still in the Queen's chamber, to concentrate on her sewing and the other maids' chatter, when all she could think about was Anton.

She wondered what he was doing today, as Queen Elizabeth had not been receiving any official business and they hadn't seen anyone all morning. Was he off skating again? Walking in the garden, where so many flirtatious ladies waited to besiege him? Or perhaps he was closeted away on his own business, that disputed estate.

Rosamund remembered Celia emerging from the Scottish apartments. It seemed she looked for her allies, no matter how unlikely. Who would stand with Anton? She could, if he would let her. If they could forget the danger of it for only an hour.

She hurried on to find the books where the Queen had left them, and turned back towards the Waterside Gallery. Anne said they were setting up the frost fair on the frozen river, and Rosamund hoped for a glimpse to distract herself, to take a moment to think how she herself could broach the estate matter to Queen Elizabeth.

She leaned against a window sill, staring out at the river scene. It was indeed crawling with activity; from this distance it looked something like a chilly anthill with every ant set to some vital task.

They were building booths for the frost fair, places to sell hot cider and candied almonds, ribbons and lace. Icy avenues were laid out between the sledding and skating. Bright streamers were being tied to the booths, loops of greenery that added to the holiday excitement.

The prospect of the fair was a merry one in the midst of a tense Court. Everyone seemed to walk on a dagger's edge, afraid of what might happen next, even as they tried to hide it beneath Christmas cheer.

Rosamund too felt on edge, but Anton was the largest part of that—not knowing his feelings for her, or even the true nature of hers for him, was difficult. And, too, the fact that she was always daydreaming about him. Surely her distraction would soon earn her a slap from the Queen? Or more, if the Queen ever discovered what was between her and Anton!

But she could not be late with the books. Rosamund took one more peek at the frozen river and hurried away back towards the Queen's chamber.

As she turned through a narrow corridor leading from the gallery to the wing connecting the Privy apartments, she saw a small group headed her way. They were led by Lady Lennox, the Queen's cousin, her stout figure swathed in her usual black satin. She looked even more pinched and unhappy than usual. Probably her petition to the Queen to let her son Darnley go to Scotland, ostensibly to visit his father, was still not progressing well.

Rosamund shrank back into a curtained alcove, having no desire to be the focus of one of the countess's gimlet stares. Or, worse, to be urged to speak to the Queen on her behalf! She was trying to avoid notice and trouble, not court it.

She peeked past the edge of the velvet drape as they drew nearer, their voices a low murmur. With Lady Lennox was the Scotsman Melville—and also Celia. She walked at the countess's side, listening closely as the countess whispered furiously to Melville.

Rosamund could make out none of their words, and they quickly passed onwards, moving out of the corridor. She waited until they were certainly gone before slipping out of her hiding place and away in the opposite direction.

She thought of what Anne's uncle had said, about how the Queen's Court was filled with dangerous foreigners and their intrigues. Yet it seemed even the Queen's own family was not averse to intrigues of their own.

She was so intent on her path that she swung swiftly around a corner, not seeing the man standing there until she collided with him. Strong hands shot out to steady her as she reeled backwards, the books tumbling to the floor.

'Rosamund!' Anton said. 'Where are you off to in such a great hurry?'

Of course it would be him, she thought with a strange mixture of delight and chagrin. He always did seem to see her at her most awkward, her most unguarded! She held onto his arms to keep herself upright, smiling at him.

He looked as if he just came from some exercise, his hair smoothed back damply from his face and his dark eyes shining like polished onyx. He wore a simple black-velvet jacket over his shirt, which was loosely laced to reveal a smooth vee of glistening skin.

Rosamund could not stop staring at that skin, she feared to her great embarrassment. Staring at it—and longing to touch it, to discover exactly what it felt like. To trace a light pattern just there with her fingertips…

'Rosamund?' he said, bemused.

She shook her head, stepping back until her hands fell away from his arms. 'I—I was just fetching some books for Her Grace,' she said, staring over his shoulder at a patch of panelled wall. 'She does hate to be kept waiting.'

'I have certainly been here at Court long enough to know the truth of *that*,' he answered. 'I will not keep you. But should we have a dance lesson tonight?'

'A dance lesson?' she said, her head still whirling.

'Aye. Our time grows short until Twelfth Night. I was playing tennis with Lord Langley this morning, he told me of a chamber near the chapel we could use. It is assigned to his cousin, who is in the country, and thus it is empty. No one would be there to see me make a fool of myself.'

They would be alone? In a chamber, after the banquet? Rosamund was quite sure that under those too-tempting circumstances, *he* would not be the one acting foolish! But she felt as if she had already leaped down into a precipice, tumbling into a dark world she didn't recognise at all and could not stop. Falling, falling, down into peril.

'Very well,' she answered. 'Your dancing could certainly use a great deal of polishing before Twelfth Night.'

He grinned at her and bowed. 'Until then, my lady.'

Rosamund started to turn away, but then swung back, remembering what she had just seen. 'Anton!' she called.

He glanced back at her. 'Aye, Rosamund?'

'Did you…?' She looked around to be sure no one was near, then tiptoed closer to whisper, 'Did you know your cousin has made friends with the Scots delegation?'

His eyes narrowed, but other than that he showed no reaction. 'Friends?'

'I saw her yesterday, coming out of their apartments,' she said. 'And just now walking with Lady Lennox and Melville. Has she some Scottish connection?'

'Not that I know of, but then I know so little of my English family.'

'Could she…?'

'Rosamund.' He took her hand in his, holding it tightly. 'I thank you for telling me this, but pray be very careful in these matters. I know not what game Celia is playing, but with all that has been happening here of late it cannot be good. I will look into it.'

'But then *you* will not be safe!'

He raised her hand to his lips, kissing her bare fingers warmly, lingeringly. 'I have been taking care of myself for a very long time. But if anything happened to you I don't think I could bear it. Promise me you will stay far away from Celia and her—friends.'

Rosamund nodded, curling her fingers around his. He kissed them once more before he let her go. 'Until tonight, then, my lady.'

'Aye,' she murmured. 'Until tonight.'

'One, *two,* three! One, *two,* three! And—jump.'

At Rosamund's words, Anton tried the cadence but landed wrongly, dragging her down with him. She fell to the floor in a tangle of silk skirts, arms and legs—again.

'Oh!' she said, laughing. 'Perhaps it is time for a rest.'

'Rosamund, I am so sorry,' Anton cried, helping her sit up. 'I knew you would come to rue the day you agreed to teach me to dance.'

'I am not quite ruing it yet,' she said, smoothing down her skirts. 'You are getting better, I think. The volta is a very difficult dance.'

'And you are much too kind,' he said, sitting down beside her on the floor, stretching his long legs out before him. 'I can only hope not to cause complete chaos when we dance before the Queen—or injure you before that.'

'As for that, I am sure I'm safer here than in the maids' apartments,' Rosamund answered. 'The Marys leap about, shouting and quarrelling all night long.'

She leaned back on her palms, studying the tapestry-lined walls around them. It was nice in here, in Lord Langley's cousin's room, quiet and peaceful, far from the maids and the rest of the Court as they went to their late-night card parties and then stumbled home drunkenly. There was no fire, but those rich tapestries, the fine rugs on the floor and the exercise kept it warm.

She wished she could just stay there with Anton, cocooned in their own little peaceful place, for the rest of the night. For days and days.

Or at least until the Scots went home, and old Lord Pomfrey ceased to burst in on the maids in the altogether.

'It is not so tumultuous in your own home, I'm sure,' Anton said. He lay down on his side next to her, propping his hand on his palm. His hair was rumpled from their dance, falling in unruly waves over his brow. His fine satin doublet was unbuttoned, revealing his white shirt dampened by their exercise. The candlelight played over the planes and angles of his handsome face.

It all felt so wondrously intimate, just to be so close to him. To feel his warm body next to her, keeping the cold night at bay as they talked. She felt she could tell him anything, share anything with him.

'Ramsay Castle is very peaceful,' she said. 'I have no brothers or sisters, and so have always had my own chamber. I could read there in the evenings with none to disrupt me. But it can be lonely too.'

'I, too, have no siblings,' he said. 'At our home, my father was often away and it was only my mother and me. And the snow and ice!'

'No wonder you are such a fine skater, then.' She wished he would tell her more, tell her all about his life. His past, his hopes, his wishes.

'Aye, for there was little else to do.' He smiled at her, but there was a melancholy tinge to it. A whisper of memories and regrets. 'It was not like a true home.'

'And that is why you want to dance well for the Queen?' Rosamund asked. 'In hopes it will persuade her to grant your petition for the estate?'

'I doubt a fine leg on the dance floor will do that,' he said ruefully. 'At least, not on its own. But to gain her attention at every opportunity can only help, don't you think?'

Rosamund laughed. 'Her Grace does seem to admire an athletic gentleman.'

'And my pretty face?' Anton teased. 'Will that help too?'

'You are pretty indeed, Master Gustavson, though I hate to inflate your pride to even greater heights by saying so. And I am not the only one to notice,' she said. 'You can't fail but gain her attention. As for your petition—if right is with you, you definitely can't fail. The Queen is just.'

'My grandfather left it to me in his will,' he said. 'Surely that means right is with me?'

'If the will is proper and legal. He must have meant you to have it. Yet you never met him?'

He shook his head, lying down flat beside her. 'Nay, though my mother spoke of him so often I felt I knew him. They used to go to Briony Manor in the summer when she was a girl, and she would ride with him and her brother over the fields and meadows. She loved it there.'

'And that is why he left it to her—to you? It was her special place?'

'I think so, and because her brother and his sons inherited their other properties and had no need of a smaller place like Briony.' He reached out to stroke the edge of her white silk skirt between his fingers, studying it closely as if some secret was writ in the fine fabric. 'Also, my mother and grandfather quarrelled about her marriage before she left England. She always regretted it, and hoped that they could reconcile. Perhaps this was his way of doing so.'

'Oh, Anton.' Rosamund slid down to lie on her side next to him, facing him. Her heart ached at his tale, at the thought of families broken apart by quarrels, by disagreements over romances and marriages. At a lonely boy growing up in the midst of ice and snow, longing for the green warmth of a land he knew only in his mother's stories.

Always searching, as she was, for a place to belong.

He turned his head to watch her, his eyes so dark, so full of swirling depths. She felt she could fall into them and be lost, like plunging beneath the winter ice to find a whole new world. A place of unimaginable beauty, worth the danger of obtaining it.

He rolled to his side, his palm reaching out to touch her face. His long fingers slid into her hair, loosened as it was by their dance, caressing, binding them together. Slowly, slowly, as if in a dream, he cupped his hand to the back of her head, drawing her closer.

Her eyes closed tightly as he kissed her, as his lips touched hers, seeking her out hungrily. As if he had longed for her, only her, for so long, a starving man granted his one life-giving wish.

Rosamund moaned softly, her lips parting as his tongue pressed forward, seeking hers. She touched the tip of hers to his lips, licking gently to taste the wine and sugared wafers from the banquet. To taste that dark bittersweetness that was Anton alone and was more intoxicating, more needful, than anything she had ever known. He tasted of the essence of life itself.

Their tongues tangled, all artifice melting away in a torrent of sheer need, of primitive desire that washed away all before it. Come what may, ruin or wonder, none of it mattered when they kissed, when they touched.

Through the shimmering, blurry haze of lust and tenderness she felt his fingers in her hair, combing free the last of the pins as he spread the pale strands over her shoulders. With a groan, his lips slid wetly from hers, and he buried his face in her hair, in the curve where her shoulder met her neck.

'Rosamund, *hjarta*,' he whispered against her bare skin. 'You are so beautiful.'

'Not as beautiful as you,' she whispered back. She reached out for him, pulling him on top of her so she could kiss him again, could press her open, hungry mouth to his jaw, his throat, to the smooth skin revealed between the laces of his shirt. He tasted of salt, of sunshine, winter ice, candle-smoke and mint. She held onto him so tightly, closing her eyes to absorb all of him, his heartbeat, his breath, the wondrous, vibrant, young strength of him.

He was beautiful, she thought, every part of him, body and soul. And she wanted him beyond all words, all rational thought. Beyond any realisation of danger or risk.

'*Alskling,*' he muttered hoarsely. His lips trailed down her bare neck, his tongue swirling in the hollow at its base where his life-blood beat. He kissed the soft edge of her breasts, pushed high by the beaded neckline of her bodice. She gasped at the waves of pleasure that followed his mouth, the touch of his hands on her bare skin.

She drove her fingers into his hair, holding him close as he licked at the line of her cleavage, nipped at her breast then soothed the sting with the tip of his tongue.

'I want to see you,' he said.

Rosamund nodded, mutely arching her back so he could loosen her bodice-lacing. The stiffened silk fell away with her thin chemise, and he drew it down until her breasts were revealed to him.

For a moment, as he stared at her avidly, she held her breath. Were they not right? Too small? Not small enough? She had not bared herself thus to another person, not even Richard when he had pleaded with her.

It had never felt right, safe, as it did now with Anton. But suddenly she was unsure.

'So beautiful,' he said roughly. 'Rosamund, you are perfect, perfect.'

She laughed, tightening her fingers in his hair and drawing him back down to her. His lips closed over her aching nipple, drawing and licking until she moaned in delight.

Her eyes closed. She pushed his unfastened doublet off his shoulders until he shrugged it away. She closed her arms around him, her palms sliding along the groove of his spine, feeling the muscled tension of his shoulders beneath the clinging shirt. Yet still it was not nearly enough.

She wanted him in every way there could be, every way she had read about, heard whispers of. She wanted only him, and it burned inside her like a bonfire.

'Please, Anton,' she whispered, throwing every caution to the four winter winds. 'Make love to me.'

He stared up at her, raising himself to his elbows on either side of her. His eyes were shadowed with a flaming desire that matched hers, a lust that was out of control. But there was also a flash of caution, and that she did *not* want. Not now. Not when she finally knew exactly what she wanted: him.

'Rosamund,' he said hoarsely, his accent heavy. 'Have you been with a man before?'

She shook her head, swallowing hard. 'There was a—a gentleman at home. A neighbour. We kissed, and he—he wanted to do more. But I did not. I didn't trust him, not really. I didn't want him, as I do you.' Richard had been a bluff boy; Anton was a darkly mysterious, alluring man, and her desire for him was that of a woman. She saw that now.

'*Hjarta,*' he said. He rolled away to sit beside her, but he still held her hand. They were still connected in that magical moment of growing certitude and undeniable need. 'It will hurt the first time. And there could be— consequences. There are ways we can prevent it, but they are not certain.'

Consequences, as with Katherine Grey and Lord Hertford? That was chilling indeed. But Rosamund was not the Queen's cousin, and Anton was not an indiscreet fool. 'I know,' she said simply. 'But I want you, Anton. Do you not want me?'

'Want you?' He ran his hand roughly over his face. 'I burn for you, *hjarta.* I need you.'

'Then it is right.' She stood up, filled with the sure knowledge that this *was* right, that she and Anton were meant to be together, even if just for this one night. She reached for the tapes at her waist, intending to shed her heavy skirts, but her fingers fumbled at them. She was trembling too much.

'Here, my lady, let me,' he said softly. He rose to her side, his long fingers reaching out to deftly unknot the tapes. Her overskirt, her embroidered petticoat and the cage of her farthingale fell away. He finished unlacing her bodice too, and cast it away along with her sleeves.

She stood before him in only her chemise, stockings and her heeled shoes.

Anton slid down her body until he knelt at her feet. Gently, he removed first one shoe then the other, running his thumb caressingly over her instep, the sensitive curve of her ankle. His palm flattened and slid along her calf, the bend of her knee, slowly, slowly, until she could barely breathe.

He reached the hem of her chemise, lifting it up, dragging it over her silk stockings until he revealed her garters, the bare skin of her thighs above. His fingertips just traced that line where skin met knitted silk, and Rosamund thought she might snap from the tension, the anticipation. Her womanhood felt damp, aching with heavy need.

And then, at last, he touched her *there*. His fingers combed through the wet curls then pressed forward to circle one aching, throbbing point.

Rosamund cried out, her knees buckling beneath her with the jolt of lightning-hot pleasure. Anton caught her up in his arms, carrying her to the alcove bed waiting in the darkness.

He reached down to draw back the bedclothes before he laid her down amid the linens. As she pushed herself back against the bolsters, propped on her elbows, he pulled off his shirt, revealing his bare chest to her at last.

The candlelight on the wall outlined him in a contrast of shadows and golden glow, his bare, damp skin glistening.

He was well-muscled and lean from exercise, from a life lived outdoors, and his skin had a smooth, olive cast to it, roughened by a sprinkling of coarse dark hair. It arrowed down towards his hose, as if to draw her gaze.

And she did stare. She had to; she could not look away. He was a truly wondrous sight, powerful and beautiful, like a god from his Norse homeland.

He leaned onto the bed, bracing his palms on the mattress either side of her, holding her a willing captive. His head lowered, his mouth capturing hers in a passionate kiss. A kiss that blotted out everything else. There was no doubt or fear, only the knowledge that, tonight, she was his. And he was hers.

He broke their kiss only to draw her chemise over her

head and toss it away with his shirt. Her legs fell apart, and he eased between them, his body pressed to hers. Through the rough velvet of his hose, his penis was heavy and hard against her.

She almost giggled hysterically as she thought surely he would not look like old Lord Pomfrey! Then he kissed her again and any need to laugh, or even think, fled.

She wrapped her thighs around his hips, arching up against him, trying to feel yet more of him. His naked skin against her breasts made her cry out with need.

His moans answered hers, his mouth trailing away to press the hollow just below her ear. His hot breath against her made her shiver, mindless with desire.

'*Ledsen, hjarta,*' he whispered. 'I'm so sorry. I need you *now*.'

Rosamund nodded, closing her eyes as she felt him reach between their bodies to unfasten his hose. His penis, long and thick, sprang out against her thigh. She was surprised at how it felt on her bare skin, like velvet over iron, at how hot it was, and how thickly veined.

He gently pressed her legs further apart, and she braced her feet flat to the mattress as his fingers slid inside her.

Then his manhood followed, sliding slowly, ever so slowly, against her damp flesh. She tightened her jaw against the stretching, burning sensation, her shoulders tensing.

'I'm sorry,' he whispered against her cheek, his whole body held taut above her. 'I'm sorry.'

Then he drove forward and she felt a tearing deep inside, a flash of lightning-quick pain. She tried to hold back her cry but it escaped her lips.

'Shh,' he murmured. His body went perfectly still against hers. His breath rushed against her skin, as if he held his power tightly leashed. 'It will fade now, *hjarta*, I promise,' he soothed. 'I will make it better.'

He was right. As he lay still, their bodies joined, Rosamund felt the pain slowly fade away, leaving only a tiny curl of pleasure low in her belly.

She ran her hands down his back, feeling the hot, sweat-damp skin over his lean muscles pressing him closer to her.

He pulled slowly back and drove forward again, a bit deeper, and pleasure unfurled. Every thrust, every movement of his body against hers, every moan and sigh, drove the pleasure to greater heights. It was like a brilliant strand of sunshine unravelling inside her, blinding her with its brilliant light, its hot sparks of pure joy.

He suddenly arched above her, shouting out involuntarily as he pulled out of her.

Rosamund hardly noticed. Those sparks had blown into an enormous explosion of blue, red and white flames that threatened to consume her from within.

Then everything fell into darkness. When she opened her eyes, she found herself collapsed back onto the rumpled sheets, Anton stretched out beside her.

His arm was around her waist, holding her close. She turned her head to see that he lay on his side, his eyes closed, his breath laboured as if he too had felt the same wondrous, devastating pleasure as she.

'Anton…' she said.

'Shh,' he whispered, not opening his eyes. He just pulled her closer until their bodies were curled together. 'Just sleep for a moment, *alskling*.'

Rosamund closed her eyes again, resting her head on his shoulder as she felt the cold night air brush over her skin. She would happily sleep for a moment, happily stay just here, in his arms, for all the moments to come.

* * *

Anton held Rosamund as she slept, listening to her soft breath, feeling her stir against him as the night slipped away from them. The candles sputtered low, and the light at the window was edging from black into pale grey.

Soon, all too soon, he would have to let her go; their magical hours would end.

But they had been magical indeed. Women had always been a large part of his life. He liked them, liked to talk with them, laugh with them and, yes, make love with them. Their minds worked in such wondrously subtle, fascinating ways. He loved to listen to their voices as they sang, loved their perfume, their laughter, their elegance. And they often seemed to like him in return.

Yet never had he met a lady who made him respond as Rosamund did. He found himself so completely fixated on her, wanting to be with her all the time. When she laughed at his jests, his spirits soared. And when they kissed...

He had never imagined he could feel this way about a woman, about anything. Yet Rosamund could not have come into his life at a more complicated moment.

Even with all that faced him—his uncertain circumstances, her position, the dangers at Court—he could never regret finding her. Could never regret the night they had just shared. But he would have to find a way to keep her safe.

He drew her closer, pressing a gentle kiss to her brow. She murmured, her soft skin wrinkling in a frown as if she resented the interruption of her dreams.

'It grows late,' he whispered.

''Tis too cold,' she answered, burrowing closer to him. She laid her freezing feet against his bare leg, giggling when he jumped.

'I would like nothing more than to stay hidden here with you all night,' he said, and he found he did. More than anything he just wanted to lie there with her in his arms for ever. 'And then all day, and all night again.'

'That sounds a wondrous prospect,' she answered. 'But I don't think I could find enough excuses for such an absence!'

'Will you be missed for these last few hours?' Anton asked in concern. Would she be caught, just from this one night, because of him and his carelessness?

'Nay,' she said, shaking her head. Her hair flowed over his chest, a skein of fine silk. 'Almost all the maids vanish mysteriously at one time or another. And I'm sure Anne will tell some tale for me. She is such a romantic—or maybe just a mischief-maker!'

'Nevertheless, I never want you to find any kind of trouble,' he said, kissing her forehead. 'I'm sorry, Rosamund, I should have thought of it before time got away from us.'

Rosamund laughed. 'We were rather distracted. But I cannot be sorry.' She sat up in their bed, leaning down to kiss him. Her lips were soft, tasting of wine and their night together. 'Can you?'

Anton wrapped his arms around her waist, pulling her down on top of him as he kissed her again. 'Sorry for being with you? Never, my lady Rosamund. You are surely the greatest gift I have ever known.'

She touched his cheek gently, tracing over his skin lightly with her fingertips. Her touch feathered over his brow, his nose, his lips, studying him carefully as if to memorise him. He caught the tip of her finger between his lips, nipping and suckling at the soft skin until she gasped, and he felt his body harden again.

'I should take you back to your chamber,' he said

hoarsely, reluctant to let her go even as he knew he must.

Rosamund nodded silently. She rolled off him, sitting on the edge of the bed as she reached down for her discarded chemise. The curve of her back was wondrously beautiful, so pale and elegant as the length of her silvery hair fell forward over her shoulders.

He did not resist. He sat up behind her, kissing the soft, vulnerable nape of her neck. She shivered and curled back against him as he wrapped his arms and legs around her, holding her close.

They sat there, bound together in silence, in that one perfect moment that was out of time and belonged only to them. Where there was no duty, no danger, just them—for ever.

Chapter Ten

Feast of St Thomas, December 29

''Tidings true there be come new, sent from the Trinity by Gabriel to Nazareth, city of Galilee! Noel, Noel...'

Rosamund bent her head over her sewing, unable to contain her smile as she listened to the other ladies singing. She feared she must look like an utter imbecile, the way she kept smiling that morning, smiling and laughing at every tiny jest. Yet she could not help herself. That small, warm knot of happiness deep down inside would not be suppressed.

She'd had little sleep last night. By the time she'd crept into her own bed, Anton's cloak wrapped over her half-laced bodice, the other maids had been asleep. Even after she had shed her garments, carefully folding the cloak into her clothes chest, and slid under the blankets she'd not been able to sleep. She kept remembering, going over every little detail, every delicious sensation, in her mind.

She was a wicked woman now, surely? But being wicked seemed entirely worth it! Perhaps she would not feel this way come tomorrow, but for today it seemed she floated on a cloud of delight, of close-held secrets.

Unfortunately, that bright cloud obscured her stitchery. She glanced down to find that her seams were all puckered and uneven. She reached for her scissors, trimming away the thread before anyone could notice.

The Queen sat by her window, a book open in her hands. Yet she did not seem to be reading, for she merely stared out through the diamond-shaped panes of glass. The other ladies, the ones who did not sing, also read and sewed or played quiet card-games, like Anne and Catherine Knyvett.

It was a slow, silent day; the moments ticked away by the crackling flames in the grate. Too much time to be lost in lustful daydreams.

As Rosamund reached into her sewing box for a skein of thread, her gaze met the painted black eyes of the Queen's mother. She seemed to warn of the dangers of being wicked, even over the years. The dangers of trusting men, of putting one's heart above one's head and duty.

But it still felt so very good.

'God's breath!' Queen Elizabeth suddenly cried, tossing her book across the room. It narrowly missed one of the Privy Chamber ladies, who ducked out of the way before going back to her tapestry.

'I am bored,' the Queen said. 'I cannot stay in this room another moment. Come, help me dress! We are going down to the frost fair, and perhaps a sleigh ride.'

'Your Grace,' Mistress Parry said, her voice tinged with alarm. 'Lord Burghley says...'

'Forget Burghley,' the Queen said. 'Staying cloistered in here will achieve naught. I must be out among my people.' She threw open one of her clothes chests, tossing about piles of sleeves and petticoats as her ladies rushed to help her.

'Your Grace, please,' Mistress Parry begged. 'If you must go out, let us find your warmest garments for you.'

The Queen plumped herself back down in her chair, arms crossed. 'Be quick about it, then! Lady Rosamund?'

'Your Grace?' Rosamund cried, startled to hear her name. She leaped to her feet, dropping her sewing. Was she in trouble? Her secrets discovered?

'Lady Rosamund, go to the stables and instruct them to ready my sleighs. We will depart in an hour.'

'Yes, Your Grace.' Rosamund made a quick curtsy, hurrying out of the bedchamber.

The Privy Chamber and corridors were crowded with courtiers milling about gossiping, hoping for a glimpse of the Queen, a chance to speak to her, to catch her eye. But Rosamund was accustomed to them now, and dodged swiftly around the shifting groups to make her way down the stairs.

Amid all the people gathered there, between the swirling patterns of bright silks, glowing pearls and the wind-like rush of whispers, she caught a glimpse of Anton.

Her stomach lurched in a sudden jolt of excitement. Everything in her cried out to run to him, to throw her arms around him and kiss him. But everyone was watching, always watching, hoping for a new titbit of gossip about someone. Anyone.

Rosamund bit her lip to keep from smiling, and slowed her steps as she passed him, hoping he would see her and come to speak to her, give her some sign that he, too, remembered last night. That it had truly meant something.

He *did* see her and smile, an exuberant grin that

transformed his solemnly watchful face to youthful radiance. Her heart seemed to skip a beat at the sight, then pounded in her breast.

He excused himself from his Swedish friends, making his way past the crowds to her side. At first, his hand reached out for hers, as if he too longed for their touch. But then he seemed to recall that they were not alone, and just smiled down at her.

He looked so very handsome in the light of day, his dark waves of hair smoothed back to reveal the amethyst drop in his ear. The gold-embroidered high collar of his purple-velvet doublet set off his olive-complected skin perfectly, and he was every inch the consummate, cosmopolitan courtier.

Yet she recalled how he had looked last night as they'd kissed goodbye outside her door—his rumpled hair and sleepy, heavy-lidded eyes. The way their lips had lingered, their hands clinging together. How wonderfully beautiful he was.

'Lady Rosamund,' he said, his voice low, caressing. That voice, with its faint touch of a musical accent, its velvety texture, seemed to touch her as his hands could not. 'How do you fare this morning?'

'Very well indeed,' she answered. She gazed into his eyes, trying to send him her thoughts, her feelings. To convey all that last night truly meant. 'I hope that you are the same?'

'I have not seen a finer day yet in England,' he said. 'Perfect in every way.'

Rosamund laughed happily. 'I think Her Grace agrees. We are to visit the frost fair, then go for a sleigh ride along the river.'

'Indeed? A sleigh ride sounds most delightful on a such a perfect day.'

'But perhaps commonplace to you? You must use such conveyances often in Sweden.'

'And a taste of home would be welcome.'

'Then I am sure the Queen would be happy to see you there. Perhaps we will meet you at the frost fair?'

'Perhaps you will, Lady Rosamund.'

She curtsied as he bowed, still trying to hold back her exuberant smile, her laughter. She hurried on her errand, but could not help glancing back over her shoulder.

He still watched her.

The frost fair was truly an amazing sight. As Rosamund walked with the other maids between the booths, she feared she was gawking like a silly country-maid. But it was all too easy to be continually distracted by the sights and smells.

The booths, peddling everything from ribbons, embroidered stockings, gloves, spiced cider and warm gingerbread, were hung with bright pennants. The streamers of red, green and white snapped in the cold breeze, blending with the cries of the merchants, the laughter of the shoppers.

On the wide lanes between the booths people skated past, dodging around the strollers and gawkers. Beyond were sleds and sleighs, even people on horseback using the frozen river as a new kind of road.

It was very crowded, noisy with merriment that was a welcome respite from the hardships of such a cold winter. No one even seemed to notice the weather, especially as Queen Elizabeth came among them.

One would never have guessed that there had been any danger of late, any darkness hanging over the Queen's holiday celebrations. She went into the crowd of her subjects with a warm smile and happy words. She accepted bouquets of fresh greenery, a goblet of warm cider, kneeling down to speak to one shy little girl.

Rosamund observed the faces of the people who gathered around, all of them shining with joy to see their Queen, awestruck, hopeful, thrilled. As if Elizabeth was made of some winter magic. It was inconceivable in that moment that anyone could want to hurt her, want to mar that golden aura that surrounded her and touched all who looked on her.

No one even seemed to notice the extra guards who surrounded their little procession, who kept such close watch on the exuberant crowds and held their pikes and swords ready. Lord Leicester, especially, stayed close to the Queen's side, scowling at any who dared edge too near.

At one moment Elizabeth turned to him with a smile, tucking a sprig of holly into the fastening of his doublet. 'Do not frown so, Robin,' she murmured. 'It is Christmas!'

He smiled back at her, and in that moment Rosamund glimpsed something profound. The Queen looked at Leicester as she herself looked at Anton. There was such tenderness and longing in their smiles. How could she be trying to marry him off to the Scottish queen?

Master Macintosh seemed to feel the same. He fell into step with Rosamund as they continued on their way, and she saw that he too watched the Queen and Leicester, frowning.

But he just said, ''Tis a fine day, is it not, Lady Rosamund?'

She gave him a polite smile, not entirely trusting his sudden friendliness. 'If you like ice and chilly winds, Master Macintosh.'

'In Scotland, my lady, this would be a balmy summer's day!'

'Then I am glad I don't live in Scotland.'

'You do not enjoy the winter, then?'

Rosamund remembered Anton skating on the ice, and their warming kisses amid the frosty woods. 'Winter does have its own pleasures, I think. But spring has many more. Sunshine, green things growing…'

'Ach! You English are a delicate lot,' Macintosh scoffed.

'Not all of us, I think,' she said. 'Some of us seem most eager to travel to your windswept country, Master Macintosh. Lord Darnley, for instance.'

Macintosh's expression seemed to close, even as he still smiled at her. 'I understand he wishes to visit his father, who is in Edinburgh.'

'So I hear. It is very touching that family affection can overcome even the rough weather you speak of.'

'Indeed so, my lady.'

Rosamund remembered Celia emerging from the Scots' apartments, walking with Lady Lennox. Perhaps she was also intrigued by the Scottish weather. 'And surely there must be others among us frail English you have found to be hardy souls?'

'Well, there is you, Lady Rosamund.'

'Me?' She shook her head. 'I fear I am the least hardy among us.'

'Oh, I do not believe that, my lady,' Macintosh said. 'You seem filled with many—hidden depths.'

'Yes?' Rosamund said warily. 'My family would disagree with you. They think I am as shallow as can be.'

'Nay. I would say you are more like what lies beneath this ice under our feet,' he said, tapping at the bluish-silver ice with his boot. 'Swirling winter tides.'

'I am a simple female, Master Macintosh. I want

only what everyone wants—a home, a family.' And freedom to gain what she desired with no danger.

'And you think to find that here at your Queen's fancy Court?'

'I think to do my duty here, until I am needed at home again. It is an honour to be asked to wait on the Queen,' Rosamund said, even as she knew very well that was no longer true. She did not want to go home. She wanted to stay close to Anton for as long as possible. No matter the perils.

'So, Lady Rosamund of home and hearth,' Macintosh said, again all teasing smiles. 'What do you think of Court life?'

'I like the fashions very much indeed,' Rosamund answered lightly, holding out her velvet skirt. 'And I have heard that your Queen Mary is most stylish. Tell me, Master Macintosh, is she as tall as they say?'

They went on to speak of inconsequential matters of fashion, but still Rosamund could not quite erase the sensation that Master Macintosh wanted something from her, some nugget of information about Queen Elizabeth and her matrimonial intentions for Queen Mary. She would have to be even more careful of everything she said in the future, to be always cautious. It was easy to forget that, but she could not afford to.

Once they had walked round the whole fair, stopping to admire the wares at the various booths and watch the skaters, they all made their way back to their transport. The Queen's sleighs waited for them, piled high with blankets and furs, the horses' bridles jingling with silver bells.

As Rosamund watched Leicester hand the Queen into the grandest sleigh, the one at the head of the procession, Anton appeared at her side. She did not see him at first, but she knew he was there. His warmth seemed to surround her; his clean scent carried to her on the cold breeze like a spell.

She smiled, closing her eyes to imagine that she hugged his very presence close to her.

'My lady,' he said. 'Will you join me?'

'Of course,' she answered, turning to face him. She was quite sure she would join him wherever he cared to lead her, come what may. He held out his arm, and she slid her hand atop his woollen sleeve, resisting the urge to cling, to run her fingers up his arm to his shoulder and plunge them into his hair, to pull him close for a kiss. She had to remember her resolve to be careful, to be wary of the eyes of others.

He seemed to divine her thoughts, for his eyes darkened. He led her to the end of the line of sleighs, where one just big enough for two people waited along with a pair of beautiful white horses.

Only one vehicle was behind it, another small sleigh already occupied by Anne and Lord Langley. They seemed to have declared some sort of truce, for they were laughing together over some jest.

Rosamund glanced ahead. All the other sleighs were larger, crowded with jostling courtiers. 'How did you procure this vehicle, Master Gustavson?' she asked.

'By my wondrous charm, of course, Lady Rosamund,' he answered, giving her a jaunty grin. 'And a little bribe never hurts, either.'

She laughed, taking his hand as he helped her up onto the cushioned seat. He settled blankets and fur robes around her, tucking them close against the cold.

And, under the cover of those robes, he pressed a quick kiss to her wrist above the edge of her glove. His lips were warm, ardent, against her skin.

But his kiss was as fleeting as it was sweet. He leaped

up onto the seat beside her, taking the reins from the groom. 'Are you warm enough?' he asked roughly.

Rosamund nodded mutely. She tucked her hands into her muff, trying to hold onto his kiss as he set their sleigh into motion behind the others. The bells on all the harnesses rang out merrily, a high, silvery song in the cold air, and some of the people burst into song along with them.

'Love and joy come to you, and to you, your wassail, too! And God bless you and send you a happy new year...'

Rosamund smiled, leaning against Anton's shoulder as they lurched into movement. A few lacy snowflakes drifted from the pearly-grey sky, clinging to her eyelashes, to the fur trim of the blanket around her.

She laughed aloud, tasting the crisp snow on her lips. 'Now it truly feels like Christmas!' she said.

Anton laughed. 'You do not see snow so often, then?'

'Rarely,' she said. 'It must seem foolish to you, me getting so very excited about these tiny flurries, after the great blizzards of Sweden.'

'Oh, no,' he answered. 'I love anything that makes you smile.'

Under the cover of the robes, she linked her arm through his, feeling the tension of his lean muscles as he drove, the strong heat of him. It held her up, made her strong. Strong enough to face any danger.

'This day makes me smile,' she said. 'But what do you think of our puny English winter?'

'I think that I hope to see many more of them just like this,' he said.

They fell into a companionable silence as they flew along on the ice as if the sleigh had wings. They went under London Bridge, waving at the people above, and past the Tower. In the haze of snow and laughter, even its dark, ominous roof-lines, its thick walls, seemed muted. They rushed past Traitor's Gate, where once the Queen herself had passed through as a princess, and it was behind them.

At the docks, they went around the curve of the river and were released into the countryside. The trees along the river, thick enough to hide the fine country estates, were heavy with ice. They sparkled and glinted, like massive clusters of diamonds.

They passed a set of broad water-steps, a gate crusted with more ice, and in the distance Rosamund could see the square battlements of an old red-brick manor house. For just a moment she allowed herself a distant, impossible dream: that it was *her* house, hers and Anton's. That they would stroll along those battlements in the evening, arm in arm, looking out over their gardens before they went inside to sit by their fire.

In her dream, her parents came to dine with them, to play with their grandchildren, all quarrels forgotten, a true family once again. But then the fantasy house was past; the dream burst like a shimmering ice-bauble. Like the delicate moments she had with Anton.

'Did your mother truly quarrel with her father before she married?' Rosamund asked wistfully.

Anton glanced down at her, his brow arched in surprise. 'Indeed she did. He did not approve her choice of a Swedish diplomat she met at Court, and protested that she would go too far from home. That she would be lonely and unprotected. Sadly, he proved correct in the end.'

Rosamund bit her lip, staring out at the countryside as it flew past, a grey blur. 'It is sad when families are torn apart by disagreements. We all have so little time together as it is.'

'Rosamund, *kar*,' Anton said gently. He shifted the reins to one hand, putting his other arm around her shoulders to draw her closer. 'This is not a day for melancholy! I do so hate to see you sad.'

Rosamund smiled, resting her head on his shoulder. 'How can I be sad when I'm here with you? It's only…'

'Only what?'

'It is so difficult to admit when one is wrong and one's parents are *right*!' she said, laughing. 'Your own grandfather was surely right in a terrible way, but I admit I am glad now of my father's advice.'

'And what was his advice to you?'

Rosamund remembered her father's words: *when you find the one you truly love, you will know what your mother and I mean.* Then, it had made her so angry, so confused. Now she saw the great foresight of it. Her feelings for Richard had been nothing but a girlish infatuation, a candle flame next to the bright sunlight of Anton.

How long could their time last? A fortnight, a month? Rosamund feared it could not be long, not in such a world of uncertainty. She just had to make the most of every moment.

'My father said I would one day find my own place, the place that is right for me, and I should never settle for less,' she said.

'And have you found it at Court?'

Rosamund laughed. 'Nay, not at Court! I am not clever enough to survive long there. But I think I am close. What of you, Anton?'

He hugged her closer against him. 'I think I might just be close myself.'

The sleigh swung around a curve in the frozen river

and up over a rise, and a magical scene was revealed before them.

On the banks a flat space had been cleared and open-sided pavilions of green and white erected. The Queen's banners snapped from the poles, bright streamers of green, white, red and gold embroidered with Tudor roses. Bonfires were blazing with rising orange flames that sent out tendrils of welcome warmth even from that distance.

Under the pavilions, liveried servants rushed to and fro, bearing laden platters and jugs of wine.

'A snow banquet!' Rosamund said happily. 'How lovely. You are quite right, Anton.'

'I know I am,' he answered. 'But what am I right about just now?'

'That this is not a day for sadness. It is Christmas, after all. We must make merry.'

'Oh, yes. I am quite sure I can do *that*,' he said. He bent his head, kissing her quickly before they could be seen. His lips were warm on hers, sweet and perfect. Rosamund longed to wrap her arms around him, holding onto him tightly, but he was suddenly gone from her side.

He leaped down from the sleigh, reaching under the seat and drawing out a knapsack.

'I brought you a gift too,' he said. 'In honour of the holiday.'

'A gift?' Rosamund cried in delight. 'What is it?'

'Open it and see,' he said, grinning.

She pulled aside the sack, wondering what it could be. Jewels? Silks? Books? But out tumbled a shining pair of new skates, just like Anton's, only in miniature.

'Skates?' she said slowly, holding them up to the light.

'Made especially for you, my lady. It took a great deal of searching in London to find a blacksmith who could make them,' he answered. 'I did say I would teach you to skate.'

Rosamund smiled down at them, cradling them in her lap. 'They are beautiful,' she said. 'Thank you, Anton.'

'You will be a veritable Swede in no time at all,' he said.

She laughed. 'But I fear I have no gift for you!'

'On the contrary,' he whispered. 'You gave me a most wondrous gift last night.'

Rosamund felt her cheeks burn, but Anton just kissed her again and took the skates from her hands, tucking them back under the seat. He lifted her down from the sleigh, leading her to their place in the procession into the pavilion. Once there, they were separated, Anton seated with the other Swedes and Rosamund with the maids at the table just below the Queen's.

'Your cheeks are all red, Rosamund,' Anne whispered.

'Are they? It must be the cold wind,' Rosamund answered, reaching for a goblet of wine to cover her silly urge to giggle.

'Oh, aye. The cold,' Anne said. 'We will have to start calling you "Rosie".'

'But what of you?' Rosamund said. 'You and Lord Langley seem to have mended your quarrel, whatever it was.'

Anne shrugged. 'I would not say mended. But if he makes proper amends…'

Rosamund longed to ask what was really going on between Anne and Lord Langley, longed to see her friend as happy as she was herself. But it was obvious Anne was not in a confiding mood, so she turned her attention to the food, to the fine tapestries draped around the pavilion walls to keep the wind out.

To trying not to stare at Anton like a love-sick school-girl. That was a great challenge indeed.

* * *

Anton walked along the bank of the frozen river, listening to the hum of laughter and music from the pavilion behind him. The merriment grew louder as the wine flowed, and he had found he desperately needed a breath of fresh air. A moment alone to try and break the spell he seemed to have fallen under.

The cold wind cleared his head of the music and the wine, but not of the one thing he most needed to banish. The sight of Rosamund's wide, sky-blue eyes gazing up at him as they'd dashed over the ice. Of her smile, so full of sweetness. The sweetness that was so much more alluring than any practised flirtation could ever be.

It drew him in, closer and closer, until Rosamund was all he could see, all he cared about. It was so dangerous for both of them.

Anton raked his fingers through his hair, cursing at how complicated everything had become since he'd arrived in London. He'd thought to gain his estate, start a new life free and clear—not tumble into infatuation with one of the Queen's ladies!

Anton, my dearest, he suddenly heard his mother say, the memory like a whisper on the wind. In his mind he saw her face, white with illness as she clutched at his hand. *Anton, you are so dutiful, so ambitious. But I beg you—do not let your head always rule your heart. Do not let what is really important slip by you. I regret nothing in my life, nothing I did, because I followed my heart.*

He had not understood her then, as she'd lain on her deathbed. What could be more important than duty, than bringing honour to his name? His mother had followed love and it had brought her unhappiness.

But now when he heard Rosamund laugh, when she looked at him with those eyes, he saw what his mother meant. The demands of the heart could be just as strong as those of the mind, twice as clamorous. Could he afford to listen to them?

Were they telling him what was really important in life?

Anton shook his head; he wasn't sure he knew any longer. His old, stone-solid certainty, the certainty that had carried him through battle and all the way to England, was turned to ice, liable to crack at any moment.

He turned to look back at the pavilion. Rosamund stood in the doorway, rubbing her arms against the chill as she glanced around the bleak landscape. Then she saw him and smiled.

Even from that distance it was as if the summer sun emerged from the grey cold of winter.

She waved to him, beckoning him to return to the party. Anton took one more long look at the frozen river before making his way back to her.

Surely that cracking sound he heard was his own heart, breaking open to let her peek inside for one instant before it froze up again for ever.

Chapter Eleven

Bringing in the Boar Day, December 30

'The boar's head in hand bear I, bedecked with bays and rosemary! I pray you all now, be merry, be merry, be merry…'

The gathered company in the Great Hall applauded as the roasted boar was carried in, borne aloft on a silver platter. It was a large boar, adorned with garlands of herbs and surrounded by candied fruits, a whole apple in its mouth. It was presented to Queen Elizabeth, who received it on her dais, and then paraded around the chamber.

More delicacies followed—roasted meats of all kinds, including deer and capons brought in from the Queen's hunt, pies, stewed broths and even a few fish dishes, carefully prepared with spices and sauces. These were doubly precious with the river frozen. On the multi-tiered buffets the sweets were displayed—gold-leafed gingerbread, cakes topped with candied flowers, the Queen's favourite fruit-suckets with their long-handled sucket spoons. The centrepiece was an elaborate subtlety of Whitehall itself, complete with windows, cornices, brickwork and even a blue-sugar river rippling alongside with tiny boats and barges.

Rosamund applauded along with everyone else, laughing as the Queen's jesters tumbled and gambolled between the tables. It was yet another lavish Christmas display, with everyone happily flushed with the fine malmsey wine, with flirtation and with the reckless joy of the holiday.

Yet underneath all the loud merriment there was a knife's edge of tension, of some darkness, some desperation, lurking underneath. There was always that heated blade under everything at Court, waiting for the unwary to fall onto it and destroy themselves.

Rosamund peeked over her shoulder, searching for Anton in the crowd. He sat with his Swedish friends, observing the gathering with quiet, watchful eyes. *He must feel it too,* she thought. That taut sense that something was just on the verge of happening.

What that something was, none could say. But the foreign delegations seemed the most tense of all, as if the usual perils of manoeuvring through a foreign monarch's Court were increased, even darker and deeper than usual. Like the hidden, swirling depths beneath the ice outside.

Her gaze slid along the wall, over the extra guards placed about the hall by Lord Leicester. At least no enemy could invade tonight. The merriment was safe for one more banquet.

She turned back to Anton, finding him watching her. He grinned at her, and she laughed into her serviette. She could not help it; whenever he smiled at her thus it was as if the bright sun emerged from the winter clouds. As if she soared free above any danger or worry.

That was foolish, of course, because nothing could

change their tenuous circumstances. But for one moment she could forget, could dream.

'You seem happy tonight, Rosamund,' Anne said, sipping at her wine.

'And you seem pensive,' Rosamund answered. Anne had certainly seemed happy enough on their sleigh-ride along the river, but she had received a letter on their return and was now quiet. 'I hope you did not have sad news from home?'

'Certainly not. Merely more lectures from my aunt,' Anne said. 'What of you? Have you lately heard from your parents, or your lost suitor?'

Rosamund was startled. She had almost forgotten Richard in all that had happened here at Court. He seemed almost a dream now, a ghost of sorts who had drifted into and out of her life, leaving only a mist of memories. Memories of the girl she had once been.

'Nay, to either,' she said. 'My father sends my allowance, but I have had no other word. I'm sure they want me to think only of my work here.'

'And do you?' Anne asked. 'Have you found new distractions here to make you forget the old?'

Rosamund laughed, thinking of Anton's kiss—his smile, his eyes, the way his body felt against hers as they made love. Aye, she had found ample distractions in the present to make her forget the past. Or forget the dangers of the present.

Would it break her heart all over again in the end, far worse than the smaller pain Richard's desertion had caused? She feared it would, for her feelings for Anton were a hundred times whatever the infatuation she had felt for Richard had been.

'I have enjoyed my time here,' she said. 'Haven't you, Anne?'

Anne shrugged. ''Tis better than cooling my heels at home, I dare say! At least there is dancing and music.'

And handsome men such as Lord Langley? But Rosamund said nothing, and soon the remains of the food were cleared away and the tables moved for the dancing. The Queen and Leicester led the figures for the galliard.

Anne joined the dance with one of her admirers, but Rosamund retreated into a quiet corner to watch. She was suddenly weary—weary of the feasting, the loud holiday-gaiety, the music and laughter. She longed for a warm fire to curl up next to in her dressing gown, for a book to read, a goblet of warm cider—and Anton beside her to laugh with, to kiss. To keep the endless cold winter away.

Could such dreams ever truly happen? Or was she merely fooling herself again? Perhaps Anton would go back to Sweden and disappear from her life, as Richard had. What would become of her dreams then?

Suddenly she felt a gentle touch on her arm, warm through the thin silk of her sleeve. She spun round to find Anton standing there, his eyes dark and fathomless as he watched her. As if he divined something of her strange, sad mood. He, too, seemed in a strange mood tonight.

'Are you well, my lady?' he asked quietly.

'Quite well, I thank you, Master Gustavson,' she said. 'Merely a bit tired from all the feasting.'

'It would be enough to make anyone out of sorts,' he said. 'But you seem rather melancholy.'

'Perhaps I am a bit.'

'Is it because…?' His words broke off as a rowdy crowd passed near to them, jostling and laughing drunkenly. Anton's hand tightened protectively on her arm, drawing her away from them. 'Follow me.'

He led her around the edge of the crowded hall,

keeping close to the wall where the flickering shadows hid them from view. Everyone was far too busy with their own flirtations and quarrels to notice them anyway as they ducked behind one of the tapestries.

It was the same one where they had first kissed, Rosamund saw, with her kissing bough still hung high above. The heavy cloth muffled the raucous noise of the dance, and the only light was a thin line of torch flame at their feet.

Anton held her lightly by the waist, and she wrapped her arms around his shoulders. At last that tension she had felt all night began to ebb away, like a tight cord unwinding, and she sensed a slow peace stealing over her. Perhaps he might be gone from her soon, but they were together tonight. As alone as they could be at Whitehall, closed around by their own shelter of quiet.

'Tell me why you are sad, Rosamund,' he said.

'I am not sad,' she answered. 'How could I be, when you have rescued me yet again?'

Yet he seemed unconvinced, drawing her closer in the darkness. 'Is it because of what happened between us?'

Because of their love-making? How could that be, when it had been the finest, most glorious thing that had ever happened to her? 'Nay! I could never regret *that*. Why? Do you?'

Anton laughed, kissing her brow. 'Regret being with the most beautiful woman in all of England? Oh, *alskling*, never. I *am* a man, after all.'

Rosamund grinned. 'That fact did not escape my notice.'

'I truly hope not! But there must be something that has you melancholy tonight.'

'I was just thinking of my home,' she said with a sigh. 'Of how I have not heard from my family for a while.'

'And you miss them?'

'Yes. That is it.' She did not want to speak of her fears for the future, of what would happen when he left. Not now, not yet. Not when every moment they were alone, like this one, was so precious.

'Well, we shall just have to make a merry holiday here ourselves,' he said, drawing her closer and closer until they were pressed against each other in the shadows.

Rosamund slid her hands around his neck, twining his hair over her fingers, tickling the nape of his neck. 'Oh? And how do you propose we do that?'

'Well, we start with this…' He softly kissed her brow and each of her eyelids as her eyes closed, and a sharp breath escaped her at the sudden, fiery rush of excitement. 'Or this.' His lips slid to her cheek, to the hollow just below her ear. 'Or—this.'

At last his lips met hers, his tongue touching hers as she shivered. It felt as if years had passed since their last kiss, as if she had been waiting, longing, for this for such a long time, fearful it would never come again. Yet it also seemed they had spent all their lives together just so, and that their kiss was a sweet homecoming.

He tasted of wine and sweet fruit, of Anton, of her lover. Rosamund held him tightly, straining up on her toes to be closer, ever closer, to him. To hold onto this moment for ever.

He groaned, his arms sliding to her hips as he pressed her back to the wall. He lifted her up as her legs wrapped around his waist, her heavy skirts falling back. As he held her there, braced against the wood panelling, she felt his hand slide to her thigh, caressing the bare skin above her stocking.

Every place he touched left like a trail of fire, of burning need and deep delight. Slowly, teasingly, his fingers trailed up then back again, ever closer to her aching, damp womanhood but never quite touching.

Only when she moaned, arching her hips toward him, did he at last give her what she longed for.

One finger delved inside her, pressing to that one sensitive spot. Pleasure shot through her like lightning, burning but icy-cold. He kissed the side of her neck, his breath hot, heavy, enticing against her skin.

'Rosamund,' he groaned.

She forgot where they were, forgot the world that waited just beyond their hiding place. She wanted only him, knew only him.

She reached between them, her hand fumbling under his doublet until she found the iron-heavy press of his erection straining against the lacings of his hose. If she could only free him, if they could only be joined…

A blast of trumpets stilled her hand, like a sudden rush of cold water. Anton also went still against her; he pressed his forehead to her shoulder, his fingers sliding from inside her to brace against the wall.

He drew back and they stared at each other in the shadows, as if shocked at how quickly they forgot everything when they were together.

Shocked at how disappointed they were to have their lustful moment ended.

Slowly, carefully, he eased her back to her feet, arranging her skirts around her again. She smoothed her hair up under her pearl-trimmed cap, but she feared she could do nothing about her flushed cheeks. 'Rosie', indeed!

'I'm sorry, *alskling*,' Anton whispered, kissing her hand. She smelled herself on his skin, and it made her shiver all over again.

'I'm not,' she whispered back, feeling wondrously

wanton, feeling marvellously unlike herself. Or perhaps more herself than she'd ever been before she'd found him.

Once they were able to stand, to walk without shaking, Anton held aside the tapestry to let her pass by him. Her legs were still weak, but she could not cease smiling.

She blinked at the sudden rush of torchlight, the dazzle of flame and noise after the sultry darkness. For an instant she could see only a blur, then the scene grew clearer. The trumpets had signalled a new arrival, and the dancing paused as everyone gathered around to see.

A new arrival in such an insular world as the Court was always an occasion of great interest. But not to Rosamund. She found the only thing of interest to her was Anton, the prospect of hiding behind the tapestry with him again, hiding all night, forever in his arms.

She glanced back, trying to be discreet, to find that he stood several feet away, watching her with that intense light in his dark eyes that always made her tremble. Now it made her want to grab his hand and drag him away from the crowd, make him hers alone. He gave her a secret smile, and she smiled back, trying to put all she thought and felt into that one little gesture.

But that was all she could do. The other ladies were gathering with Queen Elizabeth near the vast fireplace, and Rosamund's absence would be noticed. She couldn't afford trouble now, not for herself, and certainly not for Anton. If they were caught, he would surely be sent back to Sweden without his English estate, and she would be sent home in disgrace. Then she would never see Anton again, never even have the chance of a future with him.

She turned away from him, hastily straightening her bodice before she went to stand beside Anne.

Anne gave her a questioning glance, but they had no time to speak. The Queen's new guests had entered the hall.

The page that led the party bore Queen Mary's standard of a red lion-rampant on a gold background, so they were new representatives sent from Edinburgh. Behind the standard came a stern-faced man in black, and two finer-dressed young men carrying boxes that were surely Christmas gifts to Queen Elizabeth from her cousin.

And behind them…

Rosamund gasped, pressing her hand to her mouth. Nay, surely it could not be? But she rubbed at her eyes and he was still there.

It was Richard, unmistakably. His skin was less ruddy than it had been in the summer, and he wore a closer-trimmed beard. He wore fine new clothes too, of sky-blue and silver satin. But his tall, burly chested countryman's physique was the same, as was his shining cap of blond hair, the ever-watchful way his gaze darted about.

After all the months without any word, any appearance, here he was at Court—with a party of Scots! Rosamund was utterly bewildered. It was like the months had slid away and she was back in the past again. Only with all the new knowledge she possessed.

She glanced across the room to where Celia stood with Lady Lennox. Richard's sister-in-law did not seem surprised, but then she never did. Celia just watched the proceedings with her lips pressed together, while Lady Lennox smiled smugly, and her son Darnley just seemed drunk. As usual.

Rosamund's gaze flew back to Richard. He had not yet seen her; what would happen when he did? Would he smile at her, speak to her? Did he even remember what had happened between them last summer? For herself, she had no idea what she felt. She felt numb, frozen, by the sudden intrusion of the forgotten past into the present. By the sudden reminder of the girl she had been and the woman she had become.

'Rosamund?' Anne whispered, gently touching her sleeve. 'What is amiss?'

Rosamund shook her head, watching as the new Scots party, including Richard, bowed to the Queen.

'Your Grace,' the older man in black said. 'I am Lord Eggerton. We are happy to bear Christmas greetings from your cousin, Queen Mary, as well as dispatches from her and her hopes that you may soon meet in amity and family unity.'

'We wish the same, and we welcome you to our Court,' Elizabeth answered. 'Queen Mary is most generous to spare so many of her own Court at such a time of year!'

'We are most happy to attend on you, Your Grace, and to serve Queen Mary,' Lord Eggerton answered. 'May I present Lord Glasgow and Master Macdonald? And this is Master Richard Sutton, one of your own subjects, who brings word of your many friends in Edinburgh.'

'You are all most welcome,' the Queen said. 'I look forward to reading your dispatches tomorrow. Right now, though, you must be hungry after your journey. Please, partake of our banquet. My ladies will fetch wine.'

And it was then that Richard saw her; his eyes widened. A slow smile spread across his face, and he veered away from his group to grab her hand in his.

Startled, Rosamund fell back a step. His skin seemed rough on hers, his palm clammy. It gave her no sudden thrill, as Anton's touch always did. She had changed truly. The past had no hold on her at all now.

But he held on tightly, not letting her go.

'Rosamund!' he said. 'Here you are at last, my dear little neighbor. And looking prettier than ever. London life agrees with you.' He raised her hand to his lips, pressing a damp kiss to her knuckles as he smiled up into her eyes.

Nay, there was none of that old feeling left, of the old illusions.

She felt ridiculously foolish, admitting to herself that her parents *had* been right all along. And where exactly had Richard been all those months? What had he been doing in Scotland?

'So this is where you have been hiding,' he said. 'Here at the Queen's Court!'

'I have not been *hiding*,' Rosamund said, taking back her hand. She tucked it in the satin folds of her skirt. 'One is never more out in the open than in London, surely?'

'And yet your parents claimed they could not disclose your location!' said Richard. 'We thought you had been sent to some Continental nunnery.'

Rosamund had to laugh at the thought of her staunchly Protestant parents packing her off to a nunnery. Though perhaps they would prefer it to seeing her make a foolish and unhappy marriage. 'If anyone has been hiding, it is surely you. No one has had a glimpse of you since the summer.'

'And I am heartily sorry for that, Rosamund,' he said solemnly. 'I have thought of you so often.'

Somehow she doubted that. Their summer flirtation been nothing more than a passing breeze for them both, she knew that now. 'But you had important business in Edinburgh, it would seem?'

'I have. I want to tell you—'

'Lady Rosamund!' Queen Elizabeth called sharply. 'Come along.'

Rosamund backed away from Richard, not liking the glow in his eyes, the desperation she saw there. 'I must go,' she said.

Richard's hand shot out to grab hers again, holding on tightly. 'Rosamund, I must talk with you. Explain things.'

Rosamund shook her head. That was all done now. 'Explain what? I assure you, Master Sutton, there is no need…'

'Rosamund, please! Please, meet with me. Hear me out,' he begged. His hand held onto hers, and she could see he would not let her go until she agreed.

'Very well,' she murmured, knowing it would be the only thing that would make him let her leave. 'I will meet with you tomorrow.'

'Thank you, Rosamund. Beautiful, sweet Rosamund.' He kissed her hand again before letting her go at last. 'You will not regret it.'

And yet she already did. She regretted being a young, romantic fool, for fancying herself in love with the first man who had ever looked at her. A man she saw now played at some game between the Scots and English. Some game with her heart.

A man not like Anton at all. Or was he? Anton was such a mystery to her.

As she joined the Queen her gaze frantically scoured the crowd for a glimpse of Anton. She suddenly had a desperate need to see him, to know he was still there, that he was real.

But at the same time she hoped he had not seen her— had not seen Richard kiss her hand.

When she found him, though, she saw that her hopes

and fears were in vain. He stood near the doorway with Lord Langley, his arms crossed over his chest as he watched her with narrowed eyes.

She could read nothing of him at all.

Anton saw the blond, bearded man kiss Rosamund's hand and hold that hand tightly in his as he talked to her. It was no polite greeting; their hands were bent close, their eyes meeting as they spoke intimately, almost as if no one else was near.

Rosamund knew him; Anton could see that. She had looked shocked when he had walked past, her face suddenly as pale as if she had seen a spectre. And the man knew Rosamund, enough to boldly take her hand and whisper in her ear.

Where had the cursed man come from? What was he to Rosamund?

A wave of bitter jealousy rose up in him, and his hands tightened into fists he longed to drive into the man's blond, English face. He had never known such a fury before, and he wasn't sure he liked it. But it all could not be denied. He detested this man he had never met, because he had dared kiss Rosamund's hand, dared to be known to her in some way.

And Anton detested him for the smug smile he exchanged with his Scottish cohorts. He was up to something, and Anton determined to discover what it was—and what exactly he was to Rosamund, even as he knew he had no right to feel that way about her.

Anne Percy joined Lord Langley and him by the doorway.

'Nothing like a surprise appearance, yes?' she said, watching the new Scots delegates as they sat down to their repast. 'Too bad they are not more handsome. But then Queen Mary probably keeps the best of them at her own Court.'

'You do not think them handsome?' Lord Langley asked, striving to sound disinterested, but not quite achieving it.

'Not like our own Court gentlemen,' Anne teased. 'Though that blond-haired Englishman is not so very bad. But I fear his heart seems to be already claimed.'

Claimed by Rosamund? 'Do you know him, then, Mistress Percy?' Anton asked.

She gave him a shrewd glance. 'I know only his name—Richard Sutton. He seems to be some kinsman of Celia Sutton. And he also seems to admire Lady Rosamund—which I am sure *you* can understand, Master Gustavson.'

'Is she already known to him?' Anton asked, compelled to know, even as he did not want to know, not really.

Anne hesitated. 'I am not entirely sure yet, but I think…'

'Think what?' Anton urged.

'Rosamund told me once she had a suitor back at home,' Anne said. 'Someone her parents did not approve of, though she did not name him to me.'

'But you suspect this Richard Sutton is he?' Anton asked.

'Perhaps. He did seem rather closely acquainted with her,' said Anne. 'And she went quite pale when she saw him.'

'I see,' Anton said tightly. 'An ardent suitor.'

Anne suddenly laid her hand on his sleeve. 'Master Gustavson,' she said quietly. 'I am quite certain that whatever was between them is in the past.'

'Or *was* in the past,' Anton said, giving her a smile. Anne Percy loved to seem the careless Court flirt, sophisticated, knowing. But underneath she was a hopeful romantic.

Much like himself, fool that he was. It seemed he had too much of his mother in him, was too inclined to follow the demands of his heart even against duty and danger.

'Shall I set my men to discover why he is here?' Lord Langley said. 'To be mixed up with the Scots—it cannot be good.'

'Set your spies on him, you mean?' Anton said. 'There is no need, Lord Langley.'

Anton would find out what he needed to know all on his own. He would not see Rosamund hurt, no matter how 'ardent' the suitor. And no matter that he himself would most probably hurt her in the end...

Chapter Twelve

'Your Grace, I fear I must heartily disagree with these plans,' Lord Burghley said, thumping his walking stick against the parquet floor for emphasis.

'My dear Cecil,' answered the Queen, pounding her fist on her desk to make her own emphasis. 'I fear *I* must then remind you who is master here! This is *my* Court, and I shall order my own Christmas.'

'But your safety…'

'My safety? From what? A few paltry threats, that are as nothing compared to what I have faced in the past,' the Queen said. 'My father always had a masquerade ball to mark New Year's Day, and so shall I.'

Rosamund bent her head over her sewing, trying to pretend she was not there in the Queen's chamber, was not hearing her quarrel with Lord Burghley—again. There was always a quarrel between them.

Even in her short time at Court Rosamund felt she had heard this before—Queen Elizabeth insisting she would do something, and Lord Burghley arguing she should not for her own sake. Today it was the Queen's insistence that she would have a masked ball tomorrow night. Next week it would surely be something else.

It put Rosamund in mind of her own father. Did her father know Richard was here in London? Had he heard any rumours at Ramsay Castle as he and her mother celebrated their own holiday? If he had, he would surely summon her home in haste. But she knew she could not go now, not when Anton was still here. Not while she was still learning him.

Rosamund bit her lip, remembering Anton's face as he had watched her with Richard. What would he think of the way Richard had kissed her hand, had spoken to her so familiarly? What if Anton thought she did not care for him even after everything?

She had lain awake in her bed all night thinking of it, even as she feigned sleep to keep Anne from questioning her. She had to speak to Anton, and to Richard, too, to find out what he was doing at Court. Yet there was no time, as they all had to attend on the Queen.

Oh, how did all these Court ladies manage all their tangled love affairs? she thought as she stabbed at the linen with her needle. It was confusing enough with only two!

'Rosamund,' Anne whispered. 'Are you quite well?'

'Of course I am,' Rosamund whispered back. 'Why do you ask?'

'Because you have sewn that linen to your skirt.'

Rosamund looked down, startled to see that she had indeed firmly attached her embroidery to her velvet skirt. 'Oh, blast,' she muttered, reaching for her scissors.

'Here, let me,' Anne said, taking the scissors away.

'You would cut your gown to ribbons in your distracted state.'

Rosamund sat very still, watching as Anne snipped loose the threads. 'Tell me, my friend,' Anne said, under cover of the task, 'Is the new arrival your swain from back home?'

'Aye,' Rosamund muttered. 'Richard. I have not seen him since the summer, and I thought that was all ended.'

'But it is not?'

'He wants me to meet with him,' Rosamund said. 'He wishes to explain, he said.'

'Hmm. It did not appear *his* feelings were dimmed, not with the eager way he held your hand,' said Anne. 'But what of you?'

'I fear I do not feel as I once did towards him,' Rosamund admitted. And she had not for a very long time. Maybe not ever.

'Because of Anton Gustavson?'

'Perhaps. Or perhaps I have changed.' She knew she had. Anton had helped her change.

Anne snipped away the last of the threads. 'Will you meet with him?'

'I do not know. I feel as if I owe it to him to at least hear him out.'

'I don't think you owe him anything at all! Not with the way he deserted you. But you must do as you see fit.' Anne handed her the scissors. 'Just be careful, Rosamund, I beg you.'

'Of course I will be careful,' Rosamund said, straightening her sewing box. 'I hope I have learned *some* caution here at Court.'

Anne laughed. 'Not from me, I fear.'

'Mistress Percy! Lady Rosamund!' the Queen called. 'What are the two of you whispering about, pray?'

Anne sat up straight as Rosamund tried to stifle her giggles. 'Of our costumes for your masquerade, Your Grace,' Anne said.

'Ah. There, you see, Cecil?' Queen Elizabeth said. 'Everyone plans for the masquerade already. We cannot disappoint them.'

'As you wish, Your Grace,' Lord Burghley said reluctantly.

'And I must make my own plans,' Elizabeth said. 'Lady Rosamund, fetch Mistress Parry to me. She is in the Great Hall.'

'Yes, Your Grace.' Rosamund abandoned her ruined sewing and hurried out of the chamber, grateful for some task. For the chance to look for Anton.

Yet she did not see him in the crowds in the Presence and Privy chambers, or in the corridors. Nor was he in the gallery, where the choir was again rehearsing. This time it was for the wassail carols that traditionally accompanied the New Year's gift-giving that would commence at that night's banquet. The strain of that gift-giving showed on courtiers' faces. Would their gift impress the Queen? Would it bring them favour?

'Wassail, wassail, all over the town, our toast it is white and our ale it is brown! Our bowl it is made of the white maple-tree, and a wassailing bowl we'll drink unto thee!'

Rosamund listened to their wassail song, stopping to peer out of the window at the gardens below. She did not see Anton there, either, among the many people strolling the pathways under the weak, watery sunshine.

As Rosamund stared down at the garden she did not see the paths, the people bundled up in their furred cloaks or the winter greenery under the dusting of sparkling snow. She only saw Anton, saw his smile as he held her, his laughter as he twirled over the ice.

She saw the dark look in his eyes as he watched her with Richard. The danger that was already around them all the time.

She spun away from the window, only to come face to face with Richard himself.

He smiled at her, reaching for her hand. 'Rosamund! At last we meet. I have been looking for you all morning.'

'Indeed, M-Master Sutton?' Rosamund stammered, trying to take back her hand. He held it too tightly, though, and she worried people were watching. 'I have been with the Queen, as usual.'

His smile widened, his blue eyes crinkling in a way she had once found so attractive. 'You are very busy with your tasks here at Court. I see the Queen shows you much favour.'

'No more than any of her other ladies,' Rosamund said quickly. But then she relented a bit, drawn in by his eyes, by the memory they evoked of summer and home, the times they had shared. 'But it is true she has not thrown anything at me yet!'

Richard laughed. 'And that is quite an accomplishment, from what I have heard.' He raised her hand for a quick kiss, then he released her at last. 'Rosamund, will you walk with me? Just for a while?'

'I…' She glanced around the crowded gallery. 'I am meant to fetch Mistress Parry for the Queen. She is in the Great Hall.'

'Then I will walk with you there,' he said. 'Please, Rosamund. I must speak with you.'

'Very well, then. I would be glad of the company,' she answered. She would also be glad of the chance to find out where he had been all those months. Why he had left her. Why he had returned now.

They fell into step together as they made their way through the crowds, but he did not try to touch her again. It was as if he, too, sensed the new gulf between them, the distance of time and reflection. The distance of new pursuits and affections. A new truth, a new way of life.

Or perhaps it was only she herself who felt that, Rosamund thought wryly. Even as Richard smiled at her, as she felt the tug of home and memories, he seemed a stranger to her. What they had once been to each other seemed strange and foolish now. The emotions were of someone she scarcely even knew, a girl.

'You do look lovely, Rosamund,' he said quietly. 'Court life agrees with you.'

'You mean I look better in my fine gown than I did at home with loose hair and simple garments that can't be mussed by the country mud?'

His eyes crinkled again, and he leaned towards her, as if to find something of their old connection. 'You looked lovely then, too. Yet there is some new elegance about you here. You seem—changed.'

'As do you, Richard. But then, it has been a long time since last we met.'

'Not so long as all that.' He paused. 'I thought of you often, Rosamund. Did you think of me?'

'Of course I did. There was much speculation in the neighbourhood about where you had gone.'

'But did *you* think of *me*?'

She stilled her steps, facing him squarely. This had to be ended now. 'For a time. When I did not hear from you, though, I had to turn to other matters. To listen to the counsel of my family.'

'I wanted to write, but I fear I was not able to. Not from where I was.'

'And where were you?' she asked, not sure she wanted to know. Richard had secrets; she could tell. She needed no more secrets in her life.

'On an errand for my own family,' he said. But Rosamund noticed he would not quite meet her gaze. Mysteries, always mysteries; there were so many of them at Whitehall. 'I moved about too often, I fear. Yet I thought of you every day, remembered our declarations to each other.'

'The declarations of foolish children. My parents were right—I was too young to know my own mind.' She started to turn away, but he caught her arm in a tight clasp, crumpling the fine satin of her sleeve.

'Rosamund, that isn't true!' he insisted. 'I had work to do, for *us*. So I could support you as you deserve, to show your parents I was worthy.'

'I thought you worthy,' Rosamund said. She tugged at her arm, trying to free herself. There was a glow to Richard's eyes, a hard set to his jaw she did not like. It was as if the mask of the laughing summer-time Richard had fallen away, showing her the stony anger and resentment underneath. His hand tightened on her arm, painful enough to bruise.

'Let me go!' she cried, twisting her wrist. A few courtiers glanced their way, hoping for new distraction, new scandal.

The mask fell back into place, leaving a repentant visage behind. Yet there was still a red flush of anger in his cheeks. Rosamund suddenly remembered more than their sunlit kisses, remembered things she had once ignored, excused: the temper when a groom had fumbled with his horse; his railing against her parents, against the injustice of society. His unkind words about Celia, disguised as concern for his brother. Those memories only made Rosamund feel doubly foolish, especially as she rubbed at her sore arm.

'I am sorry, dear Rosamund,' he said repentantly. 'Forgive me. I just have thought of you, longed to see you, for so long…'

She shook her head. 'Please, Richard, do not. Our flirtation was sweet, but it seems so long ago. It is over,' she said, trying to be firm. Even if there had not been Anton, anything she had once felt for Richard was entirely over.

His lips tightened into a flat line. 'You *have* changed. Living here at Court, amid all these riches, these grand courtiers, has changed you.'

Aye, she had changed; Rosamund knew that. Yet it was not the glitter of Court that had changed her. It was knowing what a truly good man was like; it was Anton. A man who tried to do his duty, to protect her, even as their passion drew them closer and closer together.

'I am older now, that is all,' she said. 'Please, Richard. Can we not part as friends?'

'Part?' He looked as if he would very much like to argue, perhaps to reach for her, grab her again. But a laughing group passed close to them, jostling, and he stepped away. 'Yet we still have so much more to speak of together.'

'Nay, Richard,' she said. 'My life is here now, and yours is—wherever you have made it in these last months when I did not hear from you. We must part now.'

She took a step back, only to be brought up short when he snatched her hand again. That laughing knot of courtiers was still nearby, so she had no fear. Yet she did not like the way he looked at her now, the way he held onto her.

He jerked her to his side, whispering roughly, 'You and your parents think you are so great, so high above my family that you would refuse my suit. But soon, when I have made my fortune and great events have come to pass, you will be sorry.'

Rosamund twisted her hand away from him, hurrying down the gallery as fast as she dared. She longed to run, to dash to her chamber and wash her hands until the feel of him was erased. Until all her old memories, good and bad, were gone too.

She turned down another corridor, and at its end glimpsed Anton. He still wore his cap and cloak, and his skates were slung over his shoulder as if he'd just come in from the cold day. He saw her too, and a smile of welcome lit his face. But then a wariness took its place, dimming, dampening, as the grey clouds outside.

Rosamund did not care, though. She had to be near him, to lean into him, to feel that calm strength of his and know she was safe. Know that the past was gone, and Richard held no threat.

She hurried towards him, dodging around the ever-present crowds until she stood before him. She reached out and lightly touched his hand, tracing the little gold-and-ruby ring on his finger. His skin was cold, the frost still lingering on his woollen sleeve.

His smile returned, warmer than any fire, any sun.

'You were skating on the river?' she said, taking her hand back before anyone could notice her bold touch. Her fingers still tingled, though.

'Aye. 'Tis a fine day, Lady Rosamund, you should join me later and try those new skates.'

'I should like nothing better,' she answered. 'Yet I

fear I will be busy with the Queen this afternoon. She is finishing preparations for the gift-giving tonight.'

'Then I shall not keep you from your tasks,' he said. He glanced over her shoulder and his eyes narrowed.

Rosamund looked back to see that Richard stood at the other end of the corridor, watching them. She leaned closer to Anton, seeking his strength.

'Or perhaps you are also busy with your old friends from home?' he said slowly.

Her gaze flew back to his. He knew of Richard? Ah, but then of course he would. Everyone knew everything at Court. There were no secrets.

Almost.

'I—nay,' she said. 'That is, yes, Richard's family's estate neighbours ours, and I have known him a long time. I begin to think I was quite mistaken in his character, though. Too long a time has passed since I last saw him.'

'He seems quite pleased to see *you*,' Anton said. 'But then, who would not be?'

'Anton,' she whispered. 'Can we meet later?'

His hand brushed hers under cover of his cloak. 'When?' he said, his voice reluctant but deep with the knowledge that he could not resist. Just as she felt.

'There will be fireworks tonight after the gifts. Everyone will surely be distracted.'

'Lord Langley's cousin's chamber again?'

'Aye.' Rosamund longed to kiss him, to feel his lips on hers, and she saw from the intent look in his eyes that he must feel the same. Or was she imagining things again? She wanted to stay, to talk to him.

Yet she had her errand, and had to be content with one more quick touch, a smile. 'I will see you there.'

Then she hurried on her way, glad her path did not again take her past Richard.

* * *

Anton watched Rosamund dash out of the corridor, her velvet skirts twirling, before he turned his attention to the man: Richard Sutton.

Anne Percy had said he was a 'suitor' of Rosamund. Yet obviously he was not one her parents approved of, for she had been sent to Court rather than married to him. Was he now some danger to her?

When Rosamund had run up to Anton and taken his hand, he'd seen a flash of fear in her eyes, like that of the St Stephen's Day fox going to earth. He was glad indeed she felt she could run to him, but there was a fury that anyone should frighten her at all.

He leaned back against the wall, his arms crossed over his chest as he watched Richard Sutton. The man talked with Celia Sutton now, and she looked angry as well. Her usually solemn, stone-serene face was tense. She shook her head at whatever he was saying to her, and he flushed a dark, furious red.

The man did appear to be burlier than he, Anton had to admit—thick-chested and broad-shouldered; an English tavern-brawler. But he also showed signs of running to fat, where Anton was lean and quick from skating and sword-play. Surely he could best this harasser of ladies in a duel?

And a harasser he seemed indeed. He grabbed Celia's wrist, his fingers tightening as she shook her head again. Anton had seen enough. He pushed away from the wall, striding towards the arguing pair.

'Excuse me,' he said, sliding smoothly between them. He took the man's thick hand in a firm grip, peeling his tight clasp back from Celia's thin wrist. With his other hand he took her arm, drawing her a few steps away.

For once, she did not protest. She hardly seemed to notice who held her arm, so occupied was she in glaring at Richard Sutton.

So, Anton thought, he was not the only one she quarrelled with. 'I beg your pardon for interrupting such a cozy *tête-à-tête*,' he said. 'But I have an appointment with my fair cousin. I am sure you will excuse us, Master…?'

'This is my brother-in-law, Richard Sutton,' Celia said. 'He and I have nothing left to say to each other.'

'On the contrary, Celia,' Richard said, all false, bluff heartiness. 'We have a great deal to say to each other! And who is this foreigner, anyway?'

'He told you,' Celia said. 'He is my cousin. And also a *foreigner* who is much admired and favoured here at Court. Just ask Lady Rosamund Ramsay.'

She swung away suddenly, pulling Anton with her as he still held her arm. But he looked back at Richard, holding her still for just a moment longer.

'And also a foreigner well-educated in gallantry and courtesy to ladies,' he said lightly, but with an unmistakable threat of steel laced underneath. 'In my country, we tend to become very angry indeed when we see a woman treated with less than proper respect.'

The flush on Richard's florid face deepened. Celia smiled at him sweetly, and added, 'And that is why the ladies here are so appreciative of you, Anton. Our rough Englishmen from the countryside have little knowledge of such gallantry and fine manners.'

'Nay, for we have knowledge of far more useful matters,' Richard said. 'Such as warfare. Dispatching our enemies.'

'Tsk, tsk, brother,' Celia said. 'Such martial tendencies will never win you a fair maiden like Lady Rosamund.'

Anton arched his brow and gave Richard a mocking bow before walking away with Celia on his arm. He could feel the burn of the man's glare on the back of his neck all the way down the corridor, and it made him itch to draw his dagger.

But there were too many people about, and Celia's clasp was tight on his sleeve.

'So, that interesting person is your brother-in-law,' he said.

Celia snorted contemptuously, her steps so quick he had to pay close attention to keep up with her. They passed the open doors to the Great Hall, where much activity went on to prepare the tables meant to display that night's New Year's gifts.

'He *was* my brother-in-law, until my husband died,' she said. 'Now that family seeks to deny me my dower rights.'

As he sought to deny her her rights to Briony Manor? But he did not seem to be the focus of her ire today.

'They are a greedy lot, the Suttons,' she said. 'I would never have married into their midst if I had a choice. Lady Rosamund is most fortunate.'

'Lady Rosamund?'

'Ah, yes. I forgot you, too, admire her. Perhaps your suit will fare better with her parents than Richard's.' A tiny, cat-like smile touched her lips. 'I would like to see Richard's face if *that* happened.'

'They objected to his offer?' Anton asked, even as he cursed his curiosity, his damnable need to know everything about Rosamund.

'It never came to a formal offer. Richard and his family are quite ambitious, and they schemed for the match. I believe he even tried to woo her in secret, but I knew it would come to naught.'

'Why is that?'

'Why, cousin,' Celia said slyly. 'Who knew you would be so interested in provincial gossip?'

Anton laughed. 'I am a man of many interests.'

'Indeed you are. Foremost among them Lady Rosamund, perhaps?'

'Anyone may know my regard for her.'

'I would advise you to be sure of her affections, then, before you brave the Queen. Or the Ramsays. She is their only child, their treasure, and they quite dote on her. I knew they would never let her go to a clod like Richard.'

'Or to a foreigner?' They must know what a treasure they had, then, and would not easily let her go.

'That remains to be seen, does it not?' She abruptly came to a halt, staring up at him with those brown eyes so like his mother's. And his own. His only family, so very angry at him.

'I will say this, cousin,' she said. 'We have been rivals, but I am not entirely a fool. I can see that you are made of finer stuff than the Suttons, and that Lady Rosamund cares for you. But you should not underestimate Richard. He looks bluff and hearty, an empty-headed farmer sort of man, but he is ambitious. He hides and creeps like a snake, and he detests to be thwarted.'

'I have no fear of a man like him.' It was not Richard Sutton who kept him from Rosamund but his own duty.

'I know you do not. In truth, you remind me much of my own father. He feared nothing at all, for everyone seemed charmed by him, yet that was his undoing in the end. Just watch for Richard, that is all. Especially if you somehow succeed in gaining Lady Rosamund's hand.'

'Mistress Sutton!' a woman called. Anton looked up to find the Queen's cousin, Lady Lennox, beckoning to Celia.

'I must go now,' Celia said, turning away.

'Cousin, wait,' Anton said, catching her hand. 'Perhaps I am not the only one who needs must beware. What business do you have with Lady Lennox and the Scots?'

Celia gave him a crooked little smile. 'We all have to make our way here at Court, yes? Find what friends we may. Just remember what I said.'

Anton watched her go, frowning, as the day seemed to darken. It was true that he did not fear Richard Sutton, or any man. He had faced villains aplenty in battle, and in the austere court of the temperamental King Eric, and he had bested them all.

Yet he had only had to be concerned with himself then. Now there was Rosamund, and Celia too. And nothing made him angrier than threats to a lady.

That anger was also a sign that his own connection to Rosamund grew too great. He had told himself he was careful, that his heart would not rule his sense, that they would not get into trouble for their affair. That he could protect her.

But that had been foolish; he saw that now. He had to end it, once and for all.

All the courtiers crowded around the open windows of the Waterside Gallery, bundled in cloaks and furs against the cold. But no one seemed to notice the sharp night wind, for there was too much excited laughter, too much exultation over the success of their gifts to Queen Elizabeth, and the fineness of hers to them. The long tables of the Great Hall were piled high with jewels, lengths of velvet and brocade, feathered fans, exotic food and wines and all manner of lovely things, including the pearl-encrusted satin sleeves Rosamund's own parents had sent.

Not everyone was filled with happiness, of course. A few thought their gifts had been overlooked, or they were slighted by what the Queen had presented to them, and they thus sulked at the edges of the room. But they were few indeed. Everyone else was content with the warm, spiced wine passed among them by the royal pages, and with waiting for the fireworks Lord Leicester had so painstakingly planned to usher in 1565.

Rosamund felt all overcome with excitement, though not for the same reasons. Soon she would meet Anton again in their secret place, and they would be alone at last. She craved those moments in their secret world far too much, it was a bright moment of hope.

Yet some of that brightness dimmed when she glimpsed Richard across the gallery, watching her. At first she surprised him, and the expression on his face was darkly scowling, heavy with some discontent— perhaps that she had not answered the note he'd sent her via one of the pages? Then he smiled broadly and seemed something of the old Richard again. But she no longer trusted that smile. She turned away from him, hurrying over to the windows to stare out at the river.

The frost fair was still in force, full of activity under the glow of torches and the moon. Sleds glided along the frozen grooves of the Thames between the booths and she could hear the distant hum of music, wassail carols to bring in the New Year.

What would the year bring? she wondered. Everything she hoped for? Or heartbreak and trouble?

The night sky suddenly exploded above them, a crackling, glittering shower of red-and-white fireworks. A flare of green followed, and a long waterfall of blue stars. It was wondrously beautiful, and Rosamund stared up, open-mouthed with delight. It reflected the hope in her own heart, the hope that dared shine its tiny light even in the midst of danger.

Everyone out on the river stopped to stare, too, exclaiming at the beauty of it all. The sparks glistened on the ice, turning it all to a fantasy land far from the harsh realities of winter.

Rosamund eased away from the crowd as their attention was absorbed by the spectacle. Holding her silk skirts close to her sides, she tiptoed out of the gallery into the silent corridor. Once she was certain she wasn't followed, she dashed headlong towards her rendezvous.

The apartment was quiet and dark, yet she remembered well where everything was. The chairs and tables, the fine carpets—the bed. She felt her way to the window, pushing back the heavy curtains to let in the glow of the moon, the sparkle of the fireworks. They illuminated the space that had become such a haven against the world to her.

Dear; how cold! She rubbed at her arms in their embroidered sleeves, wishing for a cloak. But soon enough Anton's arms would be around her, and she could forget the cold, and everything else, for a time.

As she stood there, staring out at the night, she heard the door open behind her. Footsteps hurried across the floor, heavy and muffled by the carpet, and strong arms did indeed slide around her, drawing her back against a hard, velvet-covered chest.

For an instant, she remembered Richard staring at her, and she stiffened, half-fearful he might have followed her. But then she smelled Anton's scent— clean soap winter greenery—and felt his familiar caress at her waist, and she knew she was safe.

She relaxed against him, resting her head back on his shoulder as they watched the fireworks.

He softly kissed her cheek. 'Happy New Year, *alskling*,' he whispered.

Rosamund smiled. 'And Happy New Year to *you*, Master Gustavson. What is your wish for the next year?'

'Is this an English custom, then? Making a wish for the New Year?'

'Of course. Oh—but I forgot. You mustn't tell it, or it might not come true.'

She spun around in his arms, going up on tiptoe as their lips met in the first kiss of the new year. She tried to put all she wished for in that kiss, all she felt for him and hoped for in the future. That fear was left entirely behind.

He seemed to feel it, too. He groaned against her mouth, his tongue touching the tip of hers, tasting her as if she was the finest, sweetest of wines. His hands combed through her hair, discarding the pins and pearl combs as it tumbled over her shoulders.

'*Hjarta*,' he muttered, burying his face in her hair, kissing the side of her neck and the curve of her shoulder as he eased away her bodice.

Rosamund's eyes drifted closed, her head falling back as she lost herself in the delicious sensations of his caress, his kiss, the feel of his lips on her bare skin. But she wanted more, wanted to feel him too. To be closer, ever closer.

She fumbled eagerly for the fastenings of his doublet, but suddenly his hands grasped hers tightly, holding her away.

Rosamund stared up at him, bewildered. His jaw was tight, his eyes hooded, hidden from her. 'What— what?' she stammered. 'What is amiss?'

'I'm sorry,' he said hoarsely. 'I'm sorry, *alskling*, I should never have met you here tonight. Never let things go so far.'

Rosamund shook her head in puzzlement. Anton still held her hands, they still stood close together, but she felt him slipping away from her. It was as if a cold wind rushed between them, pushing them further and further apart.

'Things have gone—so far before,' she whispered.

He kissed her hand, his hair falling over his brow as he bent over her fingers. How handsome he was, she thought numbly. Like a dark Norse god. Other ladies thought so, too; they all sought him out, flirted with him. Yet she had been foolish enough to join their ranks, to think he cared for her, only her.

Had she been wrong? Had she entirely misread what was between them?

Rosamund stepped back, drawing away her hands. She could not think when he touched her. Her mind raced, going over every kiss, every glance and word. Nay; she had not been mistaken, surely? No man was such a fine actor.

Why, then, did he turn from her now?

'I know we have gone thus far before,' he said roughly, raking his hair back with his fingers. It fell into even greater disarray, and Rosamund longed to smooth it back, to feel the warm satin of his hair under her touch.

She tucked her hands into her skirts, forcing them to stay still.

'I was wrong, very wrong, to behave thus,' he continued. 'I put you in danger, and that was inexcusable. I'm sorry, Rosamund.'

'Nay, we both wanted this!' Rosamund cried. She took a stumbling step towards him, but he backed away. He was so distant from her. 'We could not help ourselves, no matter the danger.'

'Nonetheless, it was a mistake. It must end here.'

'End?' She felt an icy finger creep down her spine, making her feel suddenly numb, removed from the scene, as if she watched a scene in a mummer's play. If only it was not so terribly real, the end of her hopes.

'I have work to do here in England, work I have been too long distracted from,' he said implacably. 'And you have your own duties. I would not bring you trouble with the Queen, Rosamund.'

'I care not for work and duties! Not beside what we have, Anton, what we could have.' That numbness faded, and Rosamund felt instead the hot prickle of tears. Sad, angry, confused tears that she impatiently dashed away.

She had thought—nay, known!—he felt the same. But now he watched her with such cold distance in his dark eyes. He would not turn away from her, from what they had between them, out of sudden duty. Unless…

'You prefer someone else,' she whispered. 'Lady Essex? One of the other maids?' Someone prettier, more flirtatious. More careless with their emotions.

Anton frowned, looking away from her, but he did not deny it. 'I am sorry,' he said again. 'Sorry for all the trouble I have caused you.'

Trouble? Oh, that was not the half of all he had caused her! She had given herself, body and heart, to him and now he turned from her. What was wrong with her?

Rosamund spun around, dashing out of the chamber before those dreadful tears could fall. She would not give him the satisfaction of seeing them, of seeing the terrible pain he caused her with his strange words.

'This will be the last time I cry,' she vowed as she hurried down the dark, abandoned corridor. Men were not worth it in the least.

Anton listened to Rosamund's footsteps fade until

there was only silence, only the faint scent of her perfume still in the air. Then he doubled over, falling to the floor at the pain in his stomach.

At the agony of hurting his sweet Rosamund.

It had had to be done, even as he let himself steal one more kiss, one more caress, had let himself feel her in his arms again. Things had gone too far between them already. He could not let them fall into the dangerous whirlpool and be lost for ever. They had this one opportunity to draw away from the precipice, to turn back to their lives of duty, and he had taken it.

He had done what was right, at last. Why, then, was it such agony?

Anton straightened to his feet, tugging his doublet into place, smoothing back his hair. He had to be himself again, as he'd been before he'd met Rosamund and let himself be tempted by her sweetness and goodness, her angelic beauty. It should not be so difficult to do.

Yet it felt terribly as if some vital part of him was torn away and bleeding.

Chapter Thirteen

New Year's Day, January 1

'You were out very late last night, Rosamund,' Anne Percy said, brushing out Rosamund's hair as they prepared for the Queen's masquerade ball.

'Was I indeed?' Rosamund answered, feeling that heat creeping up in her cheeks again. Everyone had seemed soundly asleep when she'd tiptoed in before dawn, so hurt and confused she could only curl up in her bed and pray for the pain to leave her. But she should have known Anne would miss nothing.

'Did anyone else notice?' she whispered.

'Nay,' Anne said, reaching for the bowl of hairpins on the bedside table. 'I told them you were on an errand for the Queen. They were so full of wine they would not have noticed if the roof collapsed on them, anyway.'

'Thank you, Anne. You are a fine friend,' Rosamund said, sitting very still as Anne fastened her hair up tightly. Anne *was* a good friend, a comfort, even if she did not know it. 'If I can ever help you and Lord Langley to a secret meeting…'

Anne snorted. 'I doubt that shall ever happen! I may one day hold you to your promise of assistance, Rosamund, even if I must be with someone else. But are you sure naught is amiss? You seem distracted today.'

Rosamund had certainly seen the way Anne looked at Langley, and the way he looked at her. The air between them fairly crackled. But she said nothing; she was done with romance. It caused such numb hurt; Anne was well out of it. 'Nay, I am just tired.'

'And no wonder, we have been so busy with holiday festivities! Tell me something, though,' Anne said. 'When you returned, did you see anyone lurking about in the corridor?'

'Nay, I saw nothing,' Rosamund said, glad of the distraction of a change in topic. 'It was quite dark, though. Why?'

Anne shrugged, pushing in the last pin. 'When I came up here with Catherine and the Marys after the dancing, I thought we were followed. I just had that sense of being watched.'

'Oh, yes, I know that feeling,' Rosamund said, with a shiver of dangerous intimation.

'But when I looked there was no one. Only shadows.'

'Who would be lurking about so near the Queen's own chambers?' Rosamund said, still feeling that disquiet. She did remember well that sense of being watched, observed, even in the midst of a crowd. There had been that strange Lord of Misrule. 'The guards would be sure to send them off.'

'If they saw them. I think the guards had too much spiced wine too. Ah, well, it was likely naught. Now, which wig do you like? The red or the black?'

'It doesn't signify,' Rosamund said. Gowns and wigs were far from her mind. 'You choose.'

'You wear the red, then, and I will take the black. I shall be a sorceress of the night!' Anne said, combing out the wigs as she watched Rosamund sort through her jewels until she found her emerald-drop earrings. 'Those are very pretty.'

'Do you not think them too old-fashioned?' Rosamund said, looping one through her ear lobe. Their familiarity gave her some comfort, even as she was sad thinking of home and all she had lost. 'They were my grandmother's.'

'Nay, they will do well for an autumn spirit, I think.' They crowded together near the precious looking-glass, pushing Mary Howard out of the way so they could fit on their wigs, borrowed from the Queen's players for the masquerade. Rosamund laughed as Anne jostled her, trying to enter into the festive spirit of the night. She would not be the ghost at the banquet.

Once they were dressed, Anne in black-and-silver satin and Rosamund in deep-green velvet bound at the waist with a gold-and-emerald kirtle, they took out their jewelled masks and tied them over their faces. It felt excellent to hide behind it, Rosamund thought, as if she could be someone else for a while, and hide even from herself.

'Do we look suitably mysterious?' Anne said, twirling around.

'Surely no one will know us?' Rosamund declared.

'Oh, I think at least one person will know you!' Anne teased, laughing as she twined pearls around her throat. 'But, come, we will be late, and even masked the Queen will surely notice.'

They dashed down the privy stairs, joining the flow of people moving towards the Great Hall. It seemed a glittering, shining river of bright silks, sparkling jewels, masked visages. There were cats and stags, pale Venetians, parti-coloured jesters, solemn black veils and cloaks. No one knew each other, or at least pretended not to know, which led to much flirtatious laughter and guessing games.

Perhaps the Queen had been right to keep to the old tradition of the New Year's masquerade, Rosamund thought, despite Lord Burghley's misgivings. All the trepidations and uncertainties of the last few days seemed melted away in giddy excitement—except for her.

They all spilled into the Great Hall, which was also transformed for the night. Vast swaths of red-and-black satin draped from the gilded ceiling down the walls, like an exotic pavilion. The tables, benches and dais were removed, and the multi-tiered buffets were laden with delicacies, pyramids of sweets, platters of roast meats and even bowls of rare candied-fruits. The servants who offered wine were also masked, adding to the dark air of mystery and possibility.

'Look at that man there,' Anne said, taking two goblets of wine and handing one to Rosamund. 'The one who looks like a peacock. Do you suppose that to be Lord Leicester?'

Rosamund sipped at her wine below the edge of her mask. It was stronger than usual, richly spiced, deep enough to help her forget. 'Perhaps. He does seem fond of blue. I would think that man there more likely, though.' She gestured towards a tall, broad-shouldered man with dark hair, dressed like a knight of a hundred years ago. He whispered intently to a veiled lady.

'Quite so. But who does he speak with? The Queen incognito, do you think?' But it was not the Queen, as they soon found when the doors to the Great Hall opened again and a hush fell over the noisy crowd.

A golden chariot appeared, drawn by six tall footmen clad in white satin. And riding the chariot was the goddess Diana, a golden half-moon crowning her long, red hair. She wore a gown as green as the forest, a white fur-cloak over her shoulders and a gold bow in her hand. A quiver of arrows hung over her shoulder.

She wore a white-and-gold mask, but it could be no one but Queen Elizabeth. As the chariot came to a halt, a man dressed as a huntsman in green-and-brown wool stepped forward to offer his hand. She took it, stepping down as hidden musicians struck up a pavane. The huntsman led Diana to the dance, everyone else following.

'If that is not Leicester, then he must be perishing of jealousy!' Anne whispered.

Rosamund shook her head. 'But if the woodsman is Leicester, then who is the knight? And the veiled lady?'

'Just one of tonight's many mysteries, my friend,' Anne said as one of the Venetians claimed her hand for the dance.

Rosamund had not seen the one man she once wanted to dance with. She went instead to one of the heavy-laden buffets, inspecting the marzipan flowers and the gold-leafed cakes.

As she nibbled at a bit of candied fruit, a man enveloped in a black cloak embroidered with stars, his face hidden by a spangled, black mask, came to stand beside her. He was silent for a long moment, completely covered in that enveloping disguise, yet she could feel the heat of his intense regard. It made her most uneasy. But as she tried to edge away she found her path blocked by a knot of revellers.

'You do not dance, fair lady?' he asked, his voice hoarse and muffled.

'Nay,' Rosamund answered firmly, trying to shake

away shivers of sudden fear. She had had enough of dancing with strange masked men. 'Not tonight.'

'Such a great loss. But then, surely there are other, finer pleasures to be had on such a night as this? Perhaps you would care to see the moon in the garden…'

Rosamund finally saw a gap in the crowd and broke through it, just as the importunate man reached for her hand. His laughter followed her.

The dance floor was even more crowded now, the couples twirling and leaping in a wild Italian *passa-miente*. Despite the cold night outside, the room was hot, close packed, filled with smoke from the vast fireplace and the torches, and the heavy scent of expensive perfumes and fine fabrics packed in lavender. All the voices and the music blended in one loud, shrill madrigal set off by the drumbeat of dancing feet.

Rosamund suddenly could not breathe. Her chest felt tight in her closely laced bodice, and the red-and-black hangings seemed to be closing inward. Surely they would fall, enveloping them all in their suffocating folds.

Her stomach felt queasy with the wine and sweets, the heat. The sadness amidst the revelry was too overwhelming. She wanted to leave, to curl up somewhere and be alone. But as she turned away her path was blocked.

'Lady Rosamund?' the man said.

Rosamund was startled; for an instant she saw the man wore a black cloak, and she stiffened. But then she noticed that this man's cloak was plain, not embroidered with stars, and that it could be none but Lord Burghley. His only nod to a disguise was a small black mask and a knot of ribbons on his walking stick. Over his arm he held the Queen's fine white fur-cloak.

Rosamund smiled at him. 'La, my lord, but you are

not meant to recognise me! Is that not the point of a masquerade?'

· He smiled back. 'You must forgive me, then. Your disguise is most complete, and indeed I should never have known you. I am no good at masquerades at all. But Her Grace described your attire to me when she sent me to find you.'

'She knows my costume?'

'Oh, Lady Rosamund, but she knows everything!'

Not quite *everything*, she hoped. 'That she does, thanks to you. Does she need me for an errand?'

'She asks if you will be so kind as to fetch some documents to her. They are most urgent, and I fear she failed to sign them earlier as she meant to. They are in her bedchamber, on the table by the window. She said you would know where to find them.'

'Of course, Lord Burghley, I shall go at once,' Rosamund answered, glad of the distraction, the chance to leave the ball.

'She also sent this,' he said, holding out the fur cloak. 'She feared the corridors would be chilled after the heat of the dance.'

'That is most kind of Her Grace,' Rosamund said, letting him slide the soft fur over her shoulders. 'I will return directly.'

'Thank you, Lady Rosamund. She waits in the small library just through that door.'

As Burghley left her, she glanced around for Anne, finding her arguing with Lord Langley, who was clad in huntsman's garb. She hurried over to her, tugging on her black-velvet sleeve.

'Anne,' she whispered. 'I must run on a quick errand for the Queen.'

'Of course,' Anne said. 'Shall I come with you?'

Rosamund glanced at Lord Langley. 'Nay, you seem—occupied. I won't be gone long, the papers I'm to fetch are in Her Grace's bedchamber.'

She hurried out of the hall, drawing the Queen's cloak close around her. The corridors were indeed chilly, with no fires and only a few torches to light the way. They were silent, too, echoing with solitude after the great cacophony of the hall. Outside the windows, the frosty wind rushed by, sounding like ghostly whispers and moans.

Rosamund shivered, rushing even faster up the privy stairs and through the Privy and Presence Chambers. Those spaces, usually so crowded with attention-seekers, were empty except for shifting shadows. She found she wanted only to be gone from there.

In the bedchamber, candles were already lit, anticipating the Queen's return. The bedclothes were folded back, and a fire had been lit in the grate.

Rosamund eased back the fur hood, searching quickly through the documents on the table by the window. The only papers not locked away in the chests were piled up, waiting for the Queen's signature and seal.

'These must be them,' she muttered, catching them up. As she folded them, she could not help noticing Lord Darnley's name. A travel pass, for him to proceed to Edinburgh? But why would Queen Elizabeth suddenly give in to Lady Lennox's petitions, giving up pressing Lord Leicester's suit on Queen Mary?

Rosamund glanced up, meeting the painted dark eyes of Anne Boleyn. The Queen's mother seemed to laugh knowingly. *For love, of course,* she seemed to say. *She could no more part with him than you could your Anton.*

Yet sometimes life held other plans for people. The Queen, and her mother, knew that well. And Rosamund knew it now, too.

She hastily stuffed the folded papers into her sleeve, raising the hood as she dashed out of the silent chamber. She had suddenly had quite enough of ghosts. She wanted, needed, to see Anton again.

As she turned the corner out of the Presence Chamber, an arm suddenly curled out of the darkness, wrapping around her waist and jerking her off her feet. A gloved hand clapped hard over her mouth.

Rosamund twisted about, panic rising up inside her like an engulfing wave. She tasted the metallic tang of it in her mouth, thick and suffocating.

She twisted again, screaming silently, but it was as if she was bound in iron chains.

'Well, this is a lucky chance,' her captor whispered hoarsely. A black, hazy cloud obscured her vision, even her thoughts, and she could see nothing. 'Most obliging of the lady to come to us. I hope we did not interrupt an important assignation?'

'And no guards or anything,' another man said gloatingly. 'It must be Providence, aiding us in our cause.'

Rosamund managed to part her lips, biting down hard on her captor's palm so hard she tore away a piece of leather glove. She tasted the tang of blood.

'*Z'wounds!*' the man growled. 'She is a wild vixen.'

'I'd expect no less. Here, hold her down so we can bind her. There's no time to waste.'

The two men bore her down to the floor, Rosamund kicking and flailing. The heavy cloak and her velvet gown weighed her down, wrapping around her limbs, but she managed to kick one of the villains squarely on the chest as he tried to tie her feet.

'That is enough of that,' he cried, and she saw a fist descending towards her head.

Then there was a sharp, terrible pain—and nothing at all but darkness.

Anton glanced around the bacchanal of Queen Elizabeth's masquerade without much interest. The bright swirl of rich costumes and wine-soaked laughter could hold no appeal for him right now. Since he'd parted with Rosamund last night, it was as if the world had turned to shades of grey and drab brown. All colour and light was gone.

He had vowed to focus only on his work now, had told himself that in staying away from her he was keeping her safe. Letting her go on with her life. But whenever he glimpsed her from a distance it was as if the sun emerged again, if only for a fleeting moment.

Had he been wrong, then? Doubt was not a sensation he was familiar with, and yet it plagued him now. In trying to do the right thing, had he irrevocably wounded them both?

He studied each passing face, each lady's smile, but he saw no one who looked like Rosamund. The ball had started long ago; surely she should be there? After all that had happened…

Across the room, he saw Langley and a blackwigged lady in dark velvet. Most likely, Anne Percy, who was Rosamund's friend. Surely Anne would know where she was? He made his way through the crowd towards them, needing to know she was at least somewhere safe.

'Have you seen Lady Rosamund?' Anton asked Anne Percy.

'Aye, the Queen sent her on an errand,' Anne

answered, giving him a searching, suspicious glance. 'I have not seen her since, though she should have returned long ere since.'

Anton frowned, a tiny, cold prickle of unease forming in his mind. It seemed ridiculous, of course—Rosamund could be in any number of places, perfectly safe. Yet he could not quite shake away the feeling that all was not right, a sense that had once served him well on the battlefield.

'Is something amiss, Master Gustavson?' Anne asked. 'Shall Lord Langley and I help you to look for her?'

'Yes, I thank you, Mistress Percy,' Anton said. 'You know better where she might have gone on this errand.'

Anne nodded, leading him out of the Great Hall, dodging around drunken revellers who would draw them back into the dance. They traversed the long, shadowy corridors which grew quieter, emptier, the further they went. The only sound was the click of their shoes, the howl of the wind outside the windows.

Anton scowled as he noticed the lack of guards, even as they entered the Queen's own chambers. Had they been given the hour's respite, perhaps a ration of ale to celebrate the New Year? Or had something more sinister sent them away?

The darkened rooms certainly felt strangely ominous, as if ghosts hovered above them, harbingers of some wicked deed. Even Anne and Lord Langley, who usually were never quiet when they were together, were silent.

'The papers Rosamund was sent to fetch were in the bedchamber,' Anne whispered, pushing back her mask. 'In here.'

Even the Queen's own chamber was empty, a few flickering candles and a low-burning fire in the grate illuminating the dark, carved furniture and the soft cushions where the ladies usually sat. There were no papers on the table by the window.

'She must have gone back to the hall already,' Anne said. 'But how did we miss her?'

Anton was quite sure they had not missed seeing Rosamund there. The battle instinct was suddenly very strong in him, that taut, ominous feeling that came before the clash of war when the enemy's armies gathered on the horizon. Something was surely amiss with Rosamund.

Anne seemed to feel it, too. She leaned her palms on the table, shaking her head as Lord Langley laid his hand on her arm. 'I did think someone was lurking outside our apartment last night,' she murmured. 'I thought it was just one of Mary Howard's suitors—she does have such terrible judgement in men. But what if it was not?'

Lord Langley took her hand in his. 'There is always someone lurking about here, Anne. I'm sure it was not a villain lying in wait for Lady Rosamund.'

She slammed her free hand down, the crash echoing in the silence. 'But if it was? She is pretty and rich, and too trusting—valuable commodities here at Court. And that country suitor of hers...'

Anton glanced at her sharply. 'Master Sutton?'

'Aye, the very one. He certainly did not seem happy to have lost his prize.'

'Was she frightened of him?' Anton asked.

'She said he was not what she once thought,' Anne said. 'And I did not like the look of him.'

Did not like the look of him. Anton did not like the sound of that. He carefully studied the room, searching for any sign that things were not as they should be, that there had been a disturbance in the jewelled façade of the palace.

He found it in the corridor just outside the bedchamber—a glint of green fire in the darkness. He knelt down, reaching out for it, pushing back his mask to examine it more closely.

It was an earring, an emerald drop set in gold filigree.

'That's Rosamund's!' Anne gasped. 'She said they were her grandmother's. She wore them with her costume, a green gown and wig of red.'

Anton closed his fist around the earring, searching the floor for more clues. Crumpled up by the wall was a roughly torn scrap of glove leather, stiff with dried blood. Not Rosamund's—she had not worn gloves—but blood was never a good sign.

'I think she has been seized,' he said, his mind hardening, clarifying on one point—finding Rosamund as quickly as possible. And killing whoever had dared hurt her.

He showed the crumpled bit of leather to Lord Langley and Anne, who cried out.

'The stables,' Lord Langley said, holding onto her hand. 'They will have to get her away from the palace.'

'Should we tell the Queen?' Anne asked. 'Or Lord Burghley, or Leicester?'

'Not just yet,' Anton answered. 'If it is Rosamund's disappointed suitor, or some villain seeking ransom, we do not want to startle them into doing something rash. I will find them.'

Lord Langley nodded grimly. 'We will help you. I have men of my own household. They will be discreet in their search until we must tell Her Grace.'

'Thank you, Langley,' Anton said. 'Mistress Percy, if you will search the Great Hall again, and look wherever you know of hiding spots within the palace. But do not go alone!'

Anne nodded, her face pale, before she dashed out of the corridor. Anton and Lord Langley headed for the stables.

It had been quiet there all evening, the servants told them, with everyone at the Queen's revels. But one of the grooms had prepared a sleigh and horses earlier in the evening.

It was for Master Macintosh of the Scottish delegation.

'He wanted to be quiet about it, my lords,' the groom said. 'I thought he had a meeting with a lady.'

'And did he bring a lady with him when he departed?' Anton asked.

'Aye, that he did. He carried her. She was all bundled up in a white fur-cloak. And there were two other men, though one left in a different direction.'

'And Master Macintosh? Which way did he go?' Anton said.

'Towards Greenwich, I think, along the river. They were in a hurry. Eloping, were they?'

A lady in a white fur, carried off towards Greenwich. The cold, crystalline fury in Anton hardened into steel.

He turned on his heel, striding back towards the palace. He needed his skates—and his sword.

Chapter Fourteen

Snow Day, January 2

Rosamund slowly came awake, feeling as if she struggled up from some black underground cave towards a distant, tiny spot of light. Her limbs ached; they did not want to drag her one more step, and yet she struggled onward. She knew only that it was vital she reach that light, that she not sink back into darkness.

She forced her gritty eyes to open, her head aching as if it would split open. At first, she thought she was indeed in a cave, bound around by stone walls. She could see nothing, feel nothing, but a painful jolting beneath her.

Then she realised it was a cloak wrapped around her, the hood over her head. A soft fur hood, shutting out the world. And then she remembered.

She had been snatched as she'd left the Queen's chamber, grabbed by a man who had muffled her with his gloved hand. Who had knocked her unconscious when she'd kicked him. But where was she now? What did he want of her?

The hard surface beneath her jolted again, sending a wave of pain through her aching body. A cold, metallic-tasting panic rose up in her throat.

Nay, she told herself, pushing that panic back down before she could scream out with it. She would not give in to whoever had done this, would not let them hurt her. Not when she had so much to fight for. Not when she had to get back to Anton.

Slowly, her headache ebbed away a bit and she could hear the hum of voices above her, the clatter of horses' hooves moving swiftly. So, she was in some kind of conveyance being carried further and further from the palace with each second.

She eased back the hood a bit, carefully, slowly, so her captors would think her still unconscious. Fortunately, they had failed to tie her as they'd threatened.

'…a bloody great fool!' one man growled, his voice thick with a Scots burr. 'That's what comes of paying an Englishman to do something. They muck it up every time.'

'How was I to know this was not the Queen?' another man said, muffled by the piercing howl of the wind. 'She had red hair and a green gown, she's wearing the Queen's cloak. And she was coming out of the Queen's own bedchamber!'

'And how often do you see Queen Elizabeth wandering about alone? She may be a usurper of thrones, but the woman is not stupid.'

'Perhaps she had an assignation with that rogue, Leicester.'

'Who she would betroth to Queen Mary?' the Scotsman said. 'Aye, she's a lusty whore. But, still— not stupid. Unlike you. This woman, whoever she is, is too short to be the Queen.'

Rosamund frowned. She was *not* short. Just delicate!

But the Scotsman was right; the other man was a foolish knave indeed not to be sure of his quarry. It was an audacious scheme, seeking to kidnap Queen Elizabeth, and would require sharp, deft timing, as well as steely nerves.

What would they do with her now, since they had realised their terrible failure?

She felt the press of a sheet of parchment against her skin, the travel visa for Lord Darnley, tucked into her sleeve what seemed like days ago. Were they in the pay of Darnley and his mother, then? Or someone else entirely?

Her head pounded as she tried to make sense of it, as she thought of Melville, Lady Lennox and Celia Sutton. Of the Queen's scheme to marry Queen Mary to Lord Leicester. Of the poppet hanging from the tree—*thus to all usurpers.*

And she thought of Anton, of how she had to return to him. To set things right, to find out why he said what he did, and how they could go forward.

'What do we do with his girl, then?' the other man said. He sounded strangely distant, as if masked. 'She bit me!'

'And you deserve no less,' the Scotsman said wryly. 'These English females usually lack the spirit of our Scottish lasses, though. I wonder who she is. I suppose we should discover that before we decide how to correct your foolish error.'

Before Rosamund could brace herself, her hood was thrown back and her mask roughly untied and pulled away. Her wig was also hastily removed, and her own hair tumbled free of its pins.

'Well, well,' the Scotsman murmured. 'Lady Rosamund Ramsay.'

It was Master Macintosh, Rosamund realised in

shock, wrapped in the black, star-dotted cloak. She remembered those prickles of mistrust she had felt when he'd talked to her at the frost fair, and wished she had heeded their warnings.

She scrambled to sit up, sliding as far away from him as she could. She found she lay in the bottom of a sleigh, gliding swiftly along the frozen river. Macintosh knelt beside her and the other man held the reins, urging the horses to even greater speeds as the ice flew past in a sparkling silver blur. He glanced at her, and even though his face was half-wrapped in a knitted scarf she could see it was Richard. Richard—the man she had once thought she could care for!

Even through her shock, it made a sort of sense: his disappearance from home for months with no word; his sudden reappearance at Court; the hard desperation in his eyes whenever they met. The tension between him and Celia, who had her own dealings with the Scots. But why, *why*, would he involve himself in some treasonous conspiracy?

But, whatever his plot, it seemed clear he had not intended her to be a part of it. His eyes widened with surprise.

'Rosamund!' he cried. 'What are you doing here?'

White-hot anger burned away the cold shock, and Rosamund actually shouted, 'What am I doing here? I was foully kidnapped by *you*, of course. What would your parents say if they knew of this shame? You are a villain!'

Macintosh laughed, reaching out to grab Rosamund's wrist and pull her roughly towards him. 'Your Scots blood is showing, Lady Ramsay! She certainly reminded you of what is important, Richard—what your parents would say.'

'And I would bleed myself dry of every drop of Scots

blood, if this is what it means,' Rosamund said, snatching back her hand. 'Treason, threats—not to mention imbecility.'

Macintosh scowled, grabbing her by the shoulders and shaking her until her teeth rattled. Her head felt like it would explode under the onslaught, but she twisted hard under his grasp, wrenching herself away.

''Twas English imbecility brought us to this,' he said. 'Your ardent suitor here was the one who mistakenly grabbed you. You weren't meant to be involved at all.'

'Then I am glad his stupidity led him to take me and not the Queen,' she declared. 'She is safe from your evil intent.'

'We never intended evil towards her, Lady Rosamund,' Macintosh said. Somehow she could not quite believe him, with his bruising clasp digging into her shoulder. 'We merely sought to help her to a meeting with her cousin. Queen Mary is most eager to see her, and yet your Queen Elizabeth keeps delaying. Surely if she saw my Queen's regal and dignified nature, her great charm and beauty, she would give up the notion of marrying her to that stable boy, Leicester.'

'So you were going to carry her in secret all the way to Edinburgh?' Rosamund asked incredulously. It seemed there was plenty of imbecility all around.

''Tis true, it is a long voyage,' Macintosh said. 'And accidents do happen when one travels. These are perilous times.'

Then he did intend to kill Queen Elizabeth. And probably now her, as well, for getting in his way. Furious, Rosamund lunged towards him, arcing her fingernails toward his smirking face.

Macintosh ducked away, even as her nails left an angry red scratch down his cheek.

'Bloody hell!' he shouted. As he dragged her against him, his body fell into Richard, causing him to jerk hard on the reins. Confused the horses cried out and veered off their course towards the river bank. They crashed through the drifts of ice-crusted snow, coming to a halt wedged at an angle.

The cries of the horses, Macintosh's furious shouts and Rosamund's own screams tore the peace of the winter night. She elbowed him as hard as she could in the chest, and he slapped her across the face. Her head snapped back on her neck, her ears ringing.

Suddenly, burly arms seized her around the waist, dragging her from the listing sleigh. Richard held onto her even as she fought to be free, pulling her through the snow up the river bank.

Macintosh, still cursing, knelt by the river, pressing a handful of snow to his scratched cheek. 'Tie up the English witch, and don't let her out of your sight,' he growled. 'She'll pay for this foolishness.'

'Richard, what are you about?' Rosamund said as he plunked her down beneath a tree. Her thick cloak kept away some of the cold, but the wind still bit at her bruised skin. It was a terrible cold, dark night here in these unknown woods, and she couldn't shake away the nightmare quality of it all.

'They offered me money,' he muttered, leaning his palms on his knees as if he struggled to catch his breath. 'A great deal of money, and land to come. With so much, your parents could surely no longer disrespect me. They would be sorry for what they said.'

'They did *not disrespect* you! They merely thought we were a poor match, and it is obvious they were correct.' More than correct. They had seen things in Richard she could not then, but now saw so clearly.

He was not Anton, he was nothing like a man she could love.

'This was for *you*, Rosamund!'

She shook her head, sad beyond anything. 'Treason cannot be for me. Only for yourself, your own greed.'

'It was not greed! If seeing the rightful queen put on the throne could help us to be together…'

'I would not be with you for all the gold in Europe. I am loyal to Queen Elizabeth. And I love someone else. Someone who is honourable, kind, strong—a thousand times the man you are.' Rosamund slumped back against the tree, feeling heartily foolish that she had ever been deluded by Richard.

'So, you are like your parents now,' he said, straightening to glare down at her. Even through the milky moonlight she could see, feel, the force of his anger. The fury that she would dare reject him. It frightened her, and she pressed herself hard against the tree, gathering her legs under her.

'You think yourself above me, after all I've done for you, risked for you,' he said. 'You will not be so haughty when I am done with you!'

He grabbed for her, but Rosamund was ready. She leaped to her feet, ignoring her cramped muscles; her painfully cold feet in their thin shoes. She shed her cloak and ran as fast as she could through the snow, her path lit only by the moon shining on the ice. She lifted her skirts, dodging around the black, bare hulks of the winter trees.

Her breath ached in her lungs, her stomach lurching with fear. Her heart pounded in her ears, so she could barely hear Richard stumbling behind her. She did not know where to go, only that she had to get away.

She leaped over a rotten fallen log, and Richard tripped on it, landing hard on the snow.

'Witch!' he shouted.

Rosamund, panicked, suddenly remembered how she would climb trees as a child, how she could go higher and higher—until her mother had found out and put a stop to it.

She saw a tree just ahead with a low, thick branch and launched herself at it. Tucking her skirts into her gold kirtle, she jumped onto the branch, reaching up, straining until she could clasp the next branch up. Her palms slid on the rough, frosty wood, her soft skin scraping. She ignored the pain, pulling herself up.

Up and up she went, not daring to look down, to listen to Richard's shouted threats. At last she reached a vee in the trunk and wrapped her arms tightly around the tree as the wind tore at her hair, battered at her numb skin. She remembered golden moments with Anton, moments where they had kissed and made love, and she knew they were meant to be together.

She held onto the thought of him tightly now.

Help me, she thought, closing her eyes as she held on for her life. *Find me!*

Anton glided swiftly along the river, the dark countryside to either side of him flying along in a shadowed blur as he found his rhythm. The rhythm that always came as he skated, made of motion and speed, the knife-like sound of blades against ice. The cold meant nothing, nor did the darkness.

He had to find Rosamund, and soon. That was all that mattered. He loved her. He saw that so clearly now. He loved her, and nothing mattered beside that. Not his estate, not her parents, not the Queen, only their feelings for each other. He had to tell her that, to tell her how sorry he was for ever sending her away.

He followed the grooved tracks left in the ice by the runners of a sleigh. The vehicle had been heavy enough to leave a pathway, but it was already freezing over.

The thought of Rosamund out there in the cold night, shivering, frightened, alone, made him angrier than he had ever been. A flaming fury burned away all else, or surely would if he'd let it. But he knew that such fury, out of control, boundless, would not serve him well now. He needed sharp, cold focus. The anger would come later, when Rosamund was safe.

He remembered how he had felt on the battlefield, enclosed by an invisible shield of ice that distanced him from the death and horror. Such a feeling kept fear away, so he could fight on and stay alive.

Now it would help him find his Rosamund.

He leaned further forward, remembering her smile, the way she curled against him in bed, so trusting and loving. His beautiful, sweet winter-fairy. She was all he had thought could not exist in the bleak world, a bright spirit of hope and joy. She made him dare to think of the future as he had never done before. Made him think dreams of home and family could even be real, that loneliness could be banished from his life for ever.

And now she was gone, snatched away from the Queen's own palace with nary a trace. But he would find her, he was determined on it. Find her—and see that her kidnappers paid. That was the only thing that mattered. He listened to his heart now, as his mother had urged him to do, and it pressed him onward.

At last he noticed something, a break in the endless snowy riverbank. As he came closer, he saw it was a sleigh driven into the snow at an angle. It was empty, and for a moment Anton thought the only living things near were the horses, standing quietly in their traces. No Rosamund, no people at all. Only silence.

But then he heard a faint noise, like a muffled, muttered curse. Anton crouched low as he crept closer, drawing his short sword from its sheath.

A man in a black cloak knelt on the other side of the sleigh, scooping up handfuls of snow and pressing them to his bearded face. He half-turned towards a beam of chalky moonlight, and Anton saw it was the Scotsman, Macintosh.

A Scottish conspiracy, then. Somehow he was not surprised. The concerns of Queen Mary seemed to have permeated every corner of Whitehall of late. Now they had absorbed Rosamund, too, ensnaring her in that sticky web.

But not for long. Anton carefully slipped off his skate straps, inching closer to Macintosh in his leather-soled boots. Silently, carefully, like a cat, he came up behind the Scotsman and caught him a hard hold about the neck. He dragged him backward, pressing the blade of his sword to the man's treacherous neck.

Macintosh tensed as if to fight, but went very still at that cold touch of steel.

'Where is Lady Rosamund?' Anton demanded.

'She ran off, the stupid wench,' Macintosh said in a strangled voice. 'We never meant to grab *her*, anyway, she just got in the way.'

'You thought she was Queen Elizabeth,' Anton said, thinking of Rosamund's red wig, the fur cloak.

'I didn't want to hurt the lass, even after she clawed me,' Macintosh said. 'Not that it matters now. She'll probably freeze out there, and our errand is all undone.'

Anton's arm tightened, and Macintosh gurgled,

clawing at his sleeve. 'You let a helpless lady go off into the snow and did not even follow her?'

'That fool Sutton ran after her, wretch that he is. He's the one that took her in the first place. He was in a fury. If he catches her, she'll likely wish she froze to death first.'

So Richard Sutton was involved, determined to take some revenge on Rosamund for her rejection. A man like him, with primitive emotions and urges, would be capable of anything when angered. Anton twisted his sword closer to Macintosh's neck.

'Are you going to kill me?' the man gasped.

'Nay,' Anton answered. 'I'll leave that to the Queen. I'm sure she will have much to ask you, once you're taken to the Tower.'

'Nay!' Macintosh began frantically. He had no time to say more, for Anton brought down the hilt of his sword hard on the back of his head. He collapsed in an unconscious heap in the snow.

In the bottom of the sleigh were some thick coils of rope, no doubt meant for the Queen—or Rosamund. They served now to bind Macintosh. Anton made short work of the task, depositing the Scotsman in the bottom of the sleigh to wait for the Queen's men, before cutting the horses free so the man could not escape.

Surely Lord Langley and Anne Percy would have alerted Leicester to what had happened by now? Anton had to find Rosamund quickly. He scanned the woods just beyond the river bank, turning his sword in his hand.

At last those beams of moonlight caught on a set of blurred footprints leading into the trees. Large, booted prints, heavy, as if they dragged—or dragged something with them.

He followed their erratic pathway until he discovered a small clearing, a smudged spot just beneath a tree where perhaps someone had sat for a time. And, just beyond, a crumpled white fur-cloak, lightly covered by new snow.

He knelt down, lifting up the soft, cold fur. It still smelled of Rosamund's roses, and the Queen's richer violet-amber scent. Along its edge were a few flecks of dried blood. Macintosh's—or Rosamund's? His heart froze at the thought of her bleeding, hurt, alone.

Slowly, he stood up, examining the tracks leading away from the clearing—small, dainty feet, blurred as if she ran, zigzagging. Followed by those heavy boots. Dropping the cloak, he trailed those tracks, every sense heightened, fully aware of every sound and motion of wind in the bare branches.

Rosamund gave a good chase, he thought with pride, veering around trees, over fallen logs. Then, at last, he heard a noise breaking through that eerie, glass-like night: a man's hoarse shout, a woman's scream.

Holding his sword firmly, Anton followed the sound, running lightly through the snow until he found them. It was an astonishing sight—Rosamund was high up in a tree, balanced on the split trunk, her skirts tucked up and her white stockings glowing in the moonlight. Richard Sutton was at the base of the tree, shouting and waving his sword at her, even though she was too high for the reach of the blade.

Rosamund tottered on her perch, grabbing harder onto the trunk. The freezing wind had to be numbing her bare hands—yet another thing to kill Sutton for.

'Sutton!' Anton shouted, advancing on the man with his sword held out in challenge. 'Why don't you face someone your own size, rather than bully defenceless females?'

Richard swung towards him, waving his own sword about erratically. The steel fairly hummed in the frosty air. 'Defenceless? You are deluded, foreigner. The witch has defences aplenty, as well as a cold, fickle heart. She will desert you as sure as she did me.'

'Anton,' Rosamund sobbed, her fingers slipping on the bark.

'Hold on very tightly, Rosamund,' Anton called, struggling to hold onto his icy distance. The sight of her pale, frightened face, her tangled hair and torn gown, threatened to tear away that chilly remove as nothing else could.

But it also made him determined to protect her at all costs.

'You will never be worthy of her, not in her haughty eyes,' Richard cried. 'Nor with her family. None are good enough for the mighty Ramsays.'

'Ah, but I have something *you* will never possess,' Anton said, tossing his sword lightly from hand to hand as he advanced on his quarry.

'What might that be? Money? Land?'

'Nay. I have the lady's love.' Or he had once—and he would fight for it again for the rest of his life.

With a furious shout, Richard dived towards Anton, swinging his blade wildly. Anton brought his own sword arm-up, and the blades met with a ringing clang. He felt it reverberate down his whole arm, but he recovered swiftly, twirling his sword about to parry Richard's blows.

At first he merely defended himself, deflecting Richard's wild attacks, fighting to keep his balance on the frozen ground. But his opponent's burning fury quickly wore him down, while Anton was still fresh, still fortified with his quiet, cold anger. When Richard faltered, Anton pressed his advantage, moving forward with a series of light strikes.

He drove Richard back towards one of the looming trees, until the man clumsily lost his footing and stumbled against the trunk. With a roar, he tried to shove his sword up into Anton's chest, unprotected by armour or padding. But Anton was too quick for him, and drove his own blade through Richard's sleeve, pinning him to the tree.

'It seems I have something else you lack,' Anton said. 'A gentleman's skill with the sword.'

'Foreign whoreson!' Richard shouted. He ripped his sleeve free, driving forward again, catching Anton on the shoulder with the tip of his blade. Startled by the sting, Anton was even more shocked by what happened next. Richard took off, running through the woods, crashing like a wounded boar.

Anton ran after him, following his twisted, half-blind path as they headed back towards the river. His shoulder ached and he felt the stickiness of blood seeping through his doublet. The sweat seemed to freeze on his skin, but he hardly noticed. He ran on, chasing after Richard as the coward fled.

Richard broke free of the trees, sliding down the steep, snowy banks towards the sleigh as if he meant to drive away and escape. But the horses were gone now, broken from their traces, and Macintosh, still unconscious, lay bound in the bottom of their sleigh.

Richard, though, kept running, straight out onto the river itself. Anton pursued him, but skidded to a halt as he heard an ominous cracking sound, one he heard all too often in Swedish spring-times. He eased back up onto the bank, watching in shock as a thin patch of the river cracked beneath Richard's heavy weight. Screaming with horror, a terrible sound indeed, Richard fell down into the water below.

His head surfaced briefly, a pale dot above the jagged, diamond-like ice.

'I can't swim!' he cried. 'I can't...'

Carefully, Anton crept out onto the ice, watching for tell-tale fissures. But he was lighter than Richard, leaner, and he knew the ways of the ice. It held for him. Near the edge of the hole, he held out his sword towards the flailing man.

'Catch onto the blade!' he called. 'I can pull you out.'

Richard's hand grasped for the lifeline, but he just kept sinking down. Creeping closer, crouching down, Anton managed to grab Richard by the collar of his sodden doublet, yanking him upward. But his hands were cold, his muscles tired from the sword fight, and Richard fought against him. He tore away from Anton's grasp, sinking below the water one last time.

Anton braced his palms on the ice, exhausted, horrified, saddened. It seemed the Queen's river had exacted justice for her, before he could.

But his own task was far from finished. He made his careful way back to the bank, though it seemed the river was done with violence now, and the ice held beneath him. Once back on solid land again, he ran for Rosamund's tree.

She met him on the forest path, sobbing as she stumbled into his arms. 'I knew you would come,' she cried. 'I knew you did not mean it when you sent me away.'

Anton held her close, kissing her hair, her cheek, over and over, all quarrels forgotten, the past gone. She was alive, safe and warm and vital in his embrace. *'Alskling,'* he muttered, over and over. 'I was so scared I would not find you in time. My love, my brave, brave love.'

'Brave? Nay! I was frightened as could be. I was sure Richard would catch me, and would—oh. Richard!'

'Never fear, he won't hurt you now.'

Rosamund drew back, staring up at him with wide eyes. 'You—killed him?'

'I would have. But in the end, I did not have to. The ice did it for me.'

'How terrible.' She leaned her forehead against his chest, trembling. 'But you are hurt, Anton! Look, your shoulder.'

In truth, he had quite forgotten the wound. The cold numbed it; finding Rosamund had made it completely unimportant. ''Tis just a scratch. I cannot feel it at all. Come, my love, you will catch a terrible chill. We should find one of the horses and make our way back to the palace.'

'I *am* cold,' she murmured. 'I didn't even notice when I was in that tree, but now I'm frozen to the core. Isn't that odd?'

She was also worryingly pale, he saw. He lifted her in his arms, holding her against his unhurt shoulder as he carried her hastily out of the woods. He retrieved the Queen's cloak, wrapping it tightly around her as a meager shelter against the biting wind.

'We'll have you in your own chamber very soon,' he said. 'With a warm fire, spiced wine and plenty of blankets. Just hold on a bit longer, my love.'

'I'm not frightened now,' she responded, resting her head on his chest as her eyes drifted closed. 'I'm not even cold now. Not with you.'

'I'm sorry, my love,' he whispered. 'I'm so very sorry.'

She grew heavier in his arms, as if she sank into a

chilled stupor. For the first time, he was truly, deeply afraid. She could not be ill! Not when they were together at last.

Where were those cursed horses? He had been a fool to set them free!

At the river's edge, he saw a flicker of light in the distance—torches breaking through the darkness. It was a procession of horses, led by Lord Leicester.

'You see, *alskling*?' Anton said with a wry laugh. 'We are both rescued.'

Chapter Fifteen

⚭

January 4

Rosamund lay on her side in bed, staring out of the window at the river far below. The private bedchamber the Queen had given her was a palatial one, with fine tapestries on the walls to shut out the cold and velvet bed-hangings and blankets. A fire crackled merrily in the grate.

Yet she saw none of it. She thought only of Anton, of the way he had held her so close there in the dark, cold woods. How he had kissed her as if she was precious to him, how his words had erased all the hurt of before.

He did love her, she was so sure of it. He'd come after her because he could not live without her, as she could not live without him. And the fear of the kidnapping had been worth it, as it had brought him back to her. They could face anything to be together now.

But she had not seen him since they'd returned to the palace. She had not even had a note. She wished with all her strength she knew his thoughts now. Knew what happened in the world outside her chamber.

'Rosamund? Are you awake?' Anne Percy whispered from the doorway.

Rosamund rolled over and smiled at her friend. 'Of course I am awake. I'm not an invalid any longer, to be slumbering away at noontime.'

'Even if you are not, you should pretend to be. Being an invalid in the Queen's service has such fine concessions!' Anne teased, hurrying into the chamber Rosamund had occupied since Anton had brought her back from the forest. 'A room of your own, far away from that chattering magpie Mary Howard. Nourishing wines and meat stews. Even furs!'

She gestured towards the glossy sable wrap at the foot of the bed, as Rosamund laughed and sat up against the bolsters. 'That is all very well, but I am quite recovered now, and it is very dull to be alone here so near Twelfth Night.'

'You have books, also sent by Her Grace,' Anne said. 'And gifts such as these, which I am bid bring to you.' She put down a basket full of jellies and sweets on Rosamund's table, next to the stack of books from the Queen's library.

'Her Grace is very kind,' Rosamund said. 'But I am allowed so few guests. It is lonely.'

'The physicians say you must be quiet for at least one more day to allow your blood to warm sufficiently,' Anne said. She straightened the velvet coverlet before perching on the edge of the bed. 'You are not missing a great deal, I declare! There have been no scandalous elopements or duels at all. Things are especially quiet today, as the Queen is hunting again. Everyone feels safe again, now that you have caught the villains and foiled their wicked plot.'

'Have they all been caught, then?' Rosamund asked.

'I am sure Richard and Macintosh did not conceive such an idea themselves.'

'Secretary Melville disavows all knowledge of such a scheme, and Queen Mary has sent word of her shock and sympathy. But Macintosh is in the Tower, and Lord Burghley is on the trail. You are acclaimed the heroine of the Court!'

Rosamund shivered, remembering Richard as he'd chased her through the snow in such a fury. Picturing him sinking beneath the ice. That terrible, bitter fear, the feeling of being so cold she could never be warm again, never feel again.

But Anton had come for her, saved her—and then had not seen her again after he had left her safe at the palace. Would they quarrel again, then? Better that than be apart, surely?

'I should not be called a heroine,' she said, sinking deeper under the bedclothes. 'I did naught but run away and climb up a tree to wait.'

'You saved the Queen from being abducted!' Anne protested. 'And I should have been far too terrified to have the presence of mind to run away.'

'I doubt you have ever been terrified of anything in your life, Anne Percy! I have never known anyone bolder.'

'There is a difference between boldness and bravery.'

'Not at all. Daring to join the mummers' play and fight with Lord Langley in front of the Queen and everyone—that is bravery indeed. No other lady I know would dare such a thing.'

Anne laughed humourlessly. 'Foolishness is more like. And that act gained me naught in the end.'

'Do you and Lord Langley...' Rosamund began tentatively.

Anne shook her head. 'We are a dull subject indeed.

Not like you and your swain, the brave young Swede! Since he so daringly effected your rescue, the Court ladies are even more in love with him.'

Of course they were. How could they help it? Rosamund was no different. 'So, that is why I have not seen him of late.'

'He has been with the Queen in private council,' Anne said. 'But I think you need not fear. When he is not with Her Grace, he is hanging about in the corridor here, questioning all the physicians and servants about your health.'

A tiny light of hope flickered to life deep in Rosamund's heart. He had been there, she just had not seen him! Surely that was a good thing? 'But why has he not come in to see me?'

'You are not yet allowed visitors, remember? I am quite sure he has not forgotten you, Rosamund, nor does he pay attention to any other lady.'

Before Rosamund could question Anne further, her maid, Jane, entered the room with a curtsy. 'I beg your pardon, my lady, but you have a caller.'

'I thought I was not allowed visitors,' Rosamund said.

'They could hardly refuse *me*,' a man said, sweeping through the door. He was tall, silver-haired, and blue-eyed, still clad in a travel cloak and boots. He smiled, but his bearded face was creased with worry and tiredness.

'Father!' Rosamund cried in a rush of happiness. It was so long since she had seen her family. To see him there now was like a rush of warm, summer sunshine. She started to push back the blankets, but he rushed over to hold her there.

'Rosie, dearest, you should not exert yourself.'

Rosamund threw her arms around her father,

hugging him close as she buried her face against his shoulder, her eyes shut as she inhaled his familiar scent. He smelled of home. 'Father, you're here.'

'Of course I am,' he said, kissing the top of her head. 'I set out as soon as the Queen's messenger arrived at Ramsay Castle. Your mother is beside herself with worry. She follows in the litter, but I rode ahead as quickly as I could. We could not be easy until we had seen you ourselves.'

'I have missed you so very much,' Rosamund said, drawing back to study him closer. From the corner of her eye, she glimpsed Anne easing towards the door. 'Oh no, Anne, do not go! Come, meet my father. Father, this is Mistress Anne Percy, who has been my best friend here at Court. I could never have made my way without her.'

He stood to bow to Anne, who curtsied to him. 'You are Mildred Percy's niece, I think?' he said. 'We have heard much of you.'

'I am her niece indeed, my lord,' she answered. 'But I hope you have not heard *too* much.'

Rosamund's father laughed. 'Well, I am most grateful for your friendship to my daughter. And for looking after her in her illness.'

'She has been a great friend to me as well,' Anne said. 'I will look in on you after supper, Rosamund.'

She departed, leaving Rosamund alone again with her father. She held onto his hand, still not sure he was really there. And he held very tightly to her in turn.

'You need not worry, Father. I am quite recovered,' she said. 'And the Queen has been very attentive.'

He shook his head. 'Your mother and I thought you would be safe here at Court. What fools we were.'

'Not nearly as foolish as I was. You were quite right about Richard, Father,' Rosamund admitted.

'We had not thought him as wicked as all this. The son of our own neighbours, in a plot against the Queen!' he said sadly. 'I did not expect such a thing.'

'It was not a very well-thought-out plot, truly. But you thought him somewhat wicked, even then?'

'We heard tales of debts, of other bad behaviour that could not be acceptable in your husband. Even aside from that, his personality was not suited to yours. We knew you would not be happy with him, as your mother and I have been happy together all these years. We never imagined treason, though.'

'Nor did I,' Rosamund answered. 'Though I have to admit, Father, that even before his terrible actions I came to see Richard was not the man for me at all. You and Mama were right to send me here to Court.'

'Were we, daughter? In truth, we began to regret it as soon as you departed Ramsay Castle. Home is quiet without you there.'

'It is true that I prefer the peace of home,' she said with a laugh. 'But I have learned so much here.'

'And perhaps even found someone to replace Richard Sutton?'

She glanced at him sharply. Did he already know, then, even as her mind tumbled with ways to tell him of Anton? To persuade him that this time she had found her right match? 'You have heard tales?'

'I saw my old friend Lord Ledsen as I arrived. He told me the Court is all a-buzz with the romantic story of a handsome young Swede skating to your rescue.'

Rosamund felt her cheeks grow warm, but she pressed ahead. 'It is true, Anton did rescue me. I would surely be dead without him—or—or dishonoured by Richard.'

Her father's lips tightened, as if in deep anger. Over

Richard's threats—or her feelings for Anton? 'It seems we owe him much, then.'

'We do. And I have to tell you, Father, that even before this happened I had developed the most tender of feelings for him.' As he had for her, she hoped. Her heart had given her uncertainties before. Did it now, as well?

'Ledsen did say he has a fine reputation here at Court. But, Rosie, he is Swedish. He would take you far away from here, to a rough and cold land where you would have none of the comforts you are accustomed to,' her father said sternly.

'Perhaps he would not!' Rosamund hastened to tell him of Anton's English connections, of his estate and hopes. 'And, Father, I do care for him. You were correct when you said one day I would meet the right man for me and I would know it. Just as you and Mama knew.'

'But I did not take your mother away from everything she knew,' her father said gently, implacably. 'He does not yet have this English estate, I think.'

'Nay,' Rosamund admitted. Nor was she entirely sure he wanted her, either. 'But I am quite sure that now the Queen will…'

'Enough now, my dear.' He kissed her cheek, gently urging her to lie back against the cushions. 'I fear I have tired you, after I promised the Queen's physicians I would do no such thing. You should sleep now. I will consider what you have told me.'

Rosamund knew well enough when arguing with her father would do no good. He had to be left to do his considering, and she had to go on waiting. 'I am most glad to see you, Father. I have missed you.'

'And we have missed you. We will talk more later.'

She nodded, watching her father depart. A few moments later, Anne returned. Her friend knelt down by the bed to whisper, 'Did you tell your father of Anton, Rosie? What did he say?'

Rosamund frowned, punching at the bolster with her fist. 'He said he would consider what I have told him.'

'Consider? Is that good or ill?'

'I hardly know.'

Anton paced the corridor outside the Queen's chamber, listening closely for any word, any sound, behind that door. There was only silence. And yet he knew his entire future was in that room.

He raked his fingers through his hair impatiently, re-straining the urge to curse. He had tried to see Rosamund, yet she was closely guarded in the Queen's keeping, tucked away as she regained her health. His bribes to the physicians had gained him the knowledge that she recovered, but nothing could tell him of her heart.

Had she forgiven him for ever hurting her? Did she care for him still? She had declared she did when he'd found her in the woods, but matters had been emotional then. Would she change her mind now, back at the centre of the Court?

And what would they do if the Queen denied his suit? Could he dare to ask Rosamund to go to Sweden with him, leaving behind all she knew? Or could he find the strength to leave her once more, for ever?

Suddenly the door opened, and Lord Burghley hobbled out with his walking stick. 'You may go in now, Master Gustavson,' he said. Anton searched his lined face, but there was no hint there of his fate.

Anton smoothed his hair again, and walked into the room. It was empty of the usual gaggle of ladies, the hum of constant conversation. Queen Elizabeth sat alone at her desk, busily writing on a sheet of parchment spread before her. Anton knelt, waiting for her to speak.

At last, he heard the scratching of the quill cease and the rustle as she folded her hands on the desk, her draped sleeves falling back.

'Arise, Master Gustavson,' she said, laughing as he bowed to her. 'La, but you look as if you are being sent to the Tower! Why the great frown?'

Anton smiled reluctantly. The Queen's laughter was infectious, even as his hopes hung in the balance. 'A man cannot help but have concerns, Your Grace, when he is summoned so urgently.'

'Ah, but you are not just *any* man, Master Gustavson. You are the hero of the day. All my courtiers talk of your daring midnight ride to rescue Lady Rosamund and vanquish the villains who plotted against me.'

'I did what anyone would do in the circumstances, Your Grace.'

'Anyone? Somehow I doubt that. Many men speak of loyalty unto death, but not many have the actions to prove such poetic words.' Queen Elizabeth sat back in her chair, watching him thoughtfully. 'I am in your debt, Master Gustavson. What do you desire? Money? Jewels?'

Anton stiffened. She offered him a *reward*? Would she be willing to replace one of her ladies for the money and jewels? Or did the Queen's largesse go only so far, as everyone whispered?

Before he could answer, she smiled slyly, tapping at her chin with one long, white finger. 'Nay. I know what you truly desire. I have been reading over your petition for Briony Manor.' She gestured towards the parchment on her desk. 'I have been reading Celia Sutton's letters, as well.'

'And has Your Grace reached a conclusion?' he asked tightly.

'I do not rush into such things,' she said. 'Haste so often leads to regret, as my father and my sister often learned to their detriment. Would you crave this manor as your reward, then?'

'Of course, Your Grace.'

'Of course,' she echoed. 'But—I sense you crave another boon as well, Master Gustavson.'

Anton hardly dared move. 'Your Grace has been most generous already.'

'Indeed I have. Yet it did not escape my notice that you were in great haste to rescue Lady Rosamund—or that she is a pretty girl indeed.'

Anton's eyes narrowed as he steadily returned the Queen's stare. 'I cannot deny that she is pretty, Your Grace.'

'I do not like my ladies to leave me,' she said, reaching again for her quill as if she dismissed him. 'I must think on this a bit longer, Master Gustavson. You may go now.'

He bowed again, restraining himself from arguing as he earlier had from cursing. Quarrelling with the Queen would gain him nothing at all in this delicate, perilous dance. He played for the greatest stakes of his life, for Rosamund's love, and his every move had to be calculated to that one end.

He had to plan his next step carefully indeed, or he, like the volta he practised with Rosamund, would fall into ruin.

Chapter Sixteen

Twelfth Night, January 5

'Are you quite sure you want to do this, Rosamund?' Anne asked, fastening Rosamund's pearl necklace for her. 'You still look rather pale.'

Rosamund shook out the folds of her white-satin gown trimmed with silvery fox-fur and embroidered with twining silver flowers. Her best gown, saved for Twelfth Night. 'I could hardly miss the festivities, could I? It is the most important night of Christmas. Besides, I could not stay in bed another moment.'

All that time alone had left too much time to think. To think about Anton, and the fact that she had not seen him since their icy adventure. To think about their future, and how she would feel if she lost him for ever. Would she be able to move forward again? To forget all that he had taught her, all they had together?

Tonight felt like the end of something. But would it be a beginning, too—or a step into dark uncertainty?

She quickly pinched her cheeks, hoping to look less

pale. She had to be completely well, or risk being sent back to bed by the Queen and her infernal physicians. 'How do I look?' she asked.

'Lovely, as always,' Anne answered. 'And me?'

'Beautiful, of course,' Rosamund said, examining her friend's sable-trimmed red-velvet gown.

'Mary Howard will faint of envy when she sees us!'

'And Lord Langley will fall even more in love with you.'

'Pooh,' Anne scoffed. 'He is not in love with me, and even if he was I care not. I have found there are far grander men here at Court.'

Grander than a young, handsome, rich earl who was clearly in love with Anne? Rosamund thought not, but she knew better than to argue. Things were not always as they seemed. 'We should go down, then, and start inciting that envy.'

Anne laughed, and she and Rosamund linked arms as they hurried down the stairs and along the corridors to the Great Hall. Unlike the dark, mysterious scarlet and black of the ill-fated masquerade ball, the vast chamber was now a wintry paradise. Hangings of white and silver draped from the gilded ceiling, and the walls were lined with trees in silver pots hung with garlands of spangled-white satin to resemble ice. Silver urns held chilled white wines, and musicians in their gallery high above played soft madrigals of love.

But, unlike the real ice-wrapped forest, it was warm from the crackling fire and from the well-dressed crowds of courtiers packed all around. They all flocked to surround Rosamund when she appeared, exclaiming over her adventure.

Anton, though, was not among them, and nor was

her father, who she had not seen since they had broken their fast together that morning. She smiled and chatted, but their absence, and all the uncertainty, made her feel nervous and unhappy deep down inside. She did like to have a purpose, to know what would happen next and what her actions should be. Where she belonged.

I am not cut out for Court life, then, she thought wryly. Uncertainty was an everyday matter here. But she accepted a goblet of wine and went on with her conversation as if she had not a care in the world.

Suddenly, there was a herald of trumpets from the gallery and Queen Elizabeth appeared in the doorway, dazzling in black velvet and cloth-of-gold, her red hair entwined with a wreath of wrought-gold flowers. On her arm was the head of the Swedish delegation, Master Vernerson.

And in the procession behind her was Anton. Rosamund's breath caught at the sight of him, so very handsome in his tawny-coloured doublet sewn with black ribbons in a fashionable lattice pattern, a topaz earring in his ear. He seemed none the worse for their adventure. Indeed he seemed more hale and hearty than ever, radiating youth and life.

The Queen mounted her dais with the Swedish party, her golden train rippling behind her. Rosamund's father came to her side as they watched Queen Elizabeth, taking Rosamund's hand in his.

'You look lovely tonight, daughter,' he said with a smile. 'So much like your mother, at a Court much like this one.'

'You look fine yourself, Father,' she answered, examining his purple velvet and black-satin garments. 'I haven't seen you so well clad in ages!'

He laughed. 'There is no need for such finery at

home! Hopefully we shall be back there soon, sitting by our own fire. I am too old for this.'

The Queen raised her hand, and silence fell over the hall. 'Welcome all to our Twelfth Night celebration! We have much to celebrate, methinks, after weathering many hardships in these last days. It is cold beyond our walls, but here we have a good fire, fine food—and the best of friends.'

A cheer went up, and only as it faded did Queen Elizabeth continue. 'Some friends will remain with us,' she said, smiling at Lord Leicester who would not, after all, be travelling to Edinburgh. 'Yet we must say farewell to others. Master Vernerson and his Swedish party will be returning to King Eric, bearing our ever-lasting friendship. And Master Von Zwetkovich will return to Vienna. Our Court will soon be much less merry, I fear.'

Rosamund glanced frantically at Anton, who stood behind the Queen's shoulder. The Swedes were departing so very soon? That left them little time to make their plans. Very little time for her to persuade her father that this time she was very, very certain. That she was willing to do anything for her love.

The Queen continued. 'One of our new friends will remain with us, though, or so we hope. In thanks for his efforts to save us from a most wicked plot, and in honour of his grandfather's long service to my own father, I grant the deed of Briony Manor to Master Anton Gustavson, along with the rank of baronet.' She half-turned, holding out her hand to Anton. 'Come, then, *Sir* Anton.'

He knelt before her as she laid her bejewelled hand on his glossy dark head. 'Your Grace,' he said, 'You have my deepest thanks.'

'It is only your due, Sir Anton. Your family has long served mine, and indeed continues to do so, as Mistress Celia Sutton is going on an errand for us to Edinburgh, bearing my greetings to my cousin there. I hope I may rely on you in the future?'

'Indeed you may, Your Grace.'

Rosamund nearly laughed aloud with the sudden bright rush of joy, and she clapped her hand over her mouth. Anton was given his manor, and a title! A place in England. But what did it all mean for her, for them?

'We think you have one more task to perform, though,' the Queen said, raising Anton to his feet. 'Was there not a wager made, one concerning dancing?'

Anton smiled. 'I believe that is true, Your Grace.'

'Then we must determine a winner. Lady Rosamund Ramsay, come forward!'

The crowd parted, letting Rosamund pass. Her stomach fluttered, and she feared she could not breathe. She walked slowly, carefully, to the base of the dais, dropping into a low curtsy. 'Your Grace.'

'Lady Rosamund, are you recovered enough to dance for us?'

'I hope I am, Your Grace, thanks to your fine physicians.'

'And do you think your pupil is ready for his test?'

Rosamund laughed, daring to peek at Anton. 'We can only hope so, Your Grace.'

'Play a volta!' the Queen commanded the musicians, as Anton came to take Rosamund's hand in his. He bowed low, kissing her fingers lingeringly.

'You look well, my lady,' he murmured.

'I *feel* well,' she answered. 'Now.'

'But shall we impress the Queen with our dancing? Or were we too distracted in our lessons?'

'Do you need to impress her?' Rosamund teased. 'Are you so in need of yet more prizes?'

'Only one, I think.' He led her to the centre of the hall, where the other courtiers had made space for them and gathered around to watch.

Rosamund held tightly to Anton's hand as they took up their opening pose, smiling as if she was tranquil and happy—not quaking with fear inside. She wanted so very much for them to do well before her father and the Queen, to show that she and Anton could be truly united. But there was always the memory of the many falls they had taken in rehearsing—and the way those rehearsals had always been interrupted by kisses!

The music started, a lively tune, quicker than they were used to. Rosamund squeezed his hand and they stepped off—right, left, right, left, and jump.

To her joy, the leaping cadence went off perfectly, and they landed lightly with one foot before the other. After that, the dance went as if by magic. They jumped and twirled and spun, then whirled into the volta, facing each other.

Anton held her by the waist as they turned, Rosamund shifting onto her inside foot as she bent her knees to spring upward.

'La volta!' the crowd shouted, and Anton lifted her high, twirling her around and around as she laughed in utter joy.

Anton spun her about one last time as she laughed merrily. It had been a grand dance, perfect in every way. She hated to see it end, but it did end so splendidly, with her held tightly in Anton's arms.

He slowly lowered her to her feet, her head spinning giddily.

'Did I do that properly, then, Mistress Teacher?' he whispered.

'You are a fine pupil indeed,' she answered.

They gazed at each other, the rest of the room fading away into a mere bright blur. They seemed the only two people in all the world. All the danger, the worry, faded away, and she was sure this was where she was meant to be all along.

But they were not alone for long. Queen Elizabeth applauded, drawing them back to her. 'Very well done, Sir Anton. I think you must now concede that anyone can dance.'

'Indeed, Your Grace,' Anton said. 'If even *I* can, it is true anyone may—with a good teacher.'

'I believe you owe Lady Rosamund a boon, then,' the Queen said. 'Was that not the agreement?'

'I will give Lady Rosamund anything in my power,' he said.

'Yes? Then we have a suggestion, in which we are seconded by the lady's excellent father,' said the Queen. 'You should marry Lady Rosamund, and make her mistress of your fine new estate. Are you content with this?'

Rosamund's hand tightened on Anton's, and his fingers folded around hers. It could not be real, she thought in a daze. She had just been given all she desired, all she had hoped for so ardently. Was she dreaming?

She glanced back at her father, who smiled at her. Then she turned back to Anton and saw her own joy reflected in his beautiful dark eyes.

'I am most content with this, Your Grace,' he said.

'And you, Lady Rosamund?' the Queen said. 'Do you accept this as your wager's prize?'

'I do, Your Grace,' Rosamund whispered, sure she must be dreaming those words. 'Most heartily.'

'I do hate to lose the company of my ladies, but surely a wedding is a cause for celebration. We must all have a dance! Master Vernerson, will you partner me?' the Queen said, holding out her hand to the bowing Swede as the musicians launched into a galliard. 'It is not every day we look forward to a wedding.'

Laughing, Rosamund and Anton joined the line of dancers, twirling and leaping until they reached the end of the hall and could slip out of the doors.

There, hidden in the shadows, they were truly alone at long last.

'Is it true, then?' she whispered, holding close to his hands so he could not escape her. Not now, not so close to their dream's realisation. 'We may marry and live at our own home here in England?'

'It seems so,' Anton said, laughing. 'But do you want to marry me, Rosamund, after everything we have been through? After my foolish behaviour in letting you go? Will you be content as Lady Gustavson, far away from this grand, courtly life?'

'I will be the most content lady in all the land!' Rosamund cried. 'I only ever wanted your love, Anton.'

'And you have it, my lady. For ever.' He took the gold-and-ruby ring from his finger, sliding it onto hers. 'As you cannot yet skate, I believe you won this fairly.'

Rosamund laid her hand flat against his fine doublet, admiring the gleam of her new ring, the shining promise of it. 'And your heart?' she teased.

'You have certainly won that as well. From the first moment I saw you, it has been entirely yours.' Anton gazed down at her, his face more solemn and serious than she had ever seen it.

'As mine is yours. For ever.'

With the music of Twelfth Night in their ears, and the promise of the new year to come before them, they kissed and held each other close, knowing at last that it was truly for ever and always.

Epilogue

Briony Manor, Christmas Day, 1565

'Do you see it, Bess?' Rosamund whispered. She gently waved the newly made kissing bough above her daughter's cradle, laughing in delight as tiny Bess reached for it with her chubby rosebud hand.

Rosamund kissed those pink little fingers, marvelling at their perfection. Bess laughed, kicking her feet under the hem of her long gown. Behind them the fire crackled in the grate of the great hall, flickering on the greenery and red ribbons of the holiday.

'You know it is Christmas, don't you, my darling?' Rosamund said, swinging the bough back and forth before her daughter's fascinated gaze. The baby's eyes were dark, like her father's, but a fluff of pale-blonde hair crowned her perfect little head.

''Twas a year ago I found your father, on the coldest Christmas that ever was seen. And now this year I have you.' Her heart truly overflowed with joy, Rosamund thought. 'Christmas is the finest time of year.'

'I agree most heartily to *that*,' Anton said, bounding into the hall. He still wore his riding boots, and bore the chill of the outdoors, the crispness of green and smoke of the winter's day. But Rosamund cared naught for the dust on his boots as he kissed her.

'How are my ladies this fine afternoon?' he said, reaching for the baby's hand. Her fingers curled tight around his as she laughed and cooed.

'Quite well with our decorating, and hoping your hunt was successful,' Rosamund said, marvelling at the sight of her husband and child together—her two great loves.

'Indeed! We will have a fine feast to welcome your parents tomorrow.'

'They don't care about that. They only want to see Bess.'

'I hope you told them she is the most perfect baby in all the world.'

'In every letter since she was born. Mama writes she expects no less from *her* grandchild, and Father says we must betroth her to a duke at the very least.'

Anton laughed. 'Perhaps we should wait for her betrothal until she is walking.'

Rosamund tucked the fur-lined blanket around Bess, handing her a toy lamb to play with. 'I saw there was a letter this morning from Celia. Will we see her back in England for the holiday? She has been away on the Queen's business for so long.'

Anton shook his head. 'My cousin says her work is not yet done in Scotland. Perhaps next year.'

'Then our table will be complete. But for now we must make certain Bess's first Christmas is wondrous.'

'Just as ours is now?' he said, catching her in his arms for a long, passionate kiss. Even after a year of marriage, his kiss thrilled her to her very toes, making the cold day as warm as July.

She wrapped her arms around him, holding him close as their baby cooed and laughed. 'Oh, my dearest. There could *never* be a finer Christmas than this one!'

Author's Note

I *love* Christmas, so was very excited to dive into Rosamund and Anton's story! The history of Christmas traditions in the Renaissance is a rich—and fun!—one, especially in the reign of Elizabeth I, who certainly knew how to put on a party. Despite the lack of trees and stockings, we would be very familiar with many aspects of the holiday in the sixteenth century—the music, the feasting—though not many of us have peacock and boar's head on our tables!—the greenery and ribbon used in decoration. And the possibility of romance under the mistletoe...

I also enjoyed weaving real Elizabethan history into the story. The winter of 1564 was indeed so terribly cold that the Thames froze through and a frost fair was set up on the ice. Mary, Queen of Scots, as always for Elizabeth, was a great concern and nuisance. Her disastrous marriage to Lord Darnley was just over the horizon, despite Elizabeth's suggestion that her cousin marry Lord Leicester.

While Anton and Rosamund, as well as their families, friends and enemies, are fictional, a few real-life historical figures play a role in their story. Among them are Lord Burghley, Lord Leicester, Blanche Parry, Mistress Eglionby—who had the unenviable task of corralling the young maids of honour!—the Scots Melville and Maitland, the Austrian Adam von Zwetkovich, and the Maids Mary Howard, Mary Radcliffe and Catherine Knyvett. I also used much of Queen Elizabeth's complicated courtship politics in the story, including King Eric of Sweden—who a few years later went mad and was deposed by his brother—and Archduke Charles.

A few resources I found useful and interesting are:

Maria Hubert's *Christmas in Shakespeare's England*
Simon Thurley's *Whitehall Palace: The Official Illustrated History*. Most of Whitehall is gone now, of course, except for the Banquet Hall, but this book has old floor-plans and descriptions of the grand old palace.
Alison Sims's *Food and Feast in Tudor England*
Liza Picard's *Elizabeth's London*
Anne Somerset's *Ladies in Waiting: From the Tudors to the Present Day*
Janet Arnold's *Queen Elizabeth's Wardrobe Unlock'd* and *Patterns of Fashion 1560-1620*
Josephine Ross's *The Men Who Would Be King*, about Queen Elizabeth's many political courtships.

There are many good general biographies of Elizabeth I out there, but two I like are Alison Weir's *The Life of Elizabeth I* and Anne Somerset's *Elizabeth I*.
The manuscript of the traditional mummers' play used in Anne Percy and Lord Langley's scene came

from one performed annually at the town of Chudlington in Oxfordshire, which was first written down in 1893, but which is said to have been performed in this form for hundreds of years before that!

I hope you enjoyed Anton and Rosamund's Christmas romance! Be sure and visit my website at *http://ammandamccabe.tripod.com*, where I'll be posting lots more fun research-titbits…

* * * * *

Celebrate 60 years of pure reading
pleasure with Harlequin®!
Just in time for the holidays,
Silhouette Special Edition® is proud to present
New York Times *bestselling author*
Kathleen Eagle's
ONE COWBOY, ONE CHRISTMAS

Rodeo rider Zach Beaudry was a travelin' man—
until he broke down in middle-of-nowhere South
Dakota during a deep freeze. That's when an
angel came to his rescue....

"**D**on't die on me. Come on, Zel. You know how much I love you, girl. You're all I've got. Don't do this to me here. Not *now*."

But Zelda had quit on him, and Zach Beaudry had no one to blame but himself. He'd taken his sweet time hitting the road, and then miscalculated a shortcut. For all he knew he was a hundred miles from gas. But even if they were sitting next to a pump, the ten dollars he had in his pocket wouldn't get him out of South Dakota, which was not where he wanted to be right now. Not even his beloved pickup truck, Zelda, could get him much of anywhere on fumes. He was sitting out in the cold in the middle of nowhere. And getting colder.

He shifted the pickup into Neutral and pulled hard on the steering wheel, using the downhill slope to get her off the blacktop and into the roadside grass, where she shuddered to a standstill. He stroked the padded dash. "You'll be safe here."

But Zach would not. It was getting dark, and it was already too damn cold for his cowboy ass. Zach's battered body was a barometer, and he was feeling South Dakota, big time. He'd have given his right arm to be climbing into a hotel hot tub instead of a brutal blast of north wind. The right was his free arm anyway.

Damn thing had lost altitude, touched some part of the bull and caused him a scoreless ride last time out.

It wasn't scoring him a ride this night, either. A carload of teenagers whizzed by, topping off the insult by laying on the horn as they passed him. It was at least twenty minutes before another vehicle came along. He stepped out and waved both arms this time, damn near getting himself killed. Whatever happened to *do unto others?* In places like this, decent people didn't leave each other stranded in the cold.

His face was feeling stiff, and he figured he'd better start walking before his toes went numb. He struck out for a distant yard light, the only sign of human habitation in sight. He couldn't tell how distant, but he knew he'd be hurting by the time he got there, and he was counting on some kindly old man to be answering the door. No shame among the lame.

It wasn't like Zach was fresh off the operating table—it had been a few months since his last round of repairs—but he hadn't given himself enough time. He'd lopped a couple of weeks off the near end of the doc's estimated recovery time, rigged up a brace, done some heavy-duty taping and climbed onto another bull. Hung in there for five seconds—four seconds past feeling the pop in his hip and three seconds short of the buzzer.

He could still feel the pain shooting down his leg with every step. Only this time he had to pick the damn thing up, swing it forward and drop it down again on his own.

Pride be damned, he just hoped *somebody* would be answering the door at the end of the road. The light in the front window was a good sign.

The four steps to the covered porch might as well have been four hundred, and he was looking to climb them with a lead weight chained to his left leg. His eyes were just as screwed up as his hip. Big black spots danced around with tiny red flashers, and he couldn't tell what was real and what wasn't. He stumbled over some shrubbery, steadied himself on the porch railing and peered between vertical slats.

There in the front window stood a spruce tree with a silver star affixed to the top. Zach was pretty sure the red sparks were all in his head, but the white lights twinkling by the hundreds throughout the huge tree, those were real. He wasn't too sure about the woman hanging the shiny balls. Most of her hair was caught up on her head and fastened in a curly clump, but the light captured by the escaped bits crowned her with a golden halo. Her face was a soft shadow, her body a willowy silhouette beneath a long white gown. If this was where the mind ran off to when cold started shutting down the rest of the body, then Zach's final worldly thought was, *This ain't such a bad way to go.*

If she would just turn to the window, he could die looking into the eyes of a Christmas angel.

* * * * *

Could this woman from Zach's past get the lonesome cowboy to come in from the cold...for good?
Look for
ONE COWBOY, ONE CHRISTMAS
by Kathleen Eagle
Available December 2009
from Silhouette Special Edition®

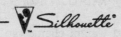

SPECIAL EDITION

We're spotlighting
a different series
every month throughout 2009
to celebrate our 60th anniversary.

This December, Silhouette Special Edition® brings you

NEW YORK TIMES BESTSELLING AUTHOR
KATHLEEN EAGLE

ONE COWBOY,
ONE CHRISTMAS

Available wherever books are sold.

Visit Silhouette Books at www.eHarlequin.com

SSE60BPA

Silhouette Desire

FROM *NEW YORK TIMES* BESTSELLING AUTHOR

DIANA PALMER

THE MAVERICK

A BRAND-NEW LONG, TALL TEXAN STORY

COMING NEXT MONTH FROM

HARLEQUIN®
HISTORICAL

Available November 24, 2009

- **HER COLORADO MAN**
by **Cheryl St.John**
(Western)
When eighteen-year-old Mariah found herself pregnant and unmarried she disappeared for a year, returning with the baby and minus the "husband." But now, with handsome adventurer Wes Burrows turning up and claiming to be the husband she invented seven years ago, Mariah's lies become flesh and blood—and her wildest dreams become a reality!

- **GALLANT OFFICER, FORBIDDEN LADY**
by **Diane Gaston**
(Regency)
Ensign Jack Vernon is haunted by the atrocities of the war in Spain. Back in London he finds the comfort he seeks in beautiful and spirited actress Ariana Blane. With Ariana pursued by a man she fears and detests, her forbidden relationship with Jack is fraught with danger—but he is a man determined to fight for his newfound love....

- **MISTLETOE MAGIC**
by **Sophia James**
(Victorian)
Miss Lillian Davenport is a paragon of good taste with an unrivaled reputation and dangerous American Lucas Clairmont challenges every rule she upholds! A confessed gambler who walks on the wrong side of right, Lucas is a man Lillian knows she should have the sense to stay well away from....

- **THE VIKING'S CAPTIVE PRINCESS**
by **Michelle Styles**
(Viking)
Renowned warrior Ivar Gunnarson is a man of deeds, not words. He certainly has no time for the ideals of love; he gets what he wants—and mysterious and enchanting Princess Thyre is no exception to that rule!